T0276919

'The enraging and galvanisi͏͏‍[...] heroine of the greatest bi[...] 20th century – the revelation of life's code. Women everywhere will be infuriated by the injustices endured by Rosalind Franklin, the scientist whose work was crucial to the discovery of DNA structure in 1953, but who was never credited by the men who stole her data and won the Nobel Prize. In this timely and important fictionalisation of Franklin's life, Mills shines a light on the grievous sexism female scientists faced in the mid-twentieth century. From being denied the degrees they had studied for alongside men, access to university common rooms, networking opportunities, travel and equal pay, to being derided, slandered and passed over for notice, *Rosalind* paints a shocking and necessary portrait of institutional misogyny in mid-century science.'

NIKKI MARMERY, author of *Lilith*

'A poignant, compelling novel that takes us into the heart and mind of Rosalind Franklin as she struggles for recognition in a man's world.'

LOUISA TREGER, author of *The Lodger*, *The Dragon Lady*, and *Madwoman*

'Loved this immersive journey into the life of a woman who changed the world's understanding of what makes us who we are. Jessica Mills shines a light on Rosalind's struggles in the dark.'

EMILY CHUNG, co-author of *The Rangoon Sisters*

'An engaging novel that intertwines the personal and the universal like braided strands of DNA. In rich historical detail, Mills captures the incredible perseverance of one woman over social, familial, and professional obstacles, and also raises the question of other equally talented women in science whose names are lost to history. The novel brilliantly emphasizes the importance of a collaborative approach to science in contrast to the "lone great man" theory. Readers are sure to follow along closely as Rosalind's discoveries unfurl in the shadow of the Second World War.'

LUNA MCNAMARA, author of *Psyche & Eros*

'A luminous, pin-sharp portrait of a true trailblazer. Mills's writing simply glows.'

ZOË HOWE, author, artist and RLF Writing Fellow at Newnham College, University of Cambridge

'Powerful, inspiring, and beautifully told, Rosalind, and the formidable woman at the heart of it, will stay with me for a long time. One of the best novels I have read this year.'

IRIS COSTELLO, author of *The Story Collector*

ROSALIND

JESSICA MILLS

Legend Press Ltd, 51 Gower Street, London, WC1E 6HJ
info@legendpress.co.uk | www.legendpress.co.uk

Print ISBN 9781915643391
Ebook ISBN 9781915643407
Set in Times.
Cover design by Rose Cooper | www.rosecooper.com

Printed in the UK by Akcent Media, 5 The Quay, St.Ives, Cambs, PE27 5AR

Jessica Mills is a journalist and author. She has written for publications such as *The Independent*, *The Wall Street Journal* and *Business Insider*, where she investigated the use of flammable cladding in hospital intensive care units in 2020.

Jessica was an editor at Dow Jones, leading the team that uncovered the misuse of funds at Abraaj and a member of the Women at Dow Jones steering committee. *Rosalind* was longlisted for the Exeter Novel Prize in 2020.

Visit Jessica
www.jessiemillsauthor.com

Follow her on Twitter
@byjessiemills

and Instagram
@jessiemillsauthor

For Tim Mills, Princy Beck and anyone else who lost their lives or loved ones during the Covid pandemic.

The chance of making a major scientific discovery is minuscule. Nearly half happen by accident. Serendipity, or mishap by another name, pulls scientists from the clutches of flat Earths and illusory sirens. Controlled experiments frame those fallacies and rescript the world's truths. At King's College London, we were specks of dust in the gargantuan cosmos, investigating the very secrets of life. Progress was not a lightning-bolt moment, it was hours of toil, in a basement that smelled of mothballs. If you had asked me then if I knew we would find the structure of DNA, I would have said, simply, that the data speaks for itself. Its voice is audible for those who listen.

The mysteries of the universe reside in the simplest of shapes. The twisted loop of a figure of eight was visible in my X-ray photographs. Two strands of the genetic code were entwined together beneath the glass, intersected at the centre, and flecked with atomic dots. I traced their smooth lines, back and forth, back, eight, back. The meandering curve of the infinity sign hides an eternity of secrets.

PROLOGUE

Norway, August 1939

As I stand in line with the other passengers, a dour-faced policeman snatches my passport from my hands. He looks up to examine me from beneath a deeply etched brow.

'English?' he asks.

His menacing eyes follow me as I walk past him and up the steps to board the ocean liner.

The port town of Bergen behind me is dotted with wooden houses in vivid hues of red and yellow. It is a different sight from the sleepy fishing village it had been on our inbound journey when the sheriff's office was closed. I wished then that we could have flown from Gressholmen Airport, in one of the new metallic Imperial Airways planes. They were as big and shiny as the Zeppelins on the banners in Paris. But Father insisted that we couldn't get the family's Austin on one.

Now, queues into the port stretch for several miles. The jetty is crawling with uniformed police in visor caps, shielding their faces from the stark Norwegian sun.

The ship has cast a deep and foreboding shadow over the sea-stair. I vault two steps at a time, levering my body until I can feel the sun's rays warm the cloth on my back.

At first, the journey out of the port is smooth. Waves undulate gently against the hull as the boat crosses the water, leaving the last sunbeams of August shimmering in the distance.

Standing on the ship's bow, I long to stay here forever. With each ripple and swell of the water, my mind drifts, first to home and then to college: I am due to return to Cambridge in less than a month.

Then suddenly, a thought grips me. At first, it is fleeting, but the more I try to suppress it, the harder it resurfaces, this time with agonising intensity. I may never return.

Seconds later, a pummelling sensation rams my stomach. The ship swings to one side, and the rail jolts against my ribs.

A Cimmerian mist quickly settles on the water's surface. Through the haze, a large vessel is just visible.

'Navy ships?' my mother asks.

My father's response is inaudible.

As we descend the poorly lit stairwell at the side of the ship, a tide of panic sweeps over me. My parents and brothers spend the rest of the journey in silence, leaving me to my thoughts, which drift to the start of term and my hopes of a career beyond the coming academic year.

Perhaps it is selfish for me to want the bourgeois life of a scientist, a so-called gentleman's profession. A life of chemistry, maths or physics would be a solipsistic existence after all. Yet while the rest of the world is upended by ideology, science remains the last bastion deserving of my faith. From the tiniest atom to the whole of the universe, science pervades every inch. It is the only language we have to make sense of the world. At the start of our family holiday to Norway there were few signs of what would transpire, or how it would change the course of our lives. At times like this, when you lose everything that you ever knew to be true, all you can do is drive forwards to keep the ghosts at bay.

I
NOW

| 1 |

Starry Night

London, January 1951

Each star in the amaranthine universe has a lifespan of its own, which always ends the same way; with those isolated stars coming together again into the collective mass of things. Maybe that is the definition of infinity; a constant loop of time, polarisation and unity, with fragments of matter dispersing and going their separate ways, before rejoining and recreating, only to begin again. It is the one concept so near to God that no man has understood it.

Could the universe be forever folding in on itself, like the infinity sign, in never-ending fractals, such as the veins on a leaf, or patterns on ice, expanding and shrinking, throughout time and space? The Einsteins, Albert and his wife Mileva, have raised the possibility. Like a star, the universe may shine most brightly before it collapses in on itself and everything around it, then expanding before retracting once more, in infinite iterations. Or else it is forever burgeoning, shining bigger and brighter with exponential complexity.

What is certain is that the world is faster to turn than many of the individuals in it.

The noticeboard in the tea room is empty except for a couple of brass drawing pins. The shiny tacks are clustered together like constellations. There are few other places to go in the university, except for the chapel. The common room is reserved only for the men. Their bluster pours out into the corridor, where they can be heard posturing about politics and sport, or *feminine charms*. Such loose talk was rife in Cambridge. There was more discretion around intimate encounters and night-time liaisons in Paris, where I have returned from four years working in France's State Chemicals Lab. There, silence could save you.

Science was meant to be my passport away from places like this. A cellar on the Strand wasn't where I envisaged I would end up while taking the Natural Sciences Tripos at Cambridge. The professors here mistake me for a student. Some don't even realise women have been let into the university. To spare their embarrassment, I dress older than my thirty years, in a plaid skirt and blouse. But I can tell from the disparaging looks on their faces; Christian Dior's latest style hasn't reached England yet.

On my first day in the lab in London, a thick fog descended on the rooftops north of Temple station. It was nearly a decade since I had left Cambridge's first all-women's college to get a job in industry. Snowflakes were floating on the breeze, and the gravestone paving was slippery with ice. William Waldorf's gothic mansion, just up from Temple, blended into obscurity on the backstreets. A few yards away, the gateway to the university was only just visible through the mist. Once it was an inlet for merchant boats on the River Thames. Now it served as a back entrance for King's College London. The throng of the Strand had moved, by necessity, from the river to the road.

Romanesque colonnades were perched incongruously on top of the arch, which plumbed the recesses below ground level. The gate didn't serve a purpose any more, except as a curiosity. On the other side of the archway was a quadrant of buildings that stood proud like tombstones; yet more vessels to entomb the history of progress.

'Have faith, Rosalind,' my father said to me as I was

leaving home that morning; I had moved back to live with my parents after returning from Paris.

Once a founding institution of the University of London, and a sister school to University College London, King's College was set up to institute the, largely Christian, faith. Perhaps it wasn't where my father had expected me to work. His own religious fervour had grown since helping my eldest brother, David, learn the Torah for his bar mitzvah two decades earlier.

'I've got plenty of faith, Father. Please let me get on or I'll be late.'

What I had wanted to say was that you didn't need to be religious to have faith, because faith is just a kind of hope, but one that you believe in instead of wish for. It has the power to knit together the disparate parts of a broken heart or to achieve the unthinkable. That sort of faith doesn't have to be in God or any other deity, it can be in a person, or in yourself. I chose to put my faith in science.

'I just worry about you, that's all,' he had said, closing the heavy black door of our stucco-fronted four-storey house behind me.

As I stood in the quad outside the university that morning, I noticed the buildings could easily be mistaken for the adjacent naval base, except the houses at Somerset House were bigger, and grander. It was my father who told me that what men prize most could be judged from the size that they build their shrines.

Just past the university gate, my foot slipped. My first thought was that it must be ice, the creeping invisible sort that has you on your back with your legs in the air before you realise it's there. But on feeling the ground with the underside of my foot, it was loose and gravelly, unlike the smooth surface of ice.

Then, looking down, I saw a pile of rubble beside a crater that stretched out for fifty feet into the distance. The crater was shrouded in a halo of mist so thick that I could taste its metallic moisture. My heart drummed an arrhythmic beat. Bomb craters weren't usually left uncovered so long after the war. There weren't any exposed like that near my family home in Notting Hill.

As I looked up past the crater, on the other side there were two men in bowler hats marching through the fog.

'Excuse me,' I began, but it was no use. They appeared not to have heard me above the howling wind. The men continued to battle against the invisible elements, sweeping their arms in ninety-degree arcs.

I stopped to adjust my hairpins. Gusts of wind had pulled apart the chignon that I had woken up half an hour early that morning to arrange. My brunette hair is several shades darker than my sister's. She and my mother are both light-haired; their tresses lightened by youth and age respectively. Everyone says I look more like my father.

After sliding two hairpins back into place and skirting around the rubble, my nylons snagged on the bitumen that had piled around the edge of the crater. Fifteen denier was the only thickness left at the haberdashery in Peter Jones on Sloane Square; I'd been lucky enough to find any stockings at all. Cupboard supplies had been scarce since the war and even a thin denier had seemed better than pencilling a seam on to the backs of my legs.

'Damned stockings.'

The gulf between me and the men was now so wide that they surely couldn't have heard me. Yet a voice interrupted my outburst, not allowing me to sit with my frustration for long.

'Doctor Franklin, welcome.'

I clasped my hand over my mouth at the thought that anyone had heard my profaning. After several seconds of looking around to see where the voice came from, I made out a silhouette. Professor Randall was standing in the lit entrance at the top of a small flight of concrete steps. He was shorter than I remembered from our first meeting a year ago, at least now that I was in inch-high brogues. He was wearing tortoiseshell glasses that accentuated his ovate forehead, with a colourful polka-dot bow tie fastening his shirt collar, and a fresh flower positioned carefully in his buttonhole. Although he was smiling, his eyes appeared to curve downwards at each corner, as if they had been etched by past disappointments.

The turnstile scraped against the floor as I pushed it open. With his hands still in his pockets, the professor then nodded, inviting me to follow his lead. Inside the university building, the steps appeared to be made of stone, possibly limestone or granite, but they were polished to the same high sheen as the marble statues on either side of the hallway. As we walked along the corridor, the professor got straight to business.

'As we discussed, Dr Franklin, I realise that we hired you to work on solutions but we think it's more important – and profitable – for you to investigate biological fibres instead.'

The professor's Lancashire accent was unmistakable.

'I received your letter, Professor…' I replied hesitantly.

'There's no need to fret, though,' he said before I could continue. 'I've reassigned you to deoxyribonucleic acid.'

'But the fellowship committee enlisted me to study solutions, not DNA.'

'That may be so, but you're needed here to work on this. We've made some fascinating progress. I have informed the fellowship committee of the change and expect they will be amenable.'

The ceilings in the main corridor of the university were vertiginous, as if they were designed to angle the students' ambitions north of their navels. The plaster was intersected by wrought-iron chandeliers midway between each buttress. Tall cabinets lined either side of the corridor. They were sparsely filled with leather-bound books. On closer inspection, these weren't encyclopaedias, but a collection of handwritten minutes from the senate. The hallowed names of science's great and good were engraved in the alabaster walls in an enclave off the main hallway. I searched among the names for Florence Nightingale.

While I was at pains not to disappoint my friend Charles Coulson, the professor had to know my doubts, in case he later found me to be a fraud; crystalline coal was a different substance entirely from organic specimens. Had I failed at the first hurdle, a chemist who had found herself unexpectedly thrust into a world of botany and flora? Familiar with my work on coal, Charles, an Oxford chemist whom I consulted with at the State Chemicals Lab in Paris, had recommended me for the job at King's College, much to the annoyance of the men in the office.

'There's something you should know,' I finally confessed.

'I know everything there is to know about your work at the Coal Board and diffraction studies in Paris. The fellowship committee was very thorough, and Charles said good things about you,' the professor replied.

'But you should also know, Professor, that I'm ignorant about anything... biological,' I stuttered, looking down at my shoes.

Professor Randall stopped and sighed. He turned to me, wearily, without lifting his hands from his pockets.

'The trouble is, Dr Franklin, biologists are ignorant about chemistry and physics. That's why we need you. They have none of the rigour that chemists and physicists have. Look,' he added, lowering his voice when someone passed us in the corridor, in a bid not to let anyone hear what he was going to say next. 'They laugh at us, you know.'

'Who, Professor?'

'The old guard. They've got no imagination at the Medical Research Council.'

He paused.

To the rest of the world, the professor's department at King's was a spectator sport, a big tent full of different disciplines. He'd assembled an eccentric melange of four biologists, two chemists, scores of biological and physical technicians, and two dozen graduates.

'We're a laughing stock to the older scientists. They call

my department "Randall's Circus". What I'm doing here is a new type of physics,' he continued. 'I call it biophysics. It's a mix of biology and physics, and it's the only way that we can get a handle on DNA's structure. If we can do that, then perhaps one day we will understand the genetic code.'

'Nucleic acids don't seem complex enough for such a grandiose purpose,' I said.

The professor started to hum to himself and walked on ahead. 'I suggest you read the work of Oswald Avery at the Rockefeller.'

'Do you mean his Frankenstein experiment?' I replied, scrambling to keep up with him.

'Precisely,' he said.

Before I had left London for Paris, it was noted in the periodicals that when Nobel nominee Oswald Avery mixed a denatured specimen of pneumonia with DNA, he'd resurrected the dead virus. The mice immediately dropped dead in his lab, and everyone was comparing him to Dr Frankenstein.

'Now, is it biblical, Dr Franklin? Or is it science?'

'But how can we be sure his sample wasn't contaminated with protein?' I asked after a second's contemplation.

'We cannot.' The professor tipped his head forward and quickened his speed. I sensed there was something he was not telling me. 'Anyway, I assure you that no other scientists here at the university are working on the DNA problem. You'll be given a doctoral student; he's already made some fine images.'

The professor talked quickly, as if he was trying to prevent me from having the time to reflect on what he was saying. The tendons in his neck protruded as he continued to drive stubbornly forwards, like a tortoise.

As he walked towards the stairwell at the other end of the corridor, the sound of his soles rapping against the parquet floor echoed in the hallway. We pivoted down the staircase, where the plaster gave way to bare brick, and the ceiling height halved.

The draught in the basement was bone-chilling and the

paint on the walls was flaking. Damp had dissolved it the same way rain macerated the trenches.

The professor's words became muffled sounds, as the walls appeared to close in around us. My throat grew dry and instinct told me to get above ground level. People often describe claustrophobia and agoraphobia as polar opposites. But while the first is the fear of enclosed spaces, and the latter the fear of the vast open world, to me they were different sides of the same coin. Fear is experienced the same: be it the fear of being alone and unable to cry for help; or the fear of being judged, or threatened, all are felt alike. When the panic strikes, in a darkroom or on the Metro, each step becomes as heavy as wading through particle soup. It feels as though people and things are pulling me into their orbits. It's only ever on a mountainside – with wide vistas all around – that I feel truly free.

'I want a specialist in X-ray diffraction. These biologists are comparatively poor at it.'

Professor Randall's voice punctured my thoughts and his face came back into sharp focus.

'You'll report directly to me,' he said. 'The samples from Switzerland give remarkably good fibre diagrams.'

The lab had sourced calf-thymus fibres from Professor Rudolf Signer at the University of Bern in Switzerland. There did not appear to be anything unusual about these remnants of the thymus gland on the surface of it, and the lab had not got particularly far in using them to decipher the structure of the DNA molecule, but through a series of controlled experiments, they could yet hold the key to life itself.

Inside a door at the near end of the basement corridor, a straight-backed man with a sandy moustache and a glint in his eye was fidgeting with his tools next to a woman leaning in his direction.

'Bruce, this is Dr Franklin. Don't mind us. We're just passing. Mary is Bruce's wife; she's preparing some herring specimens for us.'

The woman's eyes followed me around the room. Her

smile was as fixed as her no-nonsense stare. I wanted to ask if all the women in the lab were married but stopped myself before saying the words aloud. The couple glanced in each other's direction as we edged back towards the door.

'Drat.' A small voice sounded from across the corridor.

Through an open door opposite, I could see a man in spectacles twiddling the screws on a corroded brass cylinder: it looked like one of the collimators we used in Paris to focus X-ray beams onto a copper target. His curved shoulders appeared to melt into the machine. Without registering our presence, the man continued with what he was doing as if he had grown accustomed to not being noticed.

'Alec, this is Rosalind Franklin. She'll be joining our lab here at the university.'

By the time the timorous scientist acknowledged him, the professor had walked on again.

'Don't mind Stokes, he wishes to concern himself only with theory,' he muttered.

I wondered what he meant by his comment, assuming he must have thought me unworldly. But I said nothing. I did not want to portray naivety or risk having my softer side plied. I had already made that mistake, more than once.

In the middle of the far end of the corridor there was a pile of discarded cardboard. The professor had kept his surprise until last. The newly minted X-ray apparatus was standing there, gleaming, at the centre of the cellar's orbit. A spindly technician in a white lab coat asked where he should leave the empty boxes.

'The Rockefeller Institute has supplied most, if not all, of the equipment you wanted,' the professor said. 'I'll have Len set the camera to a low temperature, as you asked.'

'They haven't added a guard to the new Philips microcamera then.' I peered at the metallic apparatus, squinting at the dazzling reflections on its smooth surface.

'It appears not, though that way you can get closer to the beam,' he said.

The professor's words called to mind the warning my cousin had given me. Usually defiant, she'd begged me to heed her journalist husband's advice that the sponsors of my fellowship were manufacturing a potentially dangerous building material that had been associated with some cancers: asbestos. My research would be indebted to an industrial business in Manchester that specialised asbestos cement. Turner & Newall's proposed Midlands Works plant had recently got the go-ahead, despite a coughing spate among the builders. Until it was proven that the asbestos was causing the workers' illnesses, I could not afford to give up my research grant. I had earned it. It was a bigger disappointment than any other to learn that industry was rarely free from either politics or profit.

The professor's office at the end of the corridor was sparse except for a couple of copper taps and a ceramic sink. The desk had inbuilt gauges and dials but no drawers, and the perimeter of the room was lined with surplus worktops. He positioned himself on a wooden stool and tipped the contents from a brown envelope out onto the desk before him, then handed me a glass negative little bigger than a thumbnail.

'This, with all its spots, is your problem,' he said.

'What is it?' I peered at the tiny glass negative.

'DNA,' he replied.

The plate had come from the inside of the X-ray camera apparatus. It showed a few dispersed dots that seemed to have been positioned at random, making up a blurry image of the atoms in DNA. From this photograph alone, it would not be possible to determine the molecule's structure; at least not without clearer photographs, and more of them.

Professor Randall looked up and nodded in the direction of the doorway, where a dishevelled, flaxen-haired man was standing, looking bemused. Behind him was the timid physicist I had met minutes before.

'Get lost on your motorbike again, Gosling? Meet Dr Franklin. You'll be working with her from now on. Dr Franklin, this is Raymond Gosling.'

Raymond wasn't a large man, but he had the contented aura of someone who competed only with himself. Some scientists go into the profession because of good grades, or parental pressure, but he was in it for the thrill of the new; the adventure. He had joined the circus after all.

'What about Dr Wilkins? He's back in a few weeks,' he said.

'Dr Wilkins isn't any of your concern,' the professor replied curtly.

'These are like Professor Astbury's,' I said, thumbing the tiny glass negatives that were now scattered across the tabletop.

Dr Avery wasn't the only scientist on the circuit to have dabbled in DNA. Crystallographer Florence Bell, while toiling down the road in William Astbury's London lab – taking X-rays of keratin, the stuff of nails and hair – had said she'd unearthed the beginnings of life. She'd been mixing protein with nucleic acid from calf organs when it happened. Her supervisor, Astbury, was cautious and wary of her musings, chaining his theory firmly to the structural mechanics of the protein, absolving himself of her improbable claims. He said publicly that the ramshackle nucleotides were merely stacked like a pile of pennies.

'They're similar. We want clearer pictures,' the professor said, wringing his hands.

And so it began, my venture into unravelling some of DNA's most precious secrets.

| 2 |

Exposure

The chapel is as cool and dark as the catacombs. Gilding tinges the walls the colour of amber, the way that sunlight drenches and illuminates the inside of a pit cave. My office underneath the chapel is taller than it is wide. I hang a mirror on the wall to reflect light from the overhead windows into the room. Thin shafts of luminescence escape through the concrete barrier wall, a golden thread that connects the lab to the quad outside, which is remote from the confines of the laboratory. Dust coats the walls and the roof is leaky. Some of history's most important discoveries were made in these labs, though nobody would know to look at them now. They had little fanfare; instead, they lay in wait for future generations to find.

Joseph Lister once washed his surgical instruments with carbolic acid in the hospital wards north of the riverbank half a century ago, changing his butchering department of the healing art forever. But it wasn't until the printing press wrote of our plight that anyone on the street understood who had made the discoveries, or which felicitous geniuses had told fiction.

It is a Saturday and the only sound is of mice scuttling beneath the workbenches. I pull my cardigan tightly around my shoulders to ward off the chill. The train passengers on the

District line stood so close to each other this morning that the gravitational pull of their mass was palpable. I had forgotten the city's chill; the way no one looks each other in the eye on the Tube or apologises when they bump into you in the street. I miss the friendly faces in the City of Lights, the lively conversations, the doors held open while I was delivering four years of research papers to my supervisor.

I have saved for six months to buy a subscription to *Acta Crystallographica*, where my Paris paper will soon be published. The French State Chemical Lab's research director, Jacques. is Russian and of the view that governments should leave their citizens well alone. That extends to directors not being included in the work of their juniors. He is unlikely to want to be named in my paper. While he might admire the laissez-faire philosophy of French physiocrats, he loathes their materialism.

Since I left his lab in Paris, he has grown cool and remote, though perhaps if my paper is a triumph, then he'll have no choice but to notice me. I left when I heard of his affair. I could not stand to see the man I loved with another woman from the lab. He also has a wife, of course, but she is blind to his affairs. And yet I am unable to let go of the thought that we might one day be together. How stubborn the heart can be, though at least I am not alone in feeling like this. Take Simone de Beauvoir; although celebrity has meant that she could have her pick of lovers, she has chosen to continue to devote her affection to Jean-Paul Sartre.

What begins as a faint rattling outside my office that Saturday soon becomes impossible to ignore. In the basement corridor, the swing doors are shaking violently.

'What are you doing? I'll report you,' I tell the intruder through the shuttered doors.

'Easy, I'm a student here.'

As I unbolt the door, a man, no older than me, lifts his hands in the air feigning arrest.

'You nearly gave me a heart attack,' I say, clutching my chest. 'I didn't think anyone else was here on weekends.'

'It's the end-of-term exams coming up,' he says, hurrying down the corridor. 'I need to get something from my desk.'

I'm distracted; I have no time for an interruption.

A few minutes later the sound of footsteps – slow and measured – grows louder outside my office. My stomach and shoulders tighten. A ghostly image is reflected in the mirror above my desk. I gasp. In the periphery of my vision is a wiry figure clad in a grey suit.

'What's that dreadful sound?' The man's accent is Antipodean, with a slight Irish lilt.

'Just a student who forgot something. You must be Dr Wilkins; Raymond said you'd be returning from your holiday this week.' I stand to shake his hand.

The man's gait suggests his stoop has been moulded by frequently ducking from public view. His thick-rimmed spectacles are too large for his narrow face. He rocks his feet back and forth, straightening his shoulders, and elongating his spine. As he unfurls, his presence expands in the room, until his frame extends to a full six feet.

'Yes, and you must be Miss Franklin,' Maurice Wilkins says, tipping his head from side to side. His gaze falls on my shoulders, and up to my lips, before he looks away again.

'What's Professor Randall got you busy with? There are a few things we could use help with around here.'

There is an uncomfortable silence as I decide whether to let his address slide before he continues. 'Geoffrey and the others rarely work on weekends... I was thinking of going to the Strand Palace Hotel for lunch.' He then starts to mumble as if to cut the conversation in its tracks.

'Are you asking me to join you, Dr Wilkins?'

'Yes, I suppose I am,' he replies.

The Strand Palace Hotel, just a few hundred yards from the campus, is emblazoned in fluorescent lights. Below the sparkling pentagon-shaped façade is an opulent foyer, which is an oasis of art deco charm. Waiters flank either side of the entrance. Behind them is a pair of upholstered chaises longues. The furniture appears to be more for effect than for sitting on, as the seats remain pristine.

One of the waiters leads us through a walkway to a grand dining hall, where the chandelier inside is fit for a ballroom. We are seated opposite the roadside window. Maurice spends the first few minutes smoothing his napkin and straightening the cutlery that the waiter has painstakingly set in a line.

'Oliphant, at the University of Birmingham, first got me into science,' Maurice says, finally, breaking the silence.

He stares blankly in my direction. His eyes are glazed and his pupils have contracted to resemble tiny bullets.

'Mark Oliphant?' he repeats, imploring a response. His voice is just audible over the clatter of silver cutlery. By the time I realise that this is intended as a question, he goes on to say, 'He's working on nuclear fusion now. It could be the answer to all our energy needs. Oliphant was once lifted off the ground by a metallised balloon filled with gas. Imagine that. It took several men to stop him from floating off. It wasn't what I imagined science would be like when tinkering in the garden with my telescopes.'

Each time he speaks, I sink a little more inside. He does not wait for a reply.

When he was quite young, Maurice must have believed he could achieve anything. From the way he speaks about science, it seems he was raised to see scientists as hyaline heroes, ephemeral and untouchable. Although he says he enjoys experimentation, apathy has filtered through the crevices worn by age. He is only a few years older than me, and yet there is ennui in his voice.

'How is your meal?' the waiter asks, interrupting his diatribe.

'The starter was excellent,' I volunteer.

Maurice pushes his fork around his plate while the waiter clears the rest to make way for buttered potatoes and French beans.

'Oliphant was priest-like,' Maurice says as the main course arrives, not ceding an interruption.

'Yes?' I squirm.

'He supervised Randall at Birmingham on the magnetron, you know.'

There were rumours before I arrived in London that the physics professor had secured large quantities of funding because of his work on radar during the war.

'Do you mean Professor Randall's radar?'

'Radar won the war, you know,' Maurice says, ignoring my question.

'What about gas masks? At the Coal Board, we were making them impermeable to smoke,' I say.

I watch the cars roll past the window on the Strand. The drivers' faces are vacant, as though they are in a trance. I long to be one of them, to be at the wheel of a journey and to know my destination.

Maurice clears his throat. 'Yes, and I'm sure that was very important too, but we couldn't have won the war without the atomic bomb,' he says.

'I thought you said radar...'

'Churchill wouldn't have backed the Manhattan Project if the bomb weren't vital. Come on, Rosy.'

An image flashes on the screen of my mind of Spitfires spiralling to the ground. My hands become cold and clammy. I'm immediately transported to the time when my claustrophobia was most vivid. My parents had sent me to stay with their friends near Bexhill-on-Sea. A poster in the train station read: *Children are better off in the country; leave them there*. The thought of my parents seeing me as a child, even though I was going to turn twenty that summer, was wincing.

At first, the stay in the farmhouse was pleasant. The kitchen was lined with cracked green glazed tiles and had a big oak dining table in the middle of it. My parents' friends were often out running errands, and sometimes miscalculated their rations. They made frequent trips back and forth to the grocer.

Over breakfast one morning, I heard a strange whirring noise. It sounded like the engine of a plane. Outside the kitchen window, a Spitfire was spinning southwards like a corkscrew, leaving a trail of white smoke behind it. The plane fell in a blur of khaki, blue, red and yellow, and a small grey dot evacuated from its hump. There was no time to run outside to the Anderson shelter. So I hid under the table and watched as the sky turned black.

I could just make out, within the smoke, a second fighter plane spinning as it fell. My heart felt as though it would jump out of my chest. I was overcome with dread: a suffocating sensation, almost as if an invisible hand were pressing me into its palm.

Unable to scream, the beating in my ears was loud and palpable; it could only have been the force of survival. Then a thunderous noise tore through the atmosphere. The house quaked as a third plane seemed to crash into it with force. A deathly silence fell, before the whirring noise of a propeller started up again.

I tried to call my father on the house line, but it was no use. The phone was dead. A cable must have been unearthed by the crash. I sat there for what seemed like an eternity, wondering what my parents' friends would say about the inevitable damage that had been done to the house in their absence.

Although the house was not hit directly, the affray was reported on the news that night. Reporters were talking about the 'Battle of Britain', the aerial conflict that had British forces shooting down German aircraft over southern England; I shuddered at the thought of how close the plane had been to the farmhouse. After that day, I never let anything, people included, get too close. When they did, or whenever I found myself in a small space or crowd, it felt confining, just as it had when the Spitfires had trapped me under the kitchen table that afternoon. My father soon set about marketing indoor air raid shelters in his spare time.

'Are you all right? You looked as though you wandered off there for a moment,' Maurice says.

Whether it was intentional or not, his question feels like an accusation.

'How can you defend the bomb?' I ask.

'Well,' he says, pushing his glasses back onto his nose. 'I worked on the Manhattan Project. That's how I met my wife. She was American.'

'I'm sorry for your loss, Dr Wilkins.'

'Oh no, she's not dead.'

He looks me in the eye for the first time that afternoon.

'You have her hair, you know,' he says, pulling off his glasses and blowing on to the lens.

'Whose?'

'My wife's.' He draws his elbows close to his chest.

'People are talking about neutralism in Paris,' I say, changing the subject. 'The *New Statesman* covered it.'

He shakes his head. 'Sometimes, Rosy, staying neutral just isn't an option.'

Maurice had worked on the bomb at the time when the government was pumping all of its resources into winning the war. The costly atom bomb left the country nearly destitute; millions of homes were destroyed and a quarter of homes did not have any access to running water.

Politics was such a big word for a simple concept. At its root, it was just a tussle for power. Without weapons, it would be no more sophisticated than a fight for turf at one end of a garden, or a spat between neighbours over the fence, enlarged on to a grandiose scale. It was a revolving door of dictatorships, revolutions, socialism, liberalism and conservatism, in succession. From barbarism to pluralism, every type of society was destined to repeat itself in future iterations with the constant swing of time's pendulum.

The Parisians hadn't told themselves the same bold narrative of winning the war that the British had, even though they'd lived through a land invasion. The atomic bombs at Hiroshima and Nagasaki, rather than set the world's atmosphere on fire as some had predicted, had made most people more protective of peace. Many of us wanted to keep it that way.

'Bombing won't stop conflict from flourishing in the gaps between human ideologies,' I say, plotting my excuses to leave.

'It's silly to think that Britain would be unharmed by being neutral,' Dr Wilkins replies, looking around the room for the nearest waiter.

'I hope to never again see a bomb in my lifetime,' I say, laying down my napkin to leave.

I rush out into the hotel lobby, wiping tears from my eyes. 'The ladies',' offers one of the waiters, pointing at the powder room opposite the entrance to the dining hall.

Inside the bathroom, I clutch the cool porcelain of the sink to gain my balance. But as my thoughts turn to the many lives that have been lost, and how I nearly lost my own in Bexhill, I feel the ground give way beneath me. Breathing heavily, I lean down and rest my cheek against the sink, allowing my body to collapse around it. My mind is numb; all I can feel is the cold, hard surface against my skin. Unable to face going outside, I rest my limbs against the tangible porcelain surface and wait. The lunch has taken an hour off my work.

| 3 |

Forsaken Ones

Donovan Court, 107 Drayton Gardens, Fulham, London, March 1951

My oldest brother grunts as he helps me carry the walnut chest of drawers that Father gave me up the concrete steps to number 22 Donovan Court. The chest is all I have to furnish my new flat, along with a faded puce velvet armchair and a Victorian dining table and chairs donated by my aunts. The block, which is located north of the Fulham Road on Drayton Gardens, is on the more desirable side of Fulham, but the less appealing side of Chelsea, something our cousins do not let me forget.

'Colin says he's sorry he couldn't make it up to help,' David says softly of our middle brother.

'It's not as though Father offered either,' I reply.

David stays quiet. My father had vowed never again to help me cart my books to a new apartment after I once asked him to rescue my many French textbooks from the Blitz.

'Can you believe the deposit was so high? It seems barely legal,' I say to David while heaving the underside of the chest up the steps.

'You said you could make up the rent,' he says.

'Only with a bit of help from Mother and Father.'

That night, I arrange my ornaments in a line on the overmantel of the marble fireplace. They must be just so, or I feel off-kilter. Ever since I returned to London from Paris, I have felt that I must arrange my things with precision, to bring good luck. If I don't, only I can be held responsible for any accidents or misfortune.

As night falls in Donovan Court, I lie alone on the mattress staring up at the ceiling. I can hear a faint jangling noise outside the apartment building. It is similar to the sound that my father's car keys made in his pockets when he came home from work every night to our house in Pembridge Place.

I lift a book, translated from Italian, that Colin sent me while I was living in Paris, from beside the mattress. It begins in Eboli, a coastal town in southern Italy. The doctor who wrote it, Carlo Levi, feared morality had missed all of the towns beyond the ailing train line, leaving the former idylls of Grassano and neighbouring Aliano bereft of resources. The townspeople didn't trust either the doctors or the priests, who had many and varied indiscretions. So they resorted to superstitions to keep the spread of malaria at bay. As I read the book that evening, I realise how misled they were. Religion should be a consolation for people in times of distress and on their deathbeds. Science and medicine's goal, to the contrary, is to extend life. I begin to marvel at how, since the Aztecs and pagans, superstitions have sought to combat unpredictability in the outside world, and instead only changed human behaviour. Ever since astrologers started naming stars, we've been trying to navigate our lives by them, like seafarers trying to find our way home. Customs, if they were to be believed, could influence everything from crops to marriage and childbirth, and even death. Then came science. It was the only provable way of predicting and measuring the world, and the most reliable way of staving off illnesses, including malaria. Botched operations and radium burns are only the exceptions, but they help prove the rule, not discredit it.

Exhausted, half an hour later I fold the corner of the page and throw the book onto the other side of the bed. Nothing is more delicious at that moment than to simply lie there and soak in my newfound freedom.

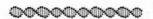

The next morning, sunlight filters through the curtains, bathing my bedroom in an amber glow. I savour the moment, brushing the underside of the Egyptian cotton sheets with my toes before getting out of bed and preparing myself for the day ahead. In Greece, people say that if you are on time, you are English. Punctuality is a preserve of the British. It leaves little scope for compromise and even less time for acting on impulse. Most days in Paris, I would get up early in the morning and paint my lips with Clarins lipstick, sometimes daubing cologne onto my neck. A few minutes here or there made little difference to my work. Indeed, it was seen as rude if I got in half an hour early to the lab, as I had done while I was working at the Coal Board before moving to Paris. Similarly, it was viewed as English if I left work before everybody else. In London, there is no time for lipstick or cologne. Besides, the crumbling transport system is far too unreliable not to plan your journey with care. My mother says I don't need make-up anyway. So the first thing I do is pin my loose curls to keep them from my eyes, and fling on a laundered lab coat.

When I get downstairs, a letter covered with French stamps is lying on the mat by the entrance to the block. The back of my neck fizzes with bubbles of elation, which travel up my spine to the crown of my head. What if it's from him? The handwriting looks familiar, but many senior scientists with tenure share a similarly illegible scrawl. There's no time to open the letter, so I put it on the mantelpiece in the hallway to read later that evening when I return from the lab.

On my cycle route along the South Bank, sunbeams have left a diffuse halo above the River Thames. There is a sweetly optimistic breeze in the air that morning.

'Your pen got lost under the X-ray tube, Dr Franklin,' Raymond says as he peeks his head around the corner of my office door, sheepishly, when I get in.

'Never mind,' I reply while reviewing my diary for the day.

Raymond's mouth drops open in disbelief at my nonchalance.

'What's the matter? Be careful the wind doesn't change, or you might stay like that,' I tell him.

I draw a circle around the crystallography conference in Stockholm on the list of international symposia for the year. American scientist Linus Pauling from the California Institute of Technology will be unveiling his new theory of proteins there. Given Florence Bell's reflections on the beginnings of life, it is only prudent to understand how keratin and nucleic acid interact. Perhaps Jacques will be there. Since seeing the letter in the hallway this morning, all I can imagine is that it's from him. I cannot let him disappoint me, again.

'What's that awful smell?' I ask Raymond while assembling my stationery.

The stench is as strong as the smell of the fish that my brothers caught in the Norwegian fjords before the war, but even more putrid.

'Mary's herrings. She's extracting their DNA,' says Raymond.

'I thought Professor Randall said no one else was working on the problem.'

'Mary and Bruce are doing their own infrared studies. No one else is on X-rays. Not now,' he says.

'What do you mean not now?'

'Not since Dr Wilkins and I were taking them,' says Raymond.

A chilling feeling that I'm not privy to some of the lab's

secrets makes my skin crawl. I begin to doubt whether I heard the professor correctly. Perhaps it's my mental acuity that's waning. Either that or the territoriality with Maurice could have perhaps been avoided. After our lunch together at the Strand, he approached me just once to discuss a paper. I could only just make out what he was saying. His eyes were darting around the room as he made repeated attempts to deflect my gaze. He said the DNA fibres stretched at the shoulder, explaining he was working on a paper with Bruce, with no mention of Mary. He was clearly reaching for answers, something that would explain the pattern of the fibres, and was presumably hoping that I could fill in the missing pieces. He seemed to be soliciting ideas for his work, for which I was unlikely to receive any credit, since it didn't sound at all like Mary would be named in their paper either.

I shut the lab door to prevent cross-contamination and set about finding the structure of DNA myself. My plan is to create a map of the molecule, though how I will do this is not yet certain. It will involve careful observation, and taking note of every chemical – indeed, every atom – in the molecule, and its position. If Astbury's assistant, Florence, is to be believed, then DNA could be significant in revealing some of the deepest mysteries of life itself – and to understand its secrets, there can be no shortcuts. Every atom, every angle of light, must be meticulously recorded, to know its shape. My colleagues have already taken the first steps by examining DNA under a microscope. I want to go one step further and take clearer X-ray photographs of the molecule than have been taken before. Existing photographs of the molecule are, by and large, fuzzy and diffuse. They cannot give us any real clues about the molecule's true structure. In order to find it, I must first record its parameters and take high-resolution pictures that will yield its true nature. My first objective is to make the humidity in the lab stable; unless the conditions are right, we will miss the anomaly. I must find and record the optimal conditions for the apparatus to perform at its best, and to ascertain DNA's structure. I will map every atom in detail, to learn its hidden configuration. Anomalies are what scientists exist for, they are the plots and coordinates to a discovery. All the minutia, from the solutions that the fibres are dissolved in, to the temperature they are heated to and how fast they are heated... all conditions affect crystal growth. Ensuring that the conditions are stable will be key to the accuracy of our experiments.

'We must deliver the hydrogen at a set temperature to regulate the humidity of the fibres,' I say.

'This'll do the trick,' Raymond replies, holding up a piece of twisted rubber.

I feel warmth rise and swell in my cheeks. 'Where did you get that?'

'Uncle Maurice gave it to me,' Raymond says, unperturbed.

A condom had been tied loosely around the apparatus with a paper clip.

'He's your uncle?'

'It's what all the students call Dr Wilkins when his head's turned.'

Shock had temporarily clouded my thinking. It is increasingly transparent that Dr Wilkins is not the shy person that everyone says he is.

The condom-bandaging technique hasn't even been rigorously applied. The apparatus is still hissing, meaning hydrogen is escaping from the edges.

'Let's try something new,' I suggest. 'The builders have left dust sheets out in the courtyard. We can use them to map out the location of the atoms.'

Raymond goes outside to find some dust sheets in the quad. Minutes after returning, he is struggling to position one of the sheets against the plaster.

'Left, a bit further.'

'How's holding a sheet up against a wall going to help us?' he asks.

'Have faith,' I say. 'Once we project the X-ray image onto

the sheet, we'll be able to see the atoms. Then we can map them out, like so.'

Our experiment quickly backfires. The image is skimming off the edge of the sheet and onto the brickwork, rendering it impossible to see the atomic configuration of the molecule.

'Stop moving,' I insist.

'I'm not, Dr Franklin. Do you want me to see if Dr Stokes can help?'

'No. I have another idea.'

In order to photograph the specimens, we must angle the camera directly at the copper target on the X-ray apparatus. Only by doing that will we be able to produce clearer photographs of the molecule. The existing photographs are diffuse, with atoms scattered unevenly around the edges. The only way to take more precise X-rays of the DNA strands is by angling the beam directly through the centre of the fibres.

The engineers stare at me gormlessly as I walk past their quarter of the cellar. I feel the same sensation that I feel every time I am underground or in a darkroom, that familiar panic. It suffocates my arms, chest and shoulders. I fix my eyes on to the horizon to allay it until my facial muscles are uncomfortably taut.

On the other side of the basement, the waft of herrings is replaced by the smell of algae from the fish tanks where they and various amphibians are bred to test drugs and use in other scientific experiments. The technicians' door is ajar. It gives the illusion that somebody is on hand around the clock. Yet, as I quickly learn, anybody who tests it is met with a condemning growl.

'Who might you be?' Deputy technician Len is astounded that anyone would break the unspoken rule.

'This is Dr Franklin.' Raymond appears behind me, catching his breath.

'Nice to make your acquaintance, s'pose,' Len says, gesturing for us to sit down.

'We met once before, do you remember? Professor Randall introduced us.'

A hint of a smile softens the corners of his eyes once he's in his seat with his familiar tools at hand, sifting through a pile of paperwork. 'How can I help you?'

'The microcamera isn't fit for purpose,' I start.

'The new Philips is giving us some problems. It's knocking the ray out of line,' Raymond says, qualifying my explanation. I can describe the problem well enough, I think, but elaborating further would only complicate things.

It does not seem to be in Len's nature to promise the world, though this may well be a force of habit from needing to manage the expectations of droves of inquisitive students. The unintended side effect is, it seems, that he under-promises.

It's not long before a drawing emerges on the page in front of him of a pyramid structure. His graphite scrawls are thick and deep.

'I'm not sure if I explained it properly. We need an adjustable camera stand,' I say.

'Leave it to me.' Len pleads for us to leave.

Outside his office, the smell of algae is as pungent as ever.

'There's something I forgot to tell you,' Raymond says as we walk back to my office.

'Was it that none of the men around here are able to look a woman in the eye, just at their stockings?'

'No, not that,' he says.

'Then what is it?'

'It's Dr Wilkins,' Raymond says, hanging his head. 'I ran into him in the corridor on the way to see Len. He asked me to tell you that the condom was working perfectly well before…'

'Are those his words?'

'He's very clever really,' Raymond whispers once we are out of earshot of the engineers.

'You also said he's shy and he doesn't seem very shy to

me. I don't think any scientist who worked on the atomic bomb can be shy.'

There is an awkward silence.

'He was in the Cambridge Anti-War Group at university,' Raymond says finally.

The last thing I expected was that the man who had spent a lunch hour trying to convince me of the virtues of the atomic bomb could possibly be against war.

'Science must be bittersweet for him then,' I say.

'He has an inner drive, you know,' Raymond replies. 'His sister ended up in a wheelchair after a bout of septicaemia. Antibiotics were the only thing that could cure it.'

Dr Wilkins hadn't mentioned anything about his family except for his ex-wife.

'Antibiotics have been used since long before the war,' I say.

'Not in New Zealand,' Raymond replies, smacking his lips firmly shut. 'His father was a schoolmaster there. Though he's never mentioned New Zealand, or communism come to that, not since what happened to Philby.'

'Philby?'

'From Cambridge, he's scarpered to Paris. Everyone thinks he's a spy. I don't mean Dr Wilkins is a spy…'

'Of course not, or Professor Randall wouldn't have sent him to the conference in Naples to represent the lab in his place.'

Dr Wilkins and the professor had had a stand-up row in the lab earlier that week. Both men raised their voices. The resident scientist towered above the diminutive professor, and that meant he often got his way.

'They get along much better than that usually,' Raymond says, bringing it up again.

'What, in the men's common room?'

He pauses.

'Yes,' he replies, looking visibly embarrassed.

'Tell me about Dr Wilkins's wife,' I ask him as we get to my office.

'An art student. Divorced him and wouldn't let him see their son. Why?'

'He said I looked like her, or that I had her hair, or some other nonsense.'

Raymond continues to fill me in as we settle back down to work. From what he says, Dr Wilkins lusted for a life that is very different to the one he inhabits. He regularly doodles on his notes, sometimes sending cartoons of our lab's experiments to his friends in Cambridge. Many of his friends are artists or dancers, though as for him, his grey suits lack any artistic flair. It is almost as though, by conforming so rigidly, he has become straitjacketed.

| 4 |

Shooting Stars

King's College London, The Strand, May 1951

'There's something I must ask you.'

The professor's body is hunched over a microscope in his study. He looks as though he's about to devour the specimen beneath it, willing the rest of the world to disappear and leave him alone with the dancing orbs under the glass. I have staked out his office all morning, reasoning that if I am right there in front of him, he will have no choice but to hear me out. Now that I have rent to pay, I cannot afford to go to the event in Stockholm without money to spare, so I resolve to remind the professor of all the reasons why he should send me to Stockholm, and not Maurice. However, intention, as ever, is lost in the face of the unexpected.

'Do you remember when I started here, you said no one else was working on DNA?'

'Did I?' Professor Randall replies, standing up from his leather chair. He lifts his jacket from the back of the seat. 'Let's walk and talk,' he says.

The professor excels at extracting himself from awkward conversations. He walks on, leaving a stride of distance between us.

Despite my earlier resolve, his actions have the effect of making me doubt whether I, a woman, can be the advocate for the lab that the professor wants. I can do the necessary work, of course, but could I persuade the sceptics in person? It already feels like an almighty trial getting anybody to listen, or give me breath enough to state the facts, even the professor.

'There's a conference in Stockholm and I think it will be very beneficial if I go. Professor Pauling from the American lab will be speaking and I really would learn a lot.'

I press my notepad into my crimson skirt so the loose pages don't fall out.

The professor continues to walk on ahead.

'Maurice is perfectly capable of handling it. Where have you got to with the DNA work?' he asks.

My mind is busy with a thousand thoughts, none of which I am able to formulate out loud. At the sight of the common room, I feel a lump in my throat.

'We need a camera stand,' I say, swallowing.

'Well, when that's working, then come and speak to me,' the professor says. 'Maurice is somewhat *mature*; I want him to represent the lab. It's not personal,' he adds, walking nose first into the men-only coffee room.

I am unable to gather my arguments on the spot in the face of what seem like insurmountable deflections. Feeling dejected and unheard, I plan to write him a letter. If I can put into writing all of the things that I didn't have a chance to say to him this morning, then maybe he will choose to send me to Stockholm after all.

But, when night comes, instead of composing a letter to the professor, I fall asleep, depleted, on my bed still wearing my red skirt with my pencil on my lap.

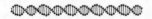

The next day, I am kneeling by the apparatus to align the microcamera with the X-ray tube, when the tranquillity in the lab is disturbed by an almighty crash. A helmet rolls across the floor in front of me until the buckle catches, visor-side up, on its rim. Raymond leans down to rescue the stray motorcycle helmet.

'I thought I was going to fall off the thing,' says Maurice, who is standing behind him.

'What do you think it was like for me carrying you on the back?' Raymond fawns.

'How was the Stazione Zoologica?' I ask, straining to reach my neck above the apparatus.

Maurice has just returned from a conference on the submicroscopic structure of protoplasm in Naples.

'Naples is a very cultured city,' he says while toying with the helmet in his hands like it's a ball.

Cultural initiations are prerequisites in some circles. Indeed, the interview for Cambridge demanded that prospective students had superfluous knowledge of the arts, notably fine art, the opera and ballet, as well as prestigious areas of the humanities, for example, niche movements in literature or politics. It wasn't enough that I understood the basic elements of science. The interview demanded that I was able to distinguish a Van Gogh from a Monet, and Mozart from Vivaldi. In truth, music gives me vertigo. Notes carry the soul adrift as if it were untethered. Listening to music feels like riding a wave or being lost at sea. I prefer the real world, the immovable mountainside and the tangible shoreline. The natural world holds more than enough secrets to keep me satiated for a lifetime.

'The galleries were formidable, and the young women were simply breathtaking,' Maurice trumpets the details of his excursion to Raymond.

I clear my throat. He is so casual with his words. This nod and a wink are subject to an exclusive membership, which relies on not being female. It is a declaration of being at the head of the food chain and everything else in it. Apart from Bruce's wife Mary, the only other woman that Maurice has ever worked with is the younger sister of a friend of his old professor, Oliphant, and he'd once asked Mary out for dinner before she and Bruce began dating.

It isn't that the women in the lab don't also talk, but you wouldn't hear Dame Honor Fell from the Strangeways Lab discussing the professors' beauty when she comes to speak to us every month. She regularly lectures the physics graduates on biology and is the only existing female adviser to the Medical Research Council. Whenever she takes us to the Strand for lunch, our conversations are never like theirs or about anything personal. That is something of a relief. I have been at the lab for just five months and there is little of my private life that I want to divulge to colleagues. There is an unspoken rule – women don't talk about our private lives at work. We have too much to lose.

Visiting professor Dame Fell has never married. I wonder now if that is a life that she has chosen for herself, rejecting any proposals that have come her way, or whether life has simply led her down that path. I know so little of her inner life and suspect the men's conversations often fall prey to bluster.

Another woman once told me that she hadn't made a single decision in her entire life. She had always gone where life had taken her. She was happy and said that she had lived a good life, yet you would never catch a man saying that he had lived a life that wasn't of his own choosing. Generous to a fault, she spent the whole of her life taking care of others until the day she died. She left this world without ever feeling that she had a say in the forces that dictated her life path. This may have been because of a belief that stirred in her soul in serendipity, kismet or fate. At her core she remained free and uncaged, her extensive bookshelf told as much. She believed that people should travel where the wind took them as freely and easily as cottonwood snow drifts on a zephyr. The people who loved her say her love still echoes in their hearts. If only she had ever felt that she had a choice.

'Did you learn anything scientific, have any meetings of minds?'

'Don't be such a prude, Rosy,' Maurice says. He purses his lips, expressing bitter disapproval.

He takes a step forward, his hands in his pockets with the helmet still wedged underneath his elbow.

'Jim Watson, a young gentleman there, was very excited about my talk. I found him to be very interesting in the calmer environs outside the conference. Luria set him up with a research gig at the Cavendish. He had a word with Bragg, you know how it is.'

From what he is saying, it seems that the distant lodestar of this Jim's career was his thesis supervisor, a microbiologist in Italy called Salvador Luria. Through him, Maurice says, the young man in Naples had met the head of the Cavendish lab in Cambridge where he now works.

Likewise, Maurice's ties with Professor Oliphant – at Birmingham – had set him up with a job for life with Professor Randall. Theirs is a network that is fortified by age.

Without access to the communal common room, getting to Stockholm seems impossible.

'Were there any women at the event?' I ask.

'Jim brought his sister, quite the beauty,' Maurice says. 'She liked our photos of DNA very much. Jim said they inspired him to look at nucleic acid.'

'He's a chemist, is he?'

'Not exactly, no. Biology's more his thing.'

Maurice continues to loom over my work, still clutching the helmet under his elbow, with his hands in his pockets.

'Are you going to offer to help?' I ask, handing him a screwdriver.

'I've just got some things to be getting on with,' he replies, gravitating towards the door.

'He must be working on his new microscope design,'

Raymond says apologetically as he picks up the screwdriver, sets his own helmet aside, and leans down to assist.

II

BEFORE

| 5 |

Exodus

Fjærland, Norway, August 1939

The cerulean sky is endless, broken only by the umbriferous mountain peaks beyond the bright outline of the cabin hotel. It is mid-August and the evergreens are coated with the same iridescent dew that's glistening on the floor of the Norwegian valley. Birds are singing above the canopy and the fish are flashing their rainbow display above the turquoise waters of the fjord. Moose live in the forest; I saw them grazing on our last trip to Fjærland. But the marshland is desolate on this unforgettable last day, without a mammal in sight.

'Last up the glacier loses,' David crows across the marsh.

My eldest brother's dimples deepen as he smiles. With the crease of his elbow, he wipes his brow and scrapes back his razor-cut fringe, slinging the day's catch of fish over his shoulder.

As I get closer, his net sack smells like seaweed that's been left out in the sun to decompose. Through the clearing, the grey silhouette of the mountains frames the burgundy cabin by the lake. My socks are still claggy from trekking through the forest, and my boots are searing the sores on my ankles.

David is planning to climb the glacier in the snow-capped mountain range this afternoon. I plan to go with him.

As we approach the cabin, the sound of Father's voice is warbling in the nearby trees. His baritone vocals echo around the pitched roof of the hotel porch.

Colin races from behind me towards the door and trips on a grassy knoll. He is sometimes mistaken for one of the refugees from Europe as his unruly mop of light hair is unlike either of my other two brothers'. He is the shortest of the three, so people presume he is the youngest, even though he's three years older than Roland. This infuriates him, and so he sticks largely to his books. Roland laughs and ruffles Colin's hair as he bends down to dust mud from his calf. Colin looks vexed.

'Serves you right, for the time you hit me with a cricket bat,' I tell him, tucking fine flyaway strands of chocolate-brown hair that have fallen in front of my eyes behind my ears.

'What, more than a decade ago?' Colin says.

'Don't worry, Roland will get his comeuppance,' David tells Colin.

'David.'

'He can take it, can't you, Roly?' David replies with a broad smile, designed to neutralise my disapproval.

Roland runs into the hotel, hungry for breakfast. The sound of his feet thudding on the wooden porch reverberates around the beams on the ceiling. Inside, the foyer is empty. It isn't unusual to see people waiting there, queuing to be checked into their rooms or to book for dinner. This new pace of life has been hard for Father to adjust to. He is sitting in the dining area near the entrance to the hotel trying to get the wireless on the window ledge to work. The transistor hasn't detected the frequency of any English-speaking station.

When growing up, I thought he was a handsome man. He wore his dark hair in a side parting, framing his round eyes and chevron moustache. Yet with age, he has the mordant temperament of a man who gave up on his dreams for a life of dutiful servitude. He sacrificed his ambitions of studying science at Oxford to lead infantry on the front line. When the Great War was over, he joined Keyser Bank in Milk Street with Grandpa.

'The BBC must have hidden its signal,' Father says.

To us, it's not surprising that the wireless doesn't work. Norway is the farthest from home we have travelled. Father shakes the wooden box. We know better than to interrupt him when he's toying with his gadgets. Doing so would usually result in a swift dressing-down. Roland collapses his bony limbs onto the wooden floor of the foyer, dissatisfied.

'Quiet, I'm getting a signal,' Father says as he twists the dial clockwise. 'If I just turn it this way.'

The crepitating transistor makes a crackling sound.

'Former enemies have… buried the hatchet,' a shrill voice screeches through the white noise. 'The Germans have struck a peace pact with Russia.'

The ivory sclera in my father's eyes bears down on his irises and his olive skin drains of colour.

'Shh,' he says, craning his neck to hear the reporter's voice.

My mother wanly arches her eyebrows as she returns my father's gaze.

Within a few minutes, one of the hotel attendants passes and whispers a few words in my father's ear. His response is sudden. 'David, pack your bags. Help your sisters. Now,' he says with one hand still on his knee.

Colin is leafing through his book, *The Family from One End Street*, undeterred, while my sister Jenifer is still eating.

'But why? We're miles from Germany,' I protest. 'Maybe now the Germans will leave Danzig alone.'

A Polish customs inspector was arrested in the autonomous state of Danzig near Poland earlier this month. To me a peace pact sounds like a good thing. Peace has been the goal of the royal tour after all. If the Germans are willing to make peace with their neighbours, perhaps it bodes well for everybody.

'Listen, Rosalind, it's not safe here,' Father says.

But then the wireless hisses, before the reporter bleats, '...a devastating blow... to Britain.'

| 6 |

Leviticus

5 Pembridge Place, Notting Hill, London, September 1939

'Did you see him?' Evi asks, grazing the elbow of her woollen jumper against the iron gate on our return several days later.

She had stayed in England with Nanny, rather than come to Norway. Father said it was too dangerous for refugees to travel to the continent.

Evi was just nine when she arrived in England to live with us earlier this year. She'd been on the waiting list at the refugee centre where my mother volunteered. When she arrived, she was alone except for a suitcase. She was sent straight upstairs to share a room with my younger sister Jenifer. We were instructed to refer to her father, who was interned at a camp in Buchenwald, only as Mr Ellis, and to never again utter the name Eisenstädter. According to Mother's friend at the refugee centre, a fifth of the camp's prisoners had gone missing. They were suspected to have died, or worse. There were whispers in polite company of the abhorrent treatment that prisoners were forced to endure at Buchenwald, the Nazis' largest concentration camp; inhumane 'experiments' sacrilegiously committed under the guise of science. Many of the people interned and enslaved at the camps were starved and shot, and anyone who had come into contact with the camp's survivors would grow pale and wild-eyed as they recounted how prisoners were poisoned by plumes of toxic gases in droves. It was enough to turn the stomachs of even those with the toughest of constitutions.

My great-uncle Herbert, whom Evi stayed with before coming to live with us, is tall and serious, with bold features that have lasted into his old age. We know better than to ask him impertinent questions. He was once leader of the Liberal Party, though we know little of his life before that. He was posted to Palestine but never spoke about it.

'Not this time, Evi,' Father replies, exchanging looks with my mother.

He slams the boot of the Austin and unwinds the canvas roof in a concertina motion.

Evi looks up at him. Her top lip is quivering.

'Maybe next time,' Father says as he hauls the luggage into the tiled hallway of our house in Notting Hill.

A few days later I go to find David to ask what I will need to take with me to university for the new term if Newnham reopens. I barely recognise his voice, which is hoarse and strained, as though he hasn't slept at all.

'Leave me alone,' he says impatiently through a crack in his bedroom door.

When I walk downstairs I find my mother dialling the rotary phone on the walnut sideboard. Her hands are shaking. After putting the receiver down, she marches into the kitchen and lights the copper kettle. The din of the wireless is audible from the hallway.

From there, I can see my father sitting in his upholstered armchair in the living room, hunched over and resting his elbows on his knees. He is looking intently at Colin, who is bolt upright on the mahogany and linen sofa. Colin's face is ashen.

'What's happened?' I whisper.

'Shh,' my mother says, with an ear to the air, as she tries to tune into the sound of the wireless.

The noise of the radio is meanwhile being drowned out by the whistling kettle.

'Chamberlain will be speaking in a minute,' she says, carrying an enamel tray laden with bone china cups and saucers into the living room.

As she puts the tray on the coffee table, Colin gets up, passing me in the hall without saying a word. My parents are too busy speaking to relatives all morning to answer any of my questions. The atmosphere is laced with electric charge.

That afternoon, the ticking noise of the overmantel clock dwarfs the thrum as Roland reaches forwards to turn on the cathedral radio. We've assembled by the wireless to listen to the prime minister speak.

'No such undertaking has been received,' Chamberlain says. An infinite pause swallows the air from the room.

Germany didn't withdraw troops from Poland, so the country is at war. The news stultifies my brothers and that night we eat in silence.

Colin puts his knife and fork down on his plate abruptly over dinner and retreats to the room he shares with Roland. David then excuses himself from the table to my father's dismay. Father watches through the open door as my brothers head upstairs before turning to me.

'Have you finished your accounts?' he asks officiously, with no mention of the bigger forces at play.

From a young age, he has tried to instil in us a sense of

responsibility, insisting regularly that we take care of our finances.

'I will, before I go back to college,' I reply, getting up to take my plate to Mother's maid in the kitchen next door.

No sooner have the words spilled from my mouth than my mother gestures for me to be silent with a wave of her hand.

'Why can't you consider a more ladylike subject?' Father asks. 'Like sociology.'

'But there's little else I'm good at other than chemistry,' I protest, placing my plate back on the table.

The purple shades in Father's face deepen. He has become rigid and conformist with age. Much of his busyness seems to deflect attention away from his own unhappiness. His own father was a banker, so his family was never short of food or clothes, but austerity after the crash made money taboo. His family had emigrated from Breslau in Poland to England two centuries ago, doing away with small luxuries. In Poland there was a common local phrase, '*przy szabasowych świecach*', meaning money is mud, but mud isn't money. Money doesn't buy happiness, but it's worse without it.

From the long silences at dinner, I surmise that Father will insist that my brothers enlist in the war effort. Roland is too young to go to the front line, at least for now. Yet from the look I saw on David's face, I have no doubt that my eldest brother will be forced to sign up, if not by my father then by the state.

| 7 |

Sisterhood

Cambridge University, October 1939

'Gentlemen,' the don brays in the august tone that marks every reverent occasion at the University of Cambridge.

I tiptoe around the edge of the mahogany-panelled auditorium. The room's hum morphs into a hive of whispers. The seats in the Maxwell theatre are arranged in rows along a sloping arc. We Newnham residents must sit at the front, the university rules dictate.

All of the men in the auditorium are wearing red and black gowns. Their drapery is a reminder that we are students of the women's college, not the university itself. As I search for an empty seat, the light above the lectern blinds me; it's as though I'm standing in the glare of every student in the room. One of the men exhales sharply though the presiding don doesn't register the insult. He can't have heard above the clamour.

Gertie's smile falters as she hesitates and turns in my direction.

'Go on,' I whisper, seeing her stop, bewildered by the crowd.

My heart leaps into my throat and a tight sensation snakes around my neck as I take my seat in the front row.

'Do we have P. L. Wilmore of King's College, Cambridge?' the don asks as he counts names on the register, pausing for the perfunctory response.

'R. E. Franklin, of Newnham?'

I stand up cautiously, gathering the hem of my skirt.

'Give us a twirl, like the girls at Homerton,' the man in the row behind sniggers.

Involuntary tremors seize my legs. I am like a rabbit in the headlights. I am prey. I freeze, speechless to defend myself. The man can't possibly know what injury his words have dealt. It is not that I wish to be invisible or go about my life without anyone taking notice. Yet such comments, made at such an unguarded moment, cast an uncomfortable spotlight that I cannot shake. I feel naked in the glare of humiliation. The men don't have to put up with such comments. They can walk down the street without interruption; free to discover the world for themselves, and make it their own. The grimace on his face makes it clear that he does not want to see me dance, except for having the grim satisfaction of forcing me to do something that suits him; the gratification of giving orders and seeing me take them. The realisation traps me and forces me to react. My heart begins to palpitate and I quickly sit before my legs give way.

My aunt Alice would have returned his scorn. However, I cannot reach for the right words. If I said anything back to him, I would likely face a reprimand from the don.

At the end of the lecture, the last dawdling footsteps echo around the empty seats at the back of the theatre. The lecture halls have been haemorrhaging students since the war began. The number of male lecturers has almost halved. Most of the men were called up for conscription. The rest, except for the scientists who are reserved for war work, will serve two more terms before they undergo military training.

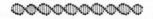

The next morning I'm woken suddenly by a knock at the door.

'Be quick or we'll miss breakfast.'

I peel myself from my inch-thin mattress. The plywood bed frame is impractically narrow so to prevent overnight visitors.

My friend Jean is standing outside my room, wearing a flutter skirt and a scarf tied around her neck. We have known each other since school, where we endured many of the same humiliations.

At Newnham College, we get just two baths a week under rationing, to save on hot water. Everyone knows that it's worth getting there early; otherwise there's a chance you might miss out, given that we are at war and everything is in short supply, including fuel. Consequently, it is rare for less than a dozen students to be queuing before breakfast, though this morning there is a queue of just one outside the bathroom.

The Goliathan student standing by the entrance is wrapped from head to toe in towels. One is tied tightly around their waist as though it is a sari and a second has been folded slipshod into a turban. The student turns to face me. It is a man, in a makeshift disguise. A resident must have smuggled him into our women-only halls. His scrunched nose reads as much of vexation as confusion.

I cover my mouth to hide my surprise.

'Don't mind my friend.' The pitch of Jean's voice rises an octave.

If the errant student whose boyfriend has stayed overnight in the dorm is found out, we all risk losing our places. Nightly visitors are a source of communal shame. While he has no right to be here, reporting the incident is pointless. The matrons have done little to stop boyfriends from visiting the halls since the war began, and I would have been singled out as a snitch, if I was even believed. The residents are making the most of the time they have left. In the mornings, the dormitory corridor is littered with stray photographs of paramours who are heading to war, left over from the tea parties the afternoons before, which harbour many a lovers' tryst. More calls for soldiers will be made before the year is out.

Once I believed that love was a waiting game and that everything in life and love would balance out in fairness eventually. There seemed to be a hermetic poetic justice in my philosophy. Now that the country is at war, I can see that others aren't taking their chances. The last thing on politicians' minds, but the first on ours, is that the number of eligible men will dwindle. Nearly a million were killed in the last war. No woman can afford to sit and wait for her lot. That had been my mother's fate. Her life was filled with housework, school committees and making sandwiches for synagogue. In all their years of marriage, she didn't deviate from making Father's favourite filling: salt beef. She warned me of the bare dance halls after the last war, and of how a woman's already meagre choices would be stripped away as women would be funnelled into menial work at the factories or employed in the care of wounded soldiers. Being able to earn my own living will be vital, or else I fear I'll be forced to marry a cousin or remain dependent on my family in some other awful way. Smart women follow the men, and science is a man's profession.

We pass a cluster of students in the hallway. Gertie from maths lectures is among them. I do not understand why she is here. She's a resident at Old Hall. It's the oldest and – in the atavistic way that only the British have of making the past an altar – the most prestigious part of the college. The boarders there call our modern building at Peile Hall and the adjacent College Hall nouveau riche by comparison.

'I don't know what you see in her – you know she's Jewish, don't you?' I overhear the hollow-cheeked girl using the slur as she talks to Gertie.

A chill ripples across my clavicle as I hear the words.

Jean has heard it too. 'Just leave it, Ros. We'll be late for breakfast.' She tugs at my sleeve.

Blood pumps loudly in my ear canal. It is my clarion call to leave. As we descend the stairs, I start to question everything that I have ever come to know. All that I thought to be true was swept from underneath me in those few minutes. I cannot be certain of anything any more, even the things I had once taken for granted. Last winter I lent my ice skates to Gertie so that she could skate on the frozen fens, and spent hours in the cold waiting for my turn. She was my friend, or at least I had believed so. Her silence now feels like a betrayal.

'There was this dark-haired chap in my art history lecture yesterday,' Jean says as we sit down to eat on one of College Hall's long trestle tables. Her eyes are smiling and wide.

College Hall is a replica of a Georgian parlour, with elaborate ceiling roses and carvings in the woodwork around the door frames and skirting boards. It is where we sit every day for breakfast, lunch and dinner.

'What, one of the men who laugh at us in lectures?' I ask.

'No, not one of those crumby Joes,' says Jean, staring into a corner of the room. 'Do you think I'm a terrible flirt, always talking about men?' she asks, noticing my inattention.

The truth is that I wish I could be as carefree as she is. I do not want to offend Jean, but do not understand why we can't talk about something more interesting, like the theory of fluorescence. At least Gertie is always happy for us to talk about maths, or science, though she has always agreed that the maths lectures aren't up to scratch.

'Oh look, here comes Ms Algebra,' Jean says.

Gertie is walking towards us. I cannot bring myself to tell her what I overheard on the stairwell minutes before. Instead, I sit there, speechless, while Jean stares at her blankly.

'There was a huge queue for the bathroom in my halls,' Gertie says before we are interrupted.

'*You* girls will be joining the auxiliary fire service.' Peile Hall's tutor, Helen Palmer, is pointing at me and several of the other students.

She has been known as 'Mrs P' ever since I arrived at

Newnham. I do not even know if she is married. Everything about Mrs P is round, including her hair, eyebrows, figure and the glasses she often forgets are perched on her head. She is always laden in knitted wool and skirts that skim her ankles.

As we line up underneath the cornice, Mrs P tells us that it is now up to us to defend the college, reminding us that it only exists because of the charity of its suffragist co-founder Millicent Fawcett.

'If you hear the alarm, you must take your post.' Her voice reverberates in the beams, just feet above our heads.

She lectures us on incendiary bombs, which are designed to cause maximum devastation by fire, telling us that we must wait for three signals: the buzzer, the alarm and the siren.

'Which should Roof Watch wait for?'

'Miss Franklin, weren't you listening? When the alarm sounds, you must heed it…'

'How will we know which is the right alarm?'

'If you have any further questions, see me in my office.' She continues to read a list of names from a sheet of paper.

When the bell sounds later that morning there are only six of us left in the hall. The kitchen staff immediately slam the lids on the porridge kegs. The milk allowance has been reduced to a quarter of a pint to share between two people, so there is little chance of filling up on tea afterwards. I feel the gnawing sensation of hunger pains in my stomach as we march in a slow procession to the shallow ditch by the cabbage patch border outside Newnham's red-turreted halls. It is autumn and the grass outside, where we must wait for hours to be counted and ticked off the register, is cold and swampy.

War has never felt more pointless. The gas masks that we carry on our nightly marches do little more than scare the evacuees who have travelled up from the cities. We repeat our marches for months, to no avail.

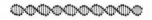

Then one freezing midnight in January, our slumber is broken by the sound of whistles. The piercing noise fills my head, like a rattling tin can, echoing and magnifying the violent noise. After a few seconds, I have a disturbing epiphany. In the last drill, the don on duty hadn't got his whistle to make a single sound, and Mrs P had lost the key to the roof. This time the whistles are punctuated by loud voices. This is not a drill.

'To the roof, ladies, quickly.' Mrs P's voice is barely raised compared to the dons'.

We walk up the stairs, past the fire buckets filled with sand. My brigade is instructed to patrol the roof and top floor of the building. Mrs P orders us to stand on lookout and watch for aircraft. Meanwhile, every instinct in my body is urging me to get beneath ground. With each step forwards, panic pulls me backwards.

'We do what we must, trust that Churchill has our best interests at heart.' Mrs P snatches at her pockets for the roof key.

When she finally finds it, and we tentatively step out onto the parapet, the roof of the building opposite is on fire. The hot furnace burns as brightly as the sun. Orange and red flames flare from its perimeter, cracking back and forth like whips. Their warmth and flicker have a distancing effect. My body is here on the roof, but my mind is drifting with the smoke plumes. I picture my father holding the front line in the Great War and hope that he would be proud of me.

Suddenly, a smoke cloud descends on us. I choke and splutter in its thick poison.

| 8 |

Nostradamus

5 Pembridge Place, Notting Hill, London, September 1940

Father is sitting at the head of the table on the night of my return from Cambridge. Last year it took me five hours to cycle home to London, but this year Father insisted that I took the train. The embossed leather chair is Father's chair. It's the only one of six dining chairs that has arms. It's his sanctuary from the demands of daily life. He is sitting on it cross-legged, leaning his elbow on the dining table as he pores over his newspaper, which he does most nights before dinner. His silence seems disapproving.

The lamp above the table spotlights his broad arms and cotton thermals, which are rolled up above his elbows. His eyes are overcast in the relief of the lamplight. The only sound as we eat is the noise of cutlery grating against china.

My mother has done away with formal clothing. There's no point wearing clothes for an occasion, she says, only to have to change them after an air raid.

'Your letters concern me,' Father says, lifting his head from his newspaper and placing his fork on the table as if it were a gauntlet. 'It seems that you've made science your religion.'

He had begged me to leave college and join the Land Army.

He then wrote to me during the term to try and convince me to take up agricultural labour if the university closed in my final year. He may not have thought that it was safe for women to live away from home in these precarious times. Yet it also seemed clear to me that he couldn't live with the shame of his daughter having the life he'd wanted for himself.

I don't look up from my plate. 'But science is life, Father,' I say.

My father's advice has always been to trust in God but I have never believed in a creator. At least not in the same way that my father does. Neither have I been able to understand why this creator had to be a man, and asked my mother this when I was nine. Why would such a creator have any interest in our tiny corner of the universe, or our even less significant lives? Science gives as much of an explanation for life as religion does, except it has the benefit of being proven.

'Your theories are pleasant to believe, but so far as I can see, they have no foundation other than they lead to a nicer view of life.' I recount what I told him in my letter, which I remember almost word for word.

'And what about after that, when this life ends?' He casts an eye over my brothers from his perch at the head of the table. 'There are some things that only God, not man, is supposed to know.'

'Winning the war won't be down to luck or fate, or God,' I say.

'*B'ezrat Hashem*. Some things will be left to the Almighty. I gave up science for this country, Rosalind, and so did your aunts.'

He thumps his fist on the dinner table so hard that the ornaments on the mantelpiece start to rattle.

When soldiers returned from the poppy fields of the last war, the Women's Land Army was forced out of work. Aunt Alice helped women who had lost their jobs to returning soldiers to find work abroad. She got a job as secretary for the Society for the Overseas Settlement of British Women.

It was Aunt Alice who once confronted Scotland Yard

when my uncle Hugh escaped from prison on compassionate leave during one of his hunger strikes. Both the jury and the other prisoners where he was detained had little sympathy for the nephew of Herbert Samuel, a Liberal cabinet minister. My aunt called Hugh's release from prison a sham, so police wouldn't have Suffragettes' blood on their hands. Grandpa thought Uncle Hugh had got in with the wrong crowd. Hugh said he couldn't stand still and watch the police beat and grope protestors at the suffrage march in 1910, on that inauspicious Friday in November, a decade before I was born. The police had raided a peaceful protest to the Houses of Parliament in support of the women's right to vote and had come armed. The day went down in history as Black Friday; inspiring more than a thousand acts of rebellion from women and men across the country. My uncle's last act of rebellion was arson; he set fire to a train carriage at Harrow, hiding out at the Bomb Shop – a bookshop on Charing Cross Road – before a dramatic arrest. He refused food more than one hundred times in resistance, before disappearing mysteriously after he was let out so the police could avoid any repercussions from his starvation.

'Alice *wanted* to go to university,' I say next.

'Is that what she told you? Sometimes, Rosalind, we must do the right thing and stand by our country,' Father says.

My mind darts chaotically from one thought to another. I can feel a tide of anger welling up inside me.

If anything is sure to elicit people's true intentions, it's a crisis. At school, my father encouraged me to complain to my teachers if they failed the pupils. Now he wants me to leave college and join the army. His real intentions are now plain.

'My contribution will be far more important as a chemist,' I say, wiping moisture from the corners of my eyes before running upstairs.

From my bedroom, I can hear my mother trying to talk him down. She has always wanted her children to live the dreams she was denied. It gives her own aspirations fresh momentum. My maternal grandfather, her father, and his father were both barristers. She didn't go to university, even though she had longed to, and she pitied others who'd had to similarly forfeit their dreams. She did what she could to help refugees and anyone else in need, but her more ambitious side has lain dormant, except for when she chairs school or local committees.

'Do you really want your daughter to end up in a factory, Ellis, like all the other women? It was ingenuity that helped win the war,' I hear her saying through my bedroom floor.

'Sweat and blood, Muriel. It was the grit and lives of thousands of men.' My father bellows so loudly that the floor shakes.

'Just think about how many lives could be saved with better equipment.'

She usually lets a minor disagreement slip, but when something is important to my mother, she can cut my father to the quick.

Later that night, I realise how the war has begun to erode family life as we know it. As I lay my necklace on my bedside table, a siren sounds outside. The noise of doors slamming and children crying emanates from the street.

My mother is standing outside my room carrying an oil lamp. She is in her nightdress.

'Put a coat on,' she says.

Still wearing my pyjamas, I wrap the blanket from my bed around my shoulders like a shawl. I hear my father loudly whispering in the hallway.

'Jenifer, Evi, coats on, quickly.'

We walk downstairs in a tired, zombie-like procession. When I reach the kitchen, I pull on a pair of wellington boots that my mother keeps by the back door. The sirens outside continue to wail. My father unlocks the back door, ushering us out into the cold and bleak, windy night. We run down the iron steps, and along the wet grass, past the rose trellis at the back of the garden. The lawn is dimly lit by the overhead lamps on the main street. The Blitz has brought with it the urgent possibility that anyone could find themselves hundreds of feet below ground, shoulder to shoulder with people they don't know huddling under blankets, at any moment. The thought of standing so close to strangers in such an enclosed space makes me feel unwashed.

The London Underground shelters are breeding grounds for disease, my parents say. I wonder whether the people in the Tube stations talk as unguardedly about homeowners who can afford shelters in their back gardens.

My father had dug a chest-height Anderson shelter at the back of the garden soon after the outbreak of war and planted grass on top of the mound to shield it from enemy forces.

'You'll be fine in here, girls,' he says now as he helps us to stoop through the hole.

The shelter is covered with corrugated iron panels that have been loosely bolted together with rusty old screws. Inside, it stinks of soil and petrol. Father has rubbed the tin roof with viscous oil, to help drive the bolts into the steel cage. The space is cramped and damp.

While crouching inside the hole that night, with the constant wail of the siren in the distance, I long to return to my halls at Cambridge. The promise of familial safety is now nowhere to be found. My face feels numb as the siren gets louder, my thoughts racing as I realise that the war has trapped us indefinitely in this cramped space at the end of the garden.

| 9 |

Sigma

Cambridge University, October 1940

Two Royal Air Force de Havilland planes whir past the window at the end of a cluttered office in the Cavendish laboratory that is owned by the University of Cambridge. The door is ajar and I can just see a desk filled with notebooks bursting with formulae, while the floor space in front of it is piled waist-high with colour-coded textbooks. Nobody seems to be in, though I call out to make sure. '*Bonjour*, Madame Weill, when do French lessons start?'

I knock for a second time. 'Madame Weill?'

There had been rumours since the beginning of the term that a student of Marie Curie's would be visiting Cambridge. The lecture hall was full on the day that the Jewish scientist who'd absconded from France was speaking. College tutors had asked the students to make donations to fund the French scientist's board. If we donated generously, we were promised free French lessons in exchange.

I sat as close to the front of the lecture theatre as possible, two rows back from Gertie. The old seating rules no longer applied. Most of the men had left for military service by my final year. They had the bonus of studying with all the best apparatus; the Cambridge laboratories had thick wooden desks, acres of space and resembled photographs of Ernest Rutherford's – the lab's director – experiments, replete with test tubes, smoke and bell jars. We could usually only see them from afar, and so the college heads had plans to set up a separate workshop at Newnham for female students. But to keep these resources from being wasted, some lecturers were now asking for us to join their classes.

Professor William Lawrence Bragg, who was introducing the lecture that day, wiped his balding forehead and fondled his greying moustache as he took the stand. He had been extremely beautiful in his youth, though that didn't matter to me or anyone else in the room in the slightest: he had won a Nobel prize with his father for X-ray diffraction, and that was *all* that mattered.

'It's a pleasure for me to welcome Mrs Adrienne Weill, an eminent scientist all the way from Paris, where she was a student of Pierre Curie – who is sadly no longer with us – and his wife Marie,' Professor Bragg said.

I pulled my glasses out of their mesh metal case and tilted my neck forward to hear as much as possible.

'Thank you, Professor Bragg, for that *thoughtful* introduction,' Madame Weill replied with a grimace, coughing and lifting a pair of glasses from her curly hair, which she then rested on her nose.

Bragg's introduction had been anything but thoughtful; he had mentioned Marie Curie solely in relation to her husband, who was the more prominent scientist of the two.

Madame Weill's accent was warm and oozed with sibilance, like the Mesdames' at the French finishing school where my parents had sent me before college.

'Today, we will be discussing metallurgy,' said the new

tutor. 'We are using X-rays to look at the structure of atoms. By doing so, we can see the structural strength of metal oxides and alloys.'

She turned on the projector. The images on the screen reminded me of evenings spent observing family photos in the drawing room at Pembridge Place, although these were nothing like any other photographs I'd ever seen. They didn't appear to belong to this world. They were of pinhead atoms scattered in fractal patterns like the veins of a leaf or cracks on ice. The images rotated in swift succession, each one a piece of art: a Henry Moore or a Matisse, in monochrome; it was a merry-go-round of masterpieces.

Was that *ferromagnetism*, or *ferrimagnetism*? Before I had a chance to raise a hand, Madame Weill was packing up her things to go. I swiftly made my way through the crowd to the lectern, but by the time I got to the front of the lecture theatre, she was gone.

'Did you forget about the college social tonight?' asked Gertie, who was alighting the stairs of the auditorium. 'Madame Weill will be speaking there too.'

The first lecture back at Cambridge since the bombing started had opened my eyes to a new microscopic world in which the hidden was now becoming seen. It seemed like kismet that our new lecturer, the person to introduce me to it, was French, so I could get French lessons.

Back in Peile Hall that evening, Mrs P was standing by one of the trestle tables, surrounded by students. The table was an assortment of sweets and cakes, hand-baked for the occasion using lard and dried fruit with what was left of rations.

'I love the English, my mother knew the former leader of the Liberals; he was a classic English gentleman,' Madame Weill said.

Her mouth was full of Victoria sponge, which Mrs P had baked herself.

'Do you mean Herbert Samuel? He's my great-uncle,' I blurted.

Everyone, including Mrs P and the new lecturer, fell silent.

'What a coincidence. My mother would have stayed with one of your relatives, Netta, was it?'

'My great-aunt; she's still alive,' I said.

As I stand outside the new lecturer's office, I'm still astounded by the coincidence from the day before; wondering how her French mother could possibly have known my great-uncle. I'm about to walk away when I hear her distinctive tones.

'They haven't stopped since I arrived.'

Madame Weill emerges from the direction of the library and seems to be shooing the planes outside the window away with her hand. She stops by the vestibule of her office lodging and drops her arms with despair as if cogitating the words I have just spoken.

'French lessons? Nobody said anything about this.'

'It was organised by the college,' I reply. 'I would rather travel to Paris, but that's impossible now.'

'Well, they did not tell me this,' she says, pacing.

'When do we start?'

'With goodbye, *au revoir, adieu*,' she says, ushering me out of her new abode.

| 10 |

Half Life

12 Mill Lane, Cambridge, August 1942

I could not have guessed that at the end of my final term at Cambridge, I would come to live with the mysterious new lecturer in the crooked brick townhouse on Mill Lane that she runs for student lodgers. On results day, I was crestfallen when my budding dreams appeared to shed away before my eyes. I passed the Natural Sciences Tripos with upper second-class honours, just a slither away from the first I wanted. My supervisor blamed my myopic focus on maths and physical chemistry, at the expense of subjects that didn't hold my attention. Madame Weill took pity on me, as I was her only French student.

Professor Norrish had offered me a research grant to investigate the kinetics of polymerisation at Cambridge. When he gave me the job, he said I would have to work for free, causing me to wonder if he'd do anything for a wageless stooge. The tyrannical lab professor now makes me work on tasks that have nothing to do with polymerisation. I must pass all of my workings by him. Gaining a science degree took me as many years to complete as the men's degree, but in Norrish's eyes, it lacks legitimacy. Newnham students are awarded decrees for the same work that earns the men at Cambridge's college degrees.

'Boys will be boys,' he says of the other researchers, the 'lab people' as I call them. There is no supposition that if he is convivial with them that it means anything more than that. Whereas, it would seem that he thinks if he shows the same affection to a woman, it might be misconstrued as something else.

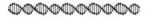

'Marie invented the word radioactivity, did you know that, Ros?' Madame Weill says one morning in the student lodging.

I lean over to take a macaron from the plate she's holding. The almonds at her local patisserie in Paris were ground to a much smoother consistency, she insists.

'What a way to put your country on the map, it's not so easy, eh?' she says.

'Where is she now?' I ask, taking a sip of coffee.

'You could say she died for her job.' Madame Weill softens her tone and stubs out her cigarette. 'There are other things in life. Love, family; you need to work out what's most important to you,' she says.

'What's the evidence she died for her job?' I say as I put my plate in the sink.

'Tesla burned his fingers on X-rays thinking it was sunburn. She didn't know what she'd found.'

'But she knew the subject inside out.'

'She spent her final days in a sanatorium. No one talks about it much,' she says. 'She took risks, but she didn't know...' Her voice trails off.

Suddenly, there's a knock at the door and Madame Weill asks me to answer it. An envelope is poking out from the letter box, thick with official stamps.

As I open the letter, which is addressed to me, the word *de-reserved* leaps out in bold type. My blood runs cold. It can mean only one thing. The letter is telling every woman scientist in the country on this day that their country needs them.

The immunity of war science no longer applies to us, just to our male colleagues, whose careers in science it seems by the wording of the letter have been preserved. We must face the doldrums alone, without our other halves, brothers, or the men we work with.

'I'll be forced to join industry!' I cry.

Madame Weill stands behind me, peering at the letter over my shoulder.

'What about your research grant?'

'Look, read here,' I say in floods of tears. 'I've got to give it up.'

'But you don't like your job anyway.'

It is not the thought of leaving Professor Norrish's lab that scares me most, but the prospect of an even worse fate. How can I resist my father's pleas to join the Land Army now? What hope is there of a woman getting a job in industry that pays?

'Don't give up so easily,' Madame Weill says as she puts her arm around my shoulders.

Lilley & Skinner (shoe shop), Southwark, London July 1945

From the West End of London to the East, there is no escaping the ration queues. The only consolation is knowing that everybody will be sent to the back of the queue without the right dates or stamps. At first, the government only planned to ration butter and sugar but that has now spread to store-cupboard staples like cereal, eggs and cheese. When my research grant ended, I moved back in with my parents and got a job at the Coal Board in London. I have spent nearly three years working there now, investigating the porosity of coal. Despite having to give up my grant, I was able to find an industrial job that would make a contribution to the war effort, which appeased my father and put paid to his attempts to make me join the Land Army. Charcoal is used in gas masks and so the work has been critical in ensuring that the filter is strong enough to resist poisonous gases. And yet coal is a simple carbon, and there are probably bigger and more complex problems I could be working on.

The ration queues this summer stretch around every corner, half a dozen deep. Elderly ladies yawn and sigh away their frustrations on the streets, surrounded by screaming babies and foolhardy young men laughing and causing mischief. Outside Lilley & Skinner, a group of boys are clamouring to get closer to the front of the line, doing tricks to skip the queue. The women have brought hessian sacks to cart their goods around in prams and are hunkering down for the long wait. Their brothers, sons, husbands and potential suitors have gone to fight, and they bear their losses on their impoverished sleeves.

In front of the shoe shop in Southwark, there's a queue of several hundred. The line goes all the way down the road and even turns the corner. It is bursting with victory rolls, mackintoshes and pencil skirts. I have walked from my parents' house in Notting Hill south of the river to buy a pair of shoes; mine have become worn from cycling and won't suffice to find another job. Shoppers are eager to get their hands on a pair of Mary Janes, courts or brogues that will last the war. As a woman in wartime Britain, there is pressure to have a pair of shoes that will fit every occasion. The war also demands that they must be comfortable enough to walk across town. Shoes are the plank on which you stand, they root you to the ground.

'Tssk, this queue ain't moved for hours,' a toothless lady hisses from the back of the line.

I migrate back north to Dolcis, where only a quarter of the number of people are queuing, and patiently wait my turn. But by the time half an hour has passed, the line has hardly moved. No one else has joined the back of the queue in many minutes. My feet haven't moved from the scrap of yellowed newspaper that's flapping underneath the sole of my shoe. I perch on my tiptoes to get a better view and see two youths in baker-boy caps weaving in and out of the line near the front. Yet more people have interspersed at various points. Hunger pangs eventually force me to leave the line and take a detour for something to eat.

The bistro where I used to go with friends before the war is still there on Talbot Road. Outside the shop, there is a strong smell of rotting cabbage and fish wafting up from the nearby market on Portobello Road. Deliveries have been delayed. With groceries in short supply, rag-and-bone men have flooded the marketplace with old trinkets and recycled clothing. Several red fire buckets are hanging up outside the Electric Cinema, in case there's another raid.

I try hopelessly to buy something to eat. The cashier – distracted by the loud clang of the door opening and closing – looks right through me as if I am invisible, as another hungry mouth pushes towards the front of the queue and shoves a ration card in his face.

Exasperated, I walk away. There is only one place where few people shop in wartime Britain and it suddenly comes to mind; the Harrods food hall, where the prices outstrip most ration allowances and so there are no queues.

The awning outside the shopfront is greener than the sunburned grass in Hyde Park which I trekked across to get there. I buy the first thing my ration card will afford me: a box of after-dinner mints.

On leaving the store, I begin to wonder if there is any way to escape London. The spacious streets and candy-coloured buildings of Westbourne Park that had once comforted me have now become a cage. The country has been at war for almost six years. Despite Victory in Europe Day, the war drags on, and so does the rationing, at least for now; how many years it will take to end is not known. And so later that day, I write to Madame Weill to ask if she knows of any jobs available in Paris.

III

BEFORE

| 11 |

Paris

Rue Garancière, Paris, February 1947

'You will sleep in the library.'

Madame Dumas is wearing a black polo-neck jumper. Her jet-black hair is scraped into a tight ponytail. She is a widow of five years. '*Cinq ans de misère*,' she says. I am unsure if she's referring to the number of years since her late husband's death or the length of their marriage. His death mask still holds vigil over the apartment on a shelf in the library, next to the plaster-winged Venus. The room is dotted with antiques and an oval-shaped tin basin stands in one corner. The widow shows me around the room and says that once the maid has finished cooking her meals, I can then use the kitchen.

The attic apartment is on the top floor of a stone building in Rue Garancière, across the road from Café de Flore, where she says Simone de Beauvoir and Jean-Paul Sartre regularly go for coffee.

'Do you have friends?' the widow asks.

'*Oui, madame*,' I reply in my best French.

'No men are allowed in your room past six.' She speaks to me in English, despite my best efforts to converse in French.

'Yes, madame.'

'You must be quiet; the door makes a terrible noise,' she adds before her maid calls to say that her *petit déjeuner* is waiting.

She thrusts out her right hand. Her polished nails are immaculate. She is holding a rusty skeleton key. I put it in my pocket for safekeeping.

The attic room is a world away from my living quarters the last time I was in France, on the foreign exchange trip I made before college. The dormitory in the big house near the river Marne was bright, with large windows that stretched from the floor to the ceiling. After supper, we bathed in the river until our bodies were silky from lolling in the cool water. The smell of damp moss infused the air on the nearby riverbank. We would crowd around the edge of the water and dip our toes in, skim stones and see how quickly we could race sticks downstream.

Most afternoons we went to Paris to hunt for materials for the next day's dressmaking class: organdie, French batiste or broderie anglaise. The new fabrics, nylon and viscose, were also beginning to be imported into France from Britain and America. Back then every experience felt bigger and more acute, and even the colours seemed to shine more brightly.

Rather than sit alone this evening in the apartment, waiting for Madame Dumas to finish her dinner, I decide to retrace my steps by visiting my favourite sights. I walk down the 1st arrondissement, past the ochre-shuttered mansions and the gated navy base. The buttery smell of chestnuts from the open-air roasters has infused the breeze with sweetness.

Meandering through Avenue des Champs-Élysées, the road that leads towards the central shopping district, I stop at the Petit Palais to seek cover from the rain.

Both the Petit Palais and its big sister the Grand Palais opposite are a short walk from my favourite spots, the Notre Dame and Arc de Triomphe. Despite its name, the Petit Palais isn't at all small, other than by comparison to the Grand Palais opposite.

As I look up at the art nouveau domes, a few droplets of

rain roll down my cheek. Water is flowing off the pitched roof of the Petit Palais and onto the rotunda below.

I join the huddle on the steps for shelter.

'Your coat please, madame,' instructs a man at the entrance.

'*De la pluie*,' I say, sheltering under my tweed jacket and pointing up towards the sky.

A woman standing in the queue behind me is surveying my stockings, pressed A-line skirt and hair. I can almost feel her stare pierce through the back of my head as I turn back to the doorman.

I would rather visit the science halls at the Palais de la Découverte in the Grand Palais opposite. But on seeing the rain gushing down the steps of the perron, I give my coat to the guard, who points towards the gallery inside.

The atrium is so enormous that the oil paintings are dwarfed by its size. In the third chamber that branches off to the right from the main atrium is a painting of a statuesque woman. She is gloved in a burgundy velvet dress worn against a black background. The plaque below it says that she is a banker's wife. She has the same uncompromising posture and sibylline eyes as my mother.

'Less self is the path to greater happiness,' is my mother's mantra. She would think that the fabric on the woman's dress was mercenary.

Farther down the hall, another woman wearing all black hoists her wares in the foreground of a busy marketplace. She was painted after the French Revolution, the sign says. From the pensive faces in the hall, all that is left of the revolution now is the smiling faces in the paintings.

The laissez-faire engine of capitalism that began to grind after the war would have been an affliction to the revolutionaries of that busy marketplace. Nobody could miss the groaning factories from the dawn of industry, but the economic age is a silent, invisible revolution. It has taken over not just the means of production, but the means of distribution too.

'This one is my favourite. Do you like it?' A baritone voice disturbs my thoughts.

On turning around, I recognise Jacques Mering, whom I had met at a conference on carbons at the Royal Institution in London the previous summer, before travelling to the Alps for a break with Jean. When I had asked Adrienne whether she knew of any jobs in France, she suggested that I go to the event as her acquaintance Marcel Mathieu, who worked for the government agency funding much of the scientific research, would be there. Marcel's friend Jacques is dressed in the same mackintosh and open-collared shirt that he was wearing that day.

'Monsieur Mering, what a surprise.' I clutch my chest. 'Do you always sneak up on people like that?'

'Think of it as an initiation,' he replies with a smile.

We stand for a moment and observe the woman in the painting. 'Since de Gaulle, the People's Revolution has become a rod for their own backs,' I say.

'I see you are just as outspoken as when we last met,' he says.

'I prefer to say *liberated,* not outspoken.'

'You did not make that gentleman's life easy at the seminar in London.'

Although Adrienne had suggested that I meet with Marcel at the seminar, I hadn't thought anything would necessarily come from it, but felt it would be worth going along anyway. And after four years of working on coal at the Coal Board in London, I had been shocked to hear one of the speakers make elementary mistakes about the subject in front of a crowd.

'Which gentleman, your friend Marcel or the man who was professing he knew everything about carbons?'

'The poor Englishman. He looked terrified, as pale as *frites*.'

'Not as terrified as we should be if his work makes it to the journals.'

'I see you are like Joan of Arc, fighting for *égalité*,' Jacques says.

I pause. 'And you, Monsieur Mering, what are you fighting for?'

'Our labours have already conquered fascism.' He laughs.

His is the French way. From the boulangeries to the shoe

stores, such verbal sparring is a game in Paris and friendship is galvanised in its furnace.

'Adrienne says you're quite the prodigy,' Jacques says.

'Do you mean Madame Weill, my French tutor?'

'*Très bien*, and you know very well she's a friend of Marcel's,' he says. I baulk at the thought that he might have known my tutor had put me up to speaking to him to get a job.

'Monsieur Mering, I don't know what you mean.'

'Please, call me Jacques.'

'I want you to know that Marcel Mathieu offered me the job on merit. My work at the Coal Board was vital to improving the function of gas masks. It showed how coal acts as a molecular sieve.'

'And where is your proof?'

'Only helium can pass through its air pockets.'

'Is that right, helium?' He cocks his head to one side.

'You look incredulous.'

'Why not hydrogen? It is half the weight,' he says.

'Coal isn't just carbon, Monsieur... Jacques. It's a hydrocarbon, it contains hydrogen. Hydrogen would have spoiled the experiment. Helium is inert.'

'Very good, Rosalind.' He fiddles with the scuffed leather strap on his Breguet watch. 'I must go to meet my wife. I will see you at the lab tomorrow.'

With that, he vanishes.

The scent of his aftershave still hangs in the air after he leaves. It is spicier and sweeter than the brand my father wears.

Each step along the Seine on the walk back to the widow's attic floats my mind in infinite directions. The February moon that evening is shimmering a thousand colours on the water's gossamer surface. The voices of women bringing in their washing from their balconies murmur above the cobbled streets. The buttery aroma of chestnuts still lingers in the air after dark; their discarded shells glisten in the gutter under the moonlight. They are the colour of Jacques's eyes, lacquered and inscrutable.

In the apartment on my return, a half-empty bottle of wine

has been left out on the dining table. I tear some bread from the baguette next to it, slather it with butter and take the snack to bed. From my mattress in the library, I can hear the widow snoring. I picture her silk eye mask askew over just one eye and hold my breath for as long as it will stifle until her heavy breathing subsides.

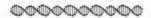

The next morning I rise at six. The first thing I do when I wake up is write down the address of the State Chemicals Lab, *12 Quai Henri IV*, and commit it to memory.

That morning the River Seine smells of pond water, not chestnuts like it did the night before. The cobbled streets are now bare and the buildings lining the river are shrouded in a blue-grey haze.

The Laboratoire Central des Services Chimiques de l'Etat has narrower, unornamented windows than the residential buildings along the Seine. The first set of doors has been cemented closed.

Jacques is standing on the roadside outside a second set of doors. His thin mop of caramel-coloured hair is combed to one side and his shirt has come untucked from his pale chinos.

'Rosalind, *ça va?*' he says with a sideways smile.

As he leans forward to kiss my cheek, he pulls me towards him, scooping his arm around my waist. I take a step back and awkwardly brush the dust off my skirt.

'Sorry I couldn't speak for long yesterday,' he says.

'I was going to say that I prefer the dynamism of Henry Moore or Giacometti,' I tell him.

'Do you paint?'

'I used to keep a scrapbook,' I say, straightening my back. 'It was very… neat.'

'The nearby café Chez Solange overlooks the exact spot where the Curies discovered radium,' Jacques says while passing an evaporating dish to staff in the lab – which everyone here in France calls the 'labo' – later that morning. The dish is filled to the brim with coffee. 'Les Cafés de PC,' he adds, pointing at the sign for the department and mouthing the words 'Physique et Chimie'. Coffee stains have marred the inside of the flask, which is balancing on a metal vice between a Bunsen burner, centrifuge and test tubes. To listen to him, anyone would think the lab itself is Café Central, where Trotsky and Lenin orchestrated their world views, from a single spot, over coffee. To him, this is his Vienna.

'Next, I will show you how to use X-rays to examine charcoal and clay,' Jacques says after lunch. 'First, you prepare the specimen. Then you mount it on the slide. The X-ray must be aligned, like so. Your turn.' He passes me a sachet filled with a powdery substance.

'Shall I fix it to the slide?' I ask.

His eyes follow the movement of my hands as I carefully set the specimen on the glass.

'Delicately done,' he says. 'But don't get happy before work is finished.'

'Jacques,' a woman calls from the other end of the room while he's still showing me how to position crystals of charcoal between two glass slides. 'I need help with something.'

'Of course, Agnes,' Jacques replies, getting up from the seat next to me.

Agnes flashes a smile of glistening teeth and sweeps a curtain of long, shiny dark hair back over her shoulder. I spend the next hour trying to decipher what she means to him, and him to her.

'So, Rosalind,' Jacques returns an hour later. His voice sounds fuller-bodied than before. 'What do you know about X-ray crystallography?'

'I was hoping you would tell me, Monsieur Mer… Jacques.'

'I'm busy today. Perhaps we can finish the experiment this evening.'

'Madame Dumas likes me to be back by six.'

'So, meet me at *dix-sept heures*.'

That afternoon, before I am due to meet Jacques, the lab staff take a break and head to the Latin Quarter. The gold and green minaret on the Grande Mosquée de Paris, next to the Panthéon, twinkles in the February sun. It was built on a network of caves used as safe houses for the French Resistance, Jacques says. Adrienne once told me her compatriots in the Resistance had laid spikes for Nazi forces on the country roads outside Paris.

Jacques stops under the oak trees on Rue-Saint Jacques.

'Sartre takes his pulpit just here.'

'When he's not in the coffee shop,' I say, bending down to remove a stone from my shoe.

When I stand up again, Vittorio is hovering his index finger over the shutter-release button on his camera. I quickly adjust my pearls for a photograph. Jacques offers to hold my handbag.

'Let me.'

'*Formaggio.*'

Vittorio recently joined the lab from Buenos Aires, where his family fled Genoa to escape Mussolini. Words flow from his mouth like rapid fire. He speaks so quickly that I have trouble making out what he is saying.

'Agnes, can you lean the other way?' he asks. 'We can't see Jacques.'

Jacques's elbow presses into my hip as Agnes clings on to his other arm. We both have dark eyes and brunette hair, though her hair is several inches longer than mine. The way we are standing on either side of Jacques is oddly symmetrical. His love of symmetry makes me wonder if he always seeks to garner the attention of two women in any room at one time.

I dig my heels into the ground, resisting the force of Agnes pushing against his other arm.

'Jacques, I didn't know you were shy,' Agnes says, broadening her smile.

Her teeth are visibly pearlescent as her lips recede.

Later on, after returning from our trip, the lab is deserted. It is only just gone 4 o'clock, but the strength of the unions means people leave before 5 o'clock in Paris. Jacques walks in and places a cup of coffee next to me, turning his fluid eyes in my direction.

'Like this.' He clasps my hand in his and adjusts the angle of the X-ray tube.

I can feel the hairs at the back of my neck stand on end as his hands grip on to mine and he sits down on the chair next to me. After a few seconds, I shake my hand away from his. I am not used to such physical attention. During my research grant in Cambridge, Professor Norrish hadn't come within an inch of me.

'I'm capable of doing it myself,' I tell him.

'There, you have it perfectly,' Jacques says.

'Do you have afternoon meetings with all of your staff?'

'Well,' he says, winding his arm backwards. His movements are slow and deliberate. 'I enjoy your company, Ros.'

'And I enjoy yours, Monsieur Mering.'

Amid the unfathomable silence, he reels himself slowly back to his feet. I do not want him to realise that I've noticed him looking back at me. Have I done something funny, made an unusual face, perhaps, that he found amusing?

'Drop by my office some time,' he says.

'When do you have in mind?' I reply, trying to catch my breath quietly without him noticing.

'How about tomorrow, after work?'

'My father will be staying. But I'm free on Saturday,' I add quickly.

'I'll be busy this weekend. It's my wife's birthday,' he says.

All of a sudden, I feel foolish for going along with his suggestion.

I glance firmly at the area above Jacques's shoulder, so he can't see me looking at him, before turning back to the X-ray apparatus. If he knew I was stealing glances at his deep eyes and broad arms, what would he think?

He is edging towards the door as if to go back to his office or to leave for the evening.

'Are you leaving?'

'First, I must find something,' he says.

'What thing?' I ask, forgetting to avert my eyes.

'People, actually. Well, I am seeking information that will help me find someone important.'

'Who?'

'My mother. I haven't seen her since the occupation.'

'By the Germans?' I ask.

'The Russians first, actually, and now,' he says. 'The Šeimena river, where I grew up, was part of Lithuania then. Communism is good for the spirit, but the tsars took the heart from the people.'

It is then that I realise what Jacques must have been hiding. He has said nothing until now about his upbringing. During the invasion, it was easier for many academics to keep their Jewishness secret. Many of us buried talk of our religion, family, loves and longings. My mother said most of the refugees in Russia couldn't afford to leave or were otherwise unable to do so. Some tried to flee the area that had once been part of Lithuania, before Stalin, but only a few had escaped. She had friends from the diaspora who had successfully managed to escape Russia. Most of them were from the autonomous oblast in the east, near the border with China. Like them, Jacques must have lived for years without identity papers.

A fleeting thought then washes over me.

Perhaps we have been brought together to heal that hidden pain that only we can see.

'What does it mean to be Lithuanian, to you?' I ask him.

'Well, it is where I am from,' he says curtly. It is clear he does not want to say anything else. Perhaps if I had asked a different question, then maybe he would have said more.

| 12 |

I Rise

Avenue de la Motte-Picquet, Paris, March 1950

'Rosalind, gallivanting is not becoming,' the widow said to me one evening after 6 o'clock. She had grown increasingly suspicious of what had gone on when she went away: her cook had taught me a slew of new recipes and at first my family, then Jean, came to stay while she was on holiday. My father was duly impressed by the dinner I cooked him one long weekend. I found Mousline potato flakes that could be curdled into a mash with milk, cheese from the fromagerie on the corner and vegetables fresh from the food stalls in the undercover markets of the Latin Quarter. Then Jean stayed with me while she was heavily pregnant and emptied the widow's fridge after one long sojourn around Paris's art galleries, during an unquenchable pregnancy craving. This heightened the intensity of the owner's audacious speculations about what went on in her absence. It was all the impetus I needed to move out.

To make up the cost of a new flat, I have moved in with a couple: Philip, a friend of Vittorio's who is widely referred to as 'the American', and his girlfriend Marion. The new apartment may afford me a room of my own, but it is crammed full of dusty furniture, tables and armchairs upholstered in baroque prints, with unnecessarily elaborate curlicues carved into the legs.

'How are you today, Ros?' Philip asks me one cold wintry night in early spring.

I got up early this morning to avoid Marion, who sleeps in late and then takes over the kitchen at lunch, only to return early in the evening to cook again.

'I have an interview in London with the fellowship committee,' I say, placing my keys on the empty mantelpiece.

'Congratulations. Champagne is in order. Marion, fetch the leftover bottle from New Year,' he calls, pausing for a response. 'She must have gone out,' he adds, going into the kitchen to get the bottle himself.

Opening champagne seems gratuitous. It is even more extravagant than my attempt at celebrating when Cambridge finally awarded me a doctorate, albeit retroactively, while I was living with the widow, a day I thought would never come.

'Listen, Vittorio says things are a little complicated in the lab,' Philip says when he returns holding a bottle of Brut.

'Don't listen to such gossip,' I reply ardently.

I silently will him to stop talking about anything involving Jacques, or my love life. My personal life, by the sheer fact of being single and female, seems to be everyone else's business, and pity only ever seems to empower the person giving it, never the person on the receiving end.

'Is it true that Jacques got together with Rachel from the labo over the summer?' he asks me, reaching for more information.

After popping the cork, he catches a glass under the spray.

'Yes, you wouldn't know it, given Agnes is still all over him.'

'Vittorio is going to Florence,' he says, handing me a flute of champagne.

The bubbles rush to the top of the glass. I take a sip to stop them from flowing over and watch them settle gently on the surface of the effervescent liquid.

'I'll let his wife know you might be keen to join them as you like Italy so much.'

'Please, I'd rather not,' I say, sensing that he has already made up his mind.

It is humiliating enough that everyone is talking about what happened in Corsica the summer before last between Jacques and Rachel, without Vittorio and his wife feeling sorry for me and inviting me to tag along on their holiday. I realise Philip is trying to help, but just because I'm alone does not mean that I am lonely. I enjoy my own company and am free to do what I wish and see whom I like.

The next day in the lab, Vittorio knocks on my door.

'The American says you're a fan of the Medici. You must come with us to Firenze,' he says.

'I wouldn't say a fan,' I reply distractedly, holding a spare dress up over my lab coat. 'What does one wear to a Jewish wedding these days? Sorry, like you'd have any idea.'

'I am Jewish, actually, but not au fait with fashion,' Vittorio says.

I feel a knot of embarrassment. I had never asked Vittorio about his religion, if he had one even or what it was. He told me he had moved to Argentina to flee Mussolini, who was a spherical dictator, regardless of religious persecution.

'The only clothing we were allowed under Mussolini was military uniform,' Vittorio says.

'Is it true that the futurist Marinetti wanted everyone to wear wool made from milk?'

'*Si*, it is,' he says. 'It stank of rotten mozzarella, but they sold it to America anyway.'

'A letter has come for you, Ros,' Jacques says when I hand him his coffee one morning that June.

He has swapped his usual slacks for a lightweight pinstripe.

'Do you know who it's from?' I ask.

I did not want to tell Jacques that I had applied for another job in England. A chemist at Oxford, Charles Coulson, said microscopes were making the world bigger, not smaller, and that King's College London, which he would be joining, needed more physicists.

'It's stamped Londres,' he replies.

On opening the letter, I am dumbstruck. It is from the fellowship committee. They have approved my research grant.

When I arrived in Paris, an interim government was still running the country. Four years on, de Gaulle is talking about putting armed forces on the streets. It could mean armoured tanks in Paris. Outside the sanctuary of the lab, fascism is gaining force once more.

After leading the French Resistance, de Gaulle was installed to oversee the interim government, but the power got to him. Within just a few years, the mood in the city shifted, as snow turns to ice. My mother feared an ensuing outbreak of civil war, given France's history of uprisings. She was begging for me to come back to London. At the State Chemicals Lab, we were the property of the government. Its direction was our fate. Recent history had taught us that. My mother was right. I had already seen the first tanks on the backstreets of Paris, with their noisy chugging engines and bright glare at night, standing down protestors and occupying most of the road space leaving little barrier between them and pedestrians.

And yet, later that night, shortly after opening a translated copy of *Christ Stopped at Eboli*, which Colin has sent me from England, I do the unexpected.

I prefer... I hesitate as the ink spills from my pen.

While writing to thank Colin, it dawns on me that I still prefer everything about Paris to London. Nationalism is something that I've never understood, and lately, it seems to afflict the

English just as much, if not more, than any other European nation. De Gaulle is a reactionary, and nothing will last for long in a country so fervently committed to public interests.

Then I start to wonder whether I can ever be as happy in Paris again as I was in those first few months. The pleasures I once enjoyed on its streets have now all but evaporated. My first years in the city were the perfect confluence of people and place, and in chasing spectres, my halcyon mind blotted out every frigid morning, every cold shoulder and every knock from a stranger. Perhaps I am longing for something that no longer exists, or maybe that never did.

Paralysed with indecision, I have only one option, to defer the fellowship in London to next year, and let the hope of tomorrow live on for another day in Paris.

IV

NOW

| 13 |

Hourglass

Fulham, London, summer 1951

The mansion block in Donovan Court in Drayton Gardens is made of the same tawny-coloured brick as many of the deco buildings built before the war. The flat has a small kitchen and ceilings that spare no extra room. Yet I am no longer sharing with an old widowed madame or an American couple where I had become the third wheel in the relationship. It is somewhere I can host dinner parties and entertain friends at last. Every morning I survey the flat and all the things that I have chosen for it, which each hold personal significance. It has a marble fireplace, where I have arranged my ornaments. I use the walnut chest that Father gave me as a bureau, and have organised a collection of the lab's X-ray photographs of DNA in a neat pile on the surface.

While trying to figure out how to decipher the structure of DNA, each neuron in my brain – flooded with new information – ignites like a rocket as it fires off its electrical impulse, exploding in supernovas and then shrinking like white dwarfs in my mind. The display has kept me satiated for hours without food, observing the visions before my eyes: the beautiful constellations of atoms in DNA. Hours have slipped through my fingers working at my desk, lost in a state of alertness. Time has dwindled as effortlessly as sand flows through an hourglass. Although that spent time, like sand, cannot be recouped.

I remain in a trance at my desk, intoxicated though sober, like a spectator at the opera. Where else would I be? Most of my friends are either married or live abroad and I have no children to occupy my time.

I lose focus at the thought, musing instead at how paradoxical it is that, as my friend Charles suggested, microscopes – and also X-rays – are making the world bigger and not smaller. As our understanding of the world around us is growing, it is enriching our experience of it. I yearn for DNA to yield its secrets; I also wish Jacques would do the same. Remembering those last heady days in Paris, I push the X-rays to one side to compose a reply to him.

When will you return to Paris? The words from his last letter still echo in my mind like the birdcalls that filled the air that spring. I had waited all day to open it and tore through the envelope as fast as I could. Blood coursed through my veins with the force and rhythmic canter of a herd of horses on seeing his signature. While I read the letter, a wave of excitement overflowed from the nape of my neck.

He had promised to come to London again to visit. He has said this several times, though our letters remain a secret just between us. I expect he would probably destroy them if anything ever happened to me.

Dear Jacques,

Sorry to have left it so long to reply. Since your letter, I have been in a quandary. The truth is that I have been grappling to come to terms with your revelations.

Sometimes, I feel as though I am falling in love with you, and that I love you desperately. None of the men in the lab in London are like you. I have never met another man that is. For every feeling you inspire, your letters stir as many ghosts.

Truth be told, I have missed ~~you~~ our time working together. You are so incisive and speak so many languages, with such deftness. Every day, ~~especially at night,~~ when we spoke in the laboratory, I felt as though it was just us in the room. You were kind and patient with me, despite my direct questions, which so often cause people to shrink. ~~I could see that you paused in my direction for what seemed like an eternity when I spoke of my grandfather and his will. Did something I said strike a chord in your heart?~~

It does not seem to make sense for a heart to beat for someone who does not reciprocate. ~~It has been hard to think of you unkindly when you intrude so gently on my daydreams. I've dared not admit this to you. You have more than your fair share of admirers. I can't tell anyone how I feel, not even my brothers, for they would tell my parents and Father would not be pleased.~~

This feeling you describe is irrational, but it is very explainable. ~~You made me feel good. You made me feel accepted.~~ Our time together was a shared space away from the conflict of daily life, away from de Gaulle and his talk of tanks. It elevated the mundane nature of existence. ~~You said it did not matter to you how dedicated I am to my work, or that I have no intention of marriage, or that I have so rarely been kissed.~~

I shall forever be grateful that you said how much you admired my work on coals, rather than challenge me on it. ~~Still now, when I am in the most solemn of moods and want to cry, I think of your letters.~~ I think ~~that I want to run, and~~ maybe it is somehow a fortuitous and beneficial thing, ~~to want to run to you~~ the friendship we share. ~~Maybe my heart knows why~~ I find ~~happiness~~ pleasure in ~~you~~ our correspondence. ~~At the same time, it brings me much anxiety, which confuses me greatly. You made me feel held in your presence, but~~ I do not know what you are ~~were~~ thinking.

I know the two of us share a bond closer than any you have with anyone else in the lab. ~~They don't know you like I~~

do, do they? I sense the pain you feel about betraying your wife, whose feelings you said you do not wish to hurt even though the flush of first love has now faded. What cruelty do you endure from her? Surely, she cannot take kindly to your affairs. Did you mean it when you said you would burn our letters if it ever came to pass? You must be prudent.

I should tell you that I hope to be at the Stockholm convention in July. Will I get to see you again before then? Perhaps I shall see you there.

Yours faithfully

Your friend from London

| 14 |

Stockholm

Stadsholmen, Stockholm, Sweden, June 1951

Stockholm at dusk is a canvas in navy blue, with the palace at its centre. In the glint of the sun at dusk, the fissures on the walls of the castle cast a crossways shadow. The stone walls still bear the scars of survival. The cobbles are lit by the evening sun, radiating like the stars in Van Gogh's *Starry Night*. He painted the picture at an asylum in Saint-Rémy-de-Provence in the south of France amid his depression. I often marvel at how he made something so colourful out of the depths of his despair. Evi had something of that same spirit. It was hope that drove her to escape the camp at Buchenwald, where she'd left her father behind without knowing what had happened to him. Her faith that she would see him again was inextinguishable. She believed that he would return one day, even after her family's assets were squandered.

'I cannot do what Maurice asks,' I say to Vittorio, who is sitting beside me on a damp mossy bench underneath the castle walls. He wants me to reveal my workings to him even though he has no apparent interest in DNA.

'He does speak his mind,' he replies.

'He treats me like I'm his lab hand,' I say.

'Can you talk to anyone else?'

'The professor refuses to intervene. I can't bring up personal feelings.'

Earlier that morning, Dr Max Perutz from the Cavendish lab in Cambridge asked me to move down several seats. It was the first time I was going to hear eminent Professor John Bernal from Birkbeck College speak. My skirt was freshly ironed, and I held it in bunches regrettably, forcing a smile as I stood up to move. It was unwise to refuse the Medical Research Council's molecular biology luminary.

He asked if I worked for Maurice, forgetting my name.

'Being Austrian, you should understand the tyranny of misinformation,' I replied, to which he forced a broad-chinned smile.

Something inside me had snapped. Nothing bothered him at that moment, however, as he was there for only one thing: American Professor Linus Pauling's talk on proteins.

When the compère then announced that the professor's speech on his new alpha helix theory of protein had been cancelled, a silver-haired black man who was sitting a few seats down from us said in an American accent, 'No, sir, it was *Herman*'s alpha.' The man laughed and slapped his knee when it was revealed that Professor Pauling had had trouble getting a passport.

'Jacques wouldn't have been sorry to have missed Pauling,' Vittorio says.

'He's coming, isn't he?'

'He's got family commitments.'

My stomach lurches into free fall at the news and my solar plexus feels as though it has taken a glancing blow. Jacques had not responded to my request to name him in my paper in *Acta Crystallographica*. His silence reduced every promise he had made to a lie. He had sworn that we would meet again, but never given a date and so it hadn't happened.

I pull my scarf tightly around my chest.

'What are you working on?' Vittorio pirouettes the conversation to a different subject.

'Nucleic acid,' I stutter, grateful he didn't delve further. My disappointment would have been impossible to hide.

'Might you go and speak to him?'

'Jacques?'

'Pauling. DNA's next on his list.'

'I'd rather speak to Bernal,' I say. 'His talk this morning was full of possibilities. Instead of asking if we've found *the* solution, he suggests it is simply *a* solution.'

'And which have you found, the solution to the structure of DNA or just a theory?'

Len has promised he will build us a tilting camera stand before we begin the next round of X-ray investigations. Yet there are no shortcuts in science, and discovering the structure of the molecule will require hours of painstaking research.

'Neither,' I admit to Vittorio. 'At least it's too early to say.'

Suddenly the silver-haired American comes to mind.

'This morning, at the crystallography conference, a man at the talk called the alpha helix "Herman's alpha". Do you know the name?' I add after a pause.

'Herman Branson? He's an associate professor in Professor Pauling's lab. Why do you ask?'

'It's probably nothing,' I say.

'I don't doubt that Herman did most of the work on the alpha helix; he's a physics genius. That might have been hard for Pauling to accept.'

'Why?' I ask Vittorio.

'It's Pauling's lab, he'll want to take the credit. And, well, it hasn't been that easy for African-American scientists to get the recognition they deserve.'

That night, inside one of the dwellings that line the edge of the battlements, a group from the Paris lab has arranged to meet for dinner. Vittorio's comment, and his trademark forthrightness, still resonate. Inside, the eatery's low ceilings are hung with wooden beams, and the backs of the chairs are laden with furs. Even in summer, Sweden's chilly gusts could pierce the skin, though it is warm enough inside the restaurant to thaw the coldest of hearts. Blood pudding and thick cream are served with smörgåsbords filled with fermented-milk products. The Swedes, it seems, have survived centuries of bitter cold through copious hot food and drink.

'We went without for so long,' I say, proposing a toast.

Anne, whose husband David used to visit our lab in Paris, clinks her glass against mine and they chime a chord. While I was living in Paris, David – a postgraduate biology student from the United States – had begun to study proteins using X-ray crystallography and wanted to learn from the best. He came to Paris to glean all that he could from Mering and his team. Anne then taught at Tuskegee, a Pennsylvania university that enrolled black students – something Harvard and Yale had done rarely since last century's Civil Rights Act was repealed and the pejorative Jim Crow laws had engulfed much of the Deep South.

Anne is plain-speaking and inventive in equal measure. She all but gave up her dreams of becoming a lawyer when she was forced to find industrial work at a radiation lab during the war years but has since instilled her appetite for justice in her pen. After marrying David and moving to England she became an editor at the Oxford University Press. We haven't seen each other since I was living near the Seine, and so arrange to visit the local patisseries together the next day.

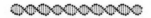

The shopfronts near the battlements offer a cornucopia of pastel-coloured delicacies. There are chocolate and cherry-filled *körsbär* chokladtårta, prinsesstårta gateau, spettekaka, and a saffron cake called saffranspannkaka. I buy several of the cakes to share with Anne.

'What do you think of them?' she asks me while teasing away a fist-sized chunk of canary-coloured saffron cake.

'The cakes?'

'No, the houses.'

Away from the battlements and the main square, the prefabricated houses on either side of the streets of Stockholm are plain, tessellated and identical, unlike the Edwardian and Victorian terraces that line the side streets of Fulham, with their elaborate porches and glass adorned with unique fretwork and stains.

'They're so dull,' I reply, speaking of the prefabs, and am instinctively reminded of Maurice.

'What, like some of your colleagues?'

I laugh at the suggestion.

'At least you don't have to argue with each other in the lab,' she says.

'You would think so,' I say, imitating Maurice's squint, 'but that's not the case. We argue constantly.'

'They're not like Jacques then,' she says.

'No.' I pause.

'Surely there's no need to fight when there's evidence to back up your findings,' she adds.

Anne spent several years submitting short stories to magazines and papers before joining academic publishing. The contrast meant she brought with her the view that science is always objective.

'At the journals, do you take everything that's sent to your desk?'

'Hardly, editors and writers rarely agree on anything,' Anne says.

Ever since it was founded in 1869, *Nature* journal has not once hired a woman as chief editor, and it has been known for friends of the editor to secure publication before others. Anne, likewise, admits to me that fewer women's bylines reach the front pages, and many more are left missing in action.

'Exactly,' I say, as my stomach clenches.

| 15 |

The Rising Tide

Cambridge, July 1951

Raymond is standing, bored, outside the Greene, King and Sons public house, which is directly opposite the gravel path up to Newnham. He is bored in the way children are; rather than seeing life as meaningless, he hungers for more of it. The chain has taken over most of Cambridge. The hanging baskets at the end of the towpath, outside the pub by the River Cam, are overflowing with pansies and marigolds in lurid colours. 'I'll go as far as Trinity,' says the student manning the nearest punt.

He talks to us while balancing one foot on the jetty and resting his other leg on the boat.

'Shall we?' I point towards the water.

'Can you let us off at the Cavendish?' Raymond asks the punter, who replies by saying it's not the first time he's been asked to make sure that students don't miss class.

'We're here for a talk on proteins *actually*,' I say, shrugging off his extended arm and stepping onto the flat-bottomed gondola, easing myself onto the damp cushion in its waterlogged well.

Raymond takes one foot off the jetty and then grabs my

shoulder to recover his balance. The punter dives forward to help him, forgetting he's still holding the oar, which slams against the side of the boat.

'Wasn't that...?' Raymond begins to ask as the punt moves away from the bank.

I nervously put on my sunglasses as he peers in the direction of Newnham.

He's facing in the direction of my old college. I don't say a word. How can I explain to him that the women's college, which I attended, gave out decrees at the time instead of degrees? Despite completing a doctorate since then, I might lose his trust, if not his respect.

The verdant lawns and lichened benches at my alma mater that morning are unchanged from my student days. Every scientist in the books I had read in its red-turreted dormitories a decade ago had stood on the shoulders of every other scientist that had gone before them. As students, we were united by our futures, which lay firmly in front of us, not behind us. That alone soldered any of the differences that would have otherwise divided us. Time stretched before us in a limitless eternity back then. Now it races ahead at breakneck speed, tethered to the ghosts that are in its wake. Perhaps one day the rising tide of success would lift all boats.

Standing at the back of the punt, the student assuredly steers by wading a single oar through the water. The punt floats effortlessly along the river, freshening our faces with back spray. The tall tree trunks cast a forgiving shade over the water, and behind it rabbits are hopping idly along the riverbank.

'Don't you think it's odd that the research council asked Maurice to speak,' Raymond says as the punt passes the pristine wickets outside Trinity College, 'when the talk is on proteins?'

'Isn't that what he's working on?' I ask.

'Never mind.' Raymond is evasive, dipping his fingers into the water rather than answering my question.

The Cavendish laboratory resembles a dilapidated baronial fortress. The building is swamped in ivy, a stark contrast to the proud Grecian columns at Trinity College. The front of the lab has been extended with a plain circular outbuilding, an import from German Bauhaus. The extension is blander than all the rest of the buildings at the School of Physical Sciences. Its only point of interest is a crocodile that has been carved onto the brickwork, which according to legend mocks Ernest Rutherford, its most illustrious professor.

The Maxwell lecture theatre inside the building is exactly how I remember it. It still has the same Belfast sink on one side, for demonstrations that go awry. But the pale glaze on the enamel sink has now cracked, and up close, the varnish on the benches has also faded and chipped. The mahogany panelled benches are otherwise still the same, though the fish tail burner lamp brackets have gone.

Standing at the entrance to the auditorium is Dr Perutz, who is greeting guests coming to Cambridge's inaugural seminar on proteins. His cheeks are pink and shiny and, above them, his thick black glasses are resting tightly on his heavy-set brow. Dr Perutz had left Austria after graduating from a university in Vienna, amid rumours that exciting new studies were being conducted at Cambridge. He has the nervous laugh of a man who's lived a life on the edge of precarity. Yet his dimples suggest that he smiles too often to hide any malevolence. All the same, I worry he will forget my name again, as he did in Stockholm.

Raymond shakes Dr Perutz's hand, as I smile and nod.

Professor Randall refused to come to today's protein symposium; he had little personal leverage with the research committee and he views the new post he's been given in Dr Perutz's molecular biology working group as a token gesture. Ever since the research council installed a committee to oversee his department, the professor has suspected ulterior motives.

After greeting the attendees, Dr Perutz sits down next to Bill Seeds, a student of Maurice's. To his right is Francis

Crick, whom Professor Randall recently refused a job. John Kendrew, a doctoral graduate who's been using X-rays to study haemoglobin, a component of blood, is sitting further down the row.

'It's wonderful to be with you today.' Maurice coughs and shuffles his papers on the lectern that is facing the sloping stairwell.

He then says something that takes me by complete surprise.

'DNA gives patterns that are basically the same,' he says, while adjusting his glasses.

I sit there unblinking, as the awareness that he's not talking about proteins at all, but about DNA, electrifies my spine. The audience is unmoved despite the fact they are here to see a talk on proteins. I cannot understand why no one is complaining.

'The Signer pattern gives a diameter of twenty angstroms,' Maurice says. 'There are one hundred million of those per millimetre...'

By the end of his talk, he is sucking his chest up towards his chin with pride like the tuxedoed men at Cambridge had done at graduation.

I head towards the exit, shielding my face with my hand in the hope he will not notice me. As I walk past the tea queue in the adjacent hall, Dr Perutz is gloating to one of the attendees about the talk.

'Rosy, what are you doing here?' Maurice stops me from leaving just as I reach the door.

My heart begins to palpitate: blood thunders through my veins. He always calls me Rosy, like I am a girl, even though just four years separate him from me. I turn thirty-one this month.

'It doesn't make sense for us to both work on DNA.' The words cascade from my mouth in a single exhalation. 'Professor Randall said no one else was working on the problem.'

Maurice frowns. 'I don't know what gave him that impression,' he says, polishing his glasses with the handkerchief he keeps in his breast pocket. 'What else would I do?' he adds, with studious control.

'Go back to your microscopes.'

After I say the words, I flee through the circular outbuilding and run towards the station, kicking the leaves that have blown from the riverside onto the road. Tears are streaming down my face. The only thing more dangerous than someone who has nothing to lose, was someone like him who has everything to gain.

| 16 |

Kings and Men

The crater in the quad is just visible from Professor Randall's office. Six years on from the war, it's an indelible sign of what has been lost. There are still fighters in Japan battling an invisible enemy in the jungle. The papers are calling them 'stragglers'. The social contract, of honour, still has an immense hold over them. Russia executed former captives when they returned home for bringing shame on their country. The Western victory may have been called a triumph over evil, but the death-or-glory stragglers in the jungle are no more evil than their adversaries. Everywhere, shades of grey left scars of crimson. The only victory to be had was in leaving the struggle behind and choosing life over warring factions.

That will soon be my choice to make.

Maurice is standing ominously by the shelves in the professor's office. His arms are folded.

He and Professor Randall, who is sitting on a stool with his elbows resting on his desk, are both staring at me inquisitively.

'It's like snow, isn't it?' Maurice says, handing me a cellophane packet full of white powder.

I couldn't imagine that the din I heard in the corridor earlier that afternoon had been over a packet of crystalline powder. There had been loud voices arguing outside my office, as was typical between Professor Randall and Maurice, who often have animated rows. Though it was most unusual for such a row to be followed by good news.

'It's more… felt-like.' I pinch the granules between my index finger and thumb and hold the bag up to the incandescent basement light. 'There's a faint yellowing. Where did you get it?'

'Dr Chargaff.'

Although I had heard the enigmatic Austrian chemist Erwin Chargaff gave samples of DNA to our lab, I haven't had the chance to meet him yet.

'Chargaff has an awesome idea. It works like this, Rosy. Complex sequences in DNA could be the gene itself.'

Maurice clasps his hands together behind his skull, in satisfaction, and leans back on his swivel chair.

'Actually, we got some results while you were away, Dr Wilkins,' I say.

'Chargaff is a very skilled scientist. He was a research fellow at Yale, you know. Studied in Vienna,' Maurice continues as though I haven't spoken.

'It seems you don't want to hear what I have to say,' I insist.

Maurice is gazing at the light streaming through the window, still oblivious to my words. He then turns slowly to face me. 'What is it, Rosy?' he says finally, with agitation.

'The structure of the atoms changes when DNA gets wet,' I stutter.

Maurice wrinkles his forehead as he examines my X-ray images.

'They're clearer, aren't they?' I say.

'They are *different*,' he says, with a guttural sound, before handing the photos back to me with an affected air of indifference.

'Changing the humidity alters the structure,' I say, scanning a finger over the images.

'From the tighter-packed structure here, A, to this here in photo B.'

'Is that what you're calling them, Rosy? They'll need a new name if these images are truly different.'

Maurice mutters something, and then turns his chair towards the professor. He's begrudged giving me the Swiss specimens ever since I arrived, though Professor Randall insisted on it when he switched my work to DNA. The fibres were extracted from the calf-thymus glands that are sold as sweetbreads at the butcher. Perhaps Maurice got bored of the problem – he didn't seem to be making much progress with getting any clearer photographs of DNA – or maybe he was too preoccupied with his mistress.

I have found that when the Signer strands, sourced from Professor Rudolf Signer at the University of Bern, were dissolved in solution the X-ray patterns were as sharp as fractal cracks on ice. The fibres changed visibly before my eyes into another state when wet; water is to ice like the saturated thymus strands are to the crystallised fibres. Much like all living organisms, it seemed that DNA was *thirsty*.

'Right, you probably know what's coming,' Professor Randall says abruptly, slapping his thighs in exasperation. 'I've been hearing far too much about the both of you. Your colleagues say that all you do is bicker and send notes between the two of you using a doctoral student as your go-between. To settle this once and for all, I suggest that Dr Franklin continues to work on crystallised DNA; this A form you speak of. Dr Wilkins, you will take B.'

'But my photographs show clearer images of the wet form,' I say, at pains to explain to him that he's proposing to hand over my discovery.

'Is that all, Dr Franklin? My labours have been focused on this matter for far too long. I have other things to be getting on with, like providing updates to our funders.'

The professor interrupts me before I have a chance to explain further.

It seems that jealousy, curiosity – call it what you will – has got the better of Maurice. Perhaps it gets all of us, in the end. Previously, I had been led to believe that he had no interest in pursuing DNA any longer, but as soon as we were making progress with solving the problem of its structure, he wanted to take the work back. Now that he's taken the work from me, we are both shackled to his mistakes. Me to his experiments at low humidity, as the crystallised form I must now work on is dry, and he to the new poorer-quality DNA fibres from Chargaff. There is little chance he will be able to use them to take my recent discoveries any further. The yellowing is a clear sign of entropy.

'Of course, Professor Randall, but it was my photographs with the fine-focus X-ray that…' I begin.

'That's the last I want to hear of this mithering,' Professor Randall says, insisting that we leave.

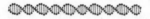

Several days later a mysterious note is pinned to the lab noticeboard. It reads *Waves at Bessel on Sea* in the unmistakably messy scrawl of Alec Stokes. We often leave jokes for each other in the lab. There's one game of chess on a table between the two rival departments that has lasted for several months.

The chessboard is still sitting in the corridor between our offices, after hitting a stalemate.

'Did you know Bessel deciphered the distance between stars?' Alec says over my shoulder.

'The parallax?'

'When a star's position is measured in different seasons, as the seasonal measurements diverge, the closer the star is to Earth,' he says.

'Light isn't a linear beam though, of course,' I say, lifting my eyes from the noticeboard momentarily.

'Which Bessel made good mathematical use of.'

'Are you talking about Bessel's functions? Daniel Bernoulli may have had something to say about that.'

'Bernoulli?' he asks.

'It was his theory of the vibrating string that Bessel applied to light.'

Russian-German polymath Friedrich Bessel had popularised the Bessel function but didn't strictly invent it. That was easy to forget. Instead of focusing on strings, he used the formula to describe the angle that light bounces off an atom, to show the direction of a wave of light.

'Bessel used his theory to measure what phase light is in, in or out, like the tide,' I say.

'I prefer to think of it as a shift in key, imperceptible to the untrained ear, it transforms the tone of a composition. It must be sheet music to a crystallographer like you,' Alec says, turning to face me.

'Stokes has a bosting idea.' Maurice appears suddenly and puts his arm around Alec.

'*This* mathematical brainbox is using Bessel functions to calculate the diffraction pattern that would be given by a helix,' he says.

'I see.'

'A bit of improvisation wouldn't go amiss, Rosy, perhaps you could learn a thing or two,' Maurice boasts.

'I've read the note.'

I tilt my head towards the noticeboard.

'What Maurice means is, Bessels will help us calculate where the atoms would be if DNA was a helix,' Stokes says in his soft, monotonous tone.

'We've been using Bessel functions to plot atomic diagrams since before the war. What's new?' I respond.

I find it hard to believe that they would go to the trouble of posting a joke on the noticeboard for everyone to see unless it moved the problem forward.

'It's marvellous how well the calculations correspond to the B diffraction pattern,' Maurice enthuses.

My heart nearly misses a beat. Could he have been looking at my photographs behind my back? I always keep them shut away in my top drawer.

'The straight grey line on the photograph, and the intensity variation, correspond perfectly,' Maurice says.

He *is* talking about one of my photographs, as clear as day. First, he took the best half of my fellowship work. Now he's stealing my X-rays.

'How dare you take my photographs and pass them off as your own!' I say, shaking at the realisation.

Maurice laughs, smugly, as I rush down the corridor to save my work.

| 17 |

Fellowship

Troy Mill was the property of King's College Cambridge for longer than any of its concomitant professors survived. The Hertfordshire mill house was part of the college estate and one of several properties meted out to generations of professors in succession. It had pitched orange roofs and too many windows for its size. Professor Randall and his wife live a stone's throw away from the old estate at The Farm House in Batchworth. The wooden gate to the farmhouse is overhung by a large tree. Behind the gate, the house is surrounded by meadow views. A river runs around the nearby town and through the adjacent crop fields.

A curvaceous woman greets me at the door. It is half past twelve, the time given on the invitation.

'You must be Rosalind,' she says. 'Let me take your coat.'

She passes canapés around to guests who are already roaming in the living area, which is adjoined to the kitchen and dining room. Bing Crosby is playing on the brass record player nestled between the sideboard and curtains. The table next door is full of distressed orange Le Creuset casserole dishes.

I wipe moisture from the back of my neck with my hand and fix my hair in the overmantel mirror.

Professor Randall is standing by a kitchen island overhung by copper pans suspended from the ceiling. He's wearing a black suit, bow tie, and a shirt half-tucked into his trousers. In his breast pocket is a corsage of flowers freshly picked from the meadow at the back of the farmhouse, to free himself from the hegemony in the echelons of all the serious professions.

'Waldo Cohn will supply us with thymidine for our nucleosides work, but we mustn't use it for anything else,' he is saying.

'He's restricting its use?' says Maurice, a glass of red wine in hand. 'Dreadful.'

'We don't know what dangers are lurking in there. Apparently, it's impure,' says the professor, moving his glasses slowly back onto the bridge of his nose.

'Rosalind, have you met Doris?' Professor Randall asks when he notices me, calling in his wife of twenty years. 'Come say hello, duck,' he says.

'I met Mrs Randall at the door. She offered to take my jacket,' I reply.

'That would have been my housekeeper, Mrs Stanley,' he says.

I do not know what to say to him. I have little interest in meeting the professor's wife, for I fear we will have nothing in common other than our gender. 'Is it worth taking the risk with impure thymidine?' I say instead.

'This is an unusual fittle,' Maurice says before the professor can answer. He lifts a white rubbery substance from the plate on the kitchen island. 'A sort of coral, is it? The New Zealand shore had all sorts, but I haven't seen this before.'

'It's intestines,' I say.

'Come on, Rosy, don't be silly.'

'It's andouille. In France it's made into a sausage, steamed, boiled, then poached,' I explain.

Maurice chokes.

'I wouldn't want to come to one of your dinner parties,' he says under his breath.

I haven't had any dinner parties since leaving Paris but did promise to treat Raymond to French onion soup one evening after the work was completed.

'Use your loaf, man. It's tripe, it's a delicacy in the north. It won't kill you,' Professor Randall says, patting Maurice on the back.

'I'm vegetarian,' he replies. His face has blanched.

The men standing around the kitchen island go quiet.

'I shall be fine with the Signer DNA,' I say, to break the silence.

'Those Faraday Society meetings haven't half come in useful, have they?' says Professor Randall.

It was at an earlier Faraday meeting that Maurice had met Signer, who'd supplied the calf thymus fibres which, since Randall split the work between us, I am using to study the structure of DNA.

Maurice coughs.

When he notices the professor is waiting for a response, he is flustered, and starts fiddling with his glasses.

'They have another meeting in September,' Maurice adds. 'It might be worth me wandering down. Perhaps Pauling might make an appearance this time.'

'Oh yes, that old codger,' Professor Randall says.

'I hope you told him to meddle elsewhere,' Maurice says.

I yearn to ask the professor what he means, but cannot reach for the words. My voice might not be heard. The way I speak is quiet but purposeful. I rarely shout loudly, like the men. Although my lungs have the capacity, it would start a needless conflict that would be hard to extricate myself from.

'Has Professor Pauling been meddling?' I ask in the end.

The men do not hear me. Their eyes remain fixed in each other's direction. I am grateful, at least, that Professor Randall has given up on introducing me to his wife.

'I intend to tell him it wouldn't be fair to the efforts of our laboratory to hand over our X-rays,' the professor says.

'Isn't he working on proteins?' I ask him.

'He thought we intended to disregard our X-rays. A certain mathematical biologist told him our lab was no longer pursuing X-ray data,' Professor Randall says while eyeballing Maurice.

'Surely not Dr Oster,' Maurice says. 'I thought he was studying ant populations.'

'Ants aren't all that's captured his imagination,' Professor Randall roars. 'Which reminds me, how are the lads getting on at Cambridge?'

'It's me who should be asking you, John, as honorary director of the research council,' Maurice says, pausing, as if for innuendo.

'Still checking up on us, are they?' Professor Randall composes himself into a more upright posture, adding inches to his height.

'The Cavendish lab has hired Jim Watson. Clever chap, he's into birdwatching,' says Maurice. 'I've invited him to our lecture next month.'

The professor raises his eyebrows. 'There's little opportunity for ornithology here,' he says, wryly.

They jostle for space for a few moments, like stags fighting to mate.

'You might regret not hiring his lab mate, Francis. He's become a rather good *friend*,' Maurice says, testily, after a pause.

Not long after Professor Randall ordered Maurice and I to split the work on DNA I was approached by Professor Bernal, who I had admired at the conference in Stockholm. He offered me a job in his lab at Birkbeck, University of London. His surprise letter seemed fortuitous, and yet I couldn't help but wonder if Randall had gone behind my back to have a word with Bernal to try and rid me from the lab. Leaving King's College and my fellowship behind would take more than a few harsh words, it would require a competing offer from another university that would enable me to transfer the placement to another lab.

Now I wait for an opportunity to take the professor aside and explain to him that Maurice has been using my X-ray photographs, but the moment never comes.

'There's no room for egos here,' the professor says, before switching the conversation back to Mrs Randall and the allotments.

| 18 |

Duplicity

Strand Campus, King's College London, November 1951

The airy lecture theatre at King's College London is unornamented, except for the polished parquet floor. A wincing draught from the far side windows has chilled the air in the room. Around the perimeter of the hall, scientists from across the university are scattered, drinking beer and talking loudly. Their huddles are thick and impregnable. Our annual colloquium shares the same Latin root as 'colloquial', but the lecture has little else in common with the military state of Rome, other than perhaps rigour.

I wind my way to the front of the crowd, avoiding the men's glances.

'I'll be on first, then Alec will go next. Rosy, you'll be speaking last.' Maurice is peering at me down the bridge of his nose.

'Isn't it better if I explain the X-ray findings first?' I whisper.

'I'll summarise that too,' he says, looking around to judge the warmth in the room.

'But I have all the data.'

Maurice chooses not to hear me. He moves swiftly through

the huddles to the front of the hall, while coughing theatrically, as if to elicit laughter or applause.

'The purpose of this colloquium is to summarise our DNA work so far,' he says, reading from a piece of paper, oblivious to whether anyone is listening. 'We also have an important visitor, one of our friends from Cambridge – he's a prodigious talent, Jim Watson.'

The words echo loudly in the brightly lit space.

A man in his early twenties, who is standing next to Maurice, laughs as though he's told a joke worthy of Broadway. His laughter is the only sound in the room. The man looks as though he hasn't had a good meal in years. His face is skeletal and his eyes are deep-set. Maurice splits from the man, holding an arm in the air to get a response from the crowd, though this falls flat to no reaction.

'I've noticed, from looking at squid sperm heads and DNA under the microscope, a familiar crossways pattern,' Maurice says.

The precipice of a cliff in the Alps suddenly tears across my vision. I had stumbled while on holiday there with Jean. Then I picture my body plummeting, like in a dream, and hitting unforgiving rocks below, as he continues to speak about DNA. I feel the intense glare of the light at the front of the lecture hall on my neck and readjust my glasses as Maurice repeats his observations… my observations.

'Chargaff has supplied us with some excellent DNA samples. He's tinkering around with the nitrogen bases, adenine, guanine, cytosine and…?' Maurice continues.

'Thymine,' I remind him, speaking through the corner of my mouth.

'Oh, thymine, yes.' Maurice blushes. 'He's looking at some sort of order for them.'

'Ratios,' I whisper.

'What was that?' Maurice gulps before addressing the audience again. 'Rosy, Ms Franklin, I mean Dr Franklin, tells us he is in fact looking at the ratios of nitrogenous bases in the nucleotides. My mistake.'

The crowd begins to dissipate as Maurice repeats the data again. After finishing his talk, Maurice pats Alec on the back, who is hanging his head despondently.

'Thank you,' Alec says several times, more quietly with each repetition, before starting his talk.

'There is only one way to trace the diffraction of light from a helix,' he says, reading from a ragged piece of lined notepaper.

His round glasses slip down the bridge of his nose, but he doesn't stop to readjust them.

'A helix or spiral shape would correlate closely to wave or cylindrical motion,' Alec continues. 'Bessel functions can be very helpful in determining the refraction of light from atoms in such a configuration.'

'There is the Patterson function,' I say under my breath, glancing down at my feet. In Stockholm, I heard the mathematical function described as the information contained in a vector map.

The audience shifts and sighs, as he is not telling them anything new, and Alec leaves the stage to scant applause. Suddenly, waiting doesn't seem so bad. I press my trembling hands into my pockets to disguise their twitch, take out my glasses and put my notes firmly against the stand. Behind the lenses of my glasses, I can hide.

'Thank you for staying with us until the end of the talk,' I begin. 'There isn't really much to add. Much of my findings have already been discussed this evening.'

The room is unreactive. But then how would they know that the previous speakers had used much of what was already in my notes? They couldn't.

'We have been working on new techniques, which mean we've been able to get clearer photographs than ever before that have allowed us to work out many aspects of DNA's structure.'

The man who is probably Jim is staring up at me from sullen eyes. He scrutinises my hair and outfit from just a few feet away. The stealth in his step and intensity of his gaze reads of a desire to possess everything he sets his eyes on. His gaze is cloying, thick and suffocating, like molasses. I shudder as he continues to move his eyes over my lips, my hair, and my neck. His mouth is agape like the caged rodents in the lab's animal enclosure when they fear being caught.

'At higher humidity, we are able to produce clearer images than ever before. We now know that the phosphate groups are located on the outside of the molecule.' I sift through my typed notes.

Given Maurice and Alec have summarised much of my findings before I had the chance to do so, as well as parroting some older findings that show little new, it is hard to know what is left to say. The helix has already been covered in quite some detail. The eyes of everyone in the room are all on me and the sound of their laughter and coughing crescendoes in my ears. I would rather be under a blanket than here, giving a talk to an inattentive group of men. They are like vultures seducing their next meal.

'I was going to speak about evidence for the helix and our other experimental findings – but I'm sure you all have homes to go to tonight,' I say.

In rare moments of abandon, I imagined that the audience, captivated by my every word, would break into raucous applause at the end of my lecture. The reality is very different. Guests are already walking towards the door at the back of the room to leave.

Jim stays behind. He is taciturn and has packed lightly, without a notebook or pen. He seems neither enlivened nor particularly bored by the talk.

'Nice of you to put your assistant on the podium,' I catch him saying to Maurice. 'If only she did something nice with her hair.'

I sweep my chocolate-brown locks behind my ears self-consciously and fold away my glasses. It seem to only ever be men who comment freely on a woman's looks, as if they are fair game. They, however, lack the same scrutiny. From puberty, our appearance is measured, dissected and masked, by our mothers and at finishing schools. We collect the profligate judgments and criticisms, wearing the deepest of the wounds, and loathe inwardly. His assumption is clearly wrong. I too made the assumption that he was young enough to be a student, and that he was probably Jim Watson, but why did Maurice not correct him?

'You must be James Watson,' I say, squashing my anger until it's a dull pain in the pit of my stomach. 'I'm Dr Franklin.'

'Tell me about Copenhagen?' Maurice interrupts, leaning in his friend's direction. Not for the first time that evening, I feel invisible.

'You can call me Jim, Ms Franklin.'

'It's Dr Franklin,' I reply.

Jim flinches. He is breathing heavily, with his eyes wide, but doesn't say anything in response.

'Jim has an interest in DNA,' Maurice says.

'Schrödinger's book *What is Life?* was neat,' Jim waxes, 'It's why I went into biology, that *and* the birds.'

'He's just got back from Copenhagen,' Maurice adds. The shadows under his eyes have deepened.

'Isn't the university there doing some work on the brain?' I ask.

'They're looking into mental defectiveness,' Jim says without compassion.

'I wouldn't have put it quite like that,' I say, taking a step back from him.

The way scientists frame difference is tainted with the same prejudice and cruelty as any other profession. While the data should be self-evident, the context of how an experiment is set up and framed are crucial to how the story is told.

Hastily making his excuses to leave, Jim asks where he can find the nearest phone. 'I'm meeting my lab partner,' he says. 'There's a train I must catch.'

'But it's only five o'clock,' Maurice says. 'Won't you stay for a drink? You can send my regards to Francis on the train up tomorrow. Why don't we get dinner at this little place I know in Soho.'

| 19 |

Maquette

The breeze has stirred up a thick cloud of atmospheric dust over London. The air here is usually tarry and stagnant compared to the Seine, but there is a pea-souper smog overhanging the city this morning. Outside the drinking houses on the backstreets up from Temple, I brush cigarette smoke away with the back of my hand but it does little to clear the air. In blustery conditions like these my steel bicycle frame has a tendency to swerve uncontrollably in the eddies, so today I took the train. When I get to the university entrance, someone unexpectedly bumps into me — probably a sky watcher observing the same phenomenon — and the collision sucks the air out of my lungs.

'Rosalind?'

Despite the knock, Dr Price's creased newspaper remains firmly tucked under his arm. He is a physics lecturer in Randall's department and a director of the university spectroscopy group, which conducts infrared studies measuring the absorption of light and radiation by matter. Although he's a Welshman, you can't tell from his accent. He's lost it the same way as Richard Burton has, so that all that's left is a deep and sonorous tone.

'I'm off to see Bruce's new model,' he says, hopping towards the stone staircase without looking back in my direction.

Light is streaming through the arched windows above the turnstile into the foyer below, casting long shadows onto the limestone. Past the marble statues of ancient Greek playwright Sophocles and opposite poetess Sappho, then up the stone staircase with the thick balustrades, I begin to quicken my pace to keep up.

'I'll join you,' I say, gasping for breath.

At the landing, I sweep my fingers along the cool metal of the century-old miniature steam train that sits on a heavy slab of stone by the window. The coolness of it reminds me of why we are here: for scientific progress.

Dr Price shoves his newspaper into my arms when we reach the door to the physics department. I don't immediately take it, startled as to why he is giving it to me until he then begins waving it in front of my eyes.

Bruce is standing at the door of his office, welcoming a group of scientists. He's wearing a neatly pressed high-buttoned shirt with the starched collar splayed over his lab coat.

'Take a look, feel free to explore,' Bruce tells them in a detached tone.

He follows each newcomer into the room with a nod of his head, ending every sentence on a low note, portraying, or indeed maybe it is truly felt, a sense of unswerving confidence. Inside his office is his new model of DNA. It has three chains of atoms, which wrap around each other tightly. The sugar bases are stacked in the middle, moulded together by chemically and mathematically impossible hydrogen bonds.

'No Maurice?' I ask him, looking around the room. We take our pews on a pair of rickety stools.

'He spent the weekend in Cambridge with the Cricks,' Bruce replies.

I recognise the name from Maurice's idolatrous riffs about the Cavendish lab's new microbiologist, Francis Crick.

'Doesn't Francis work with the man who was skulking around our lecture the other day?' I ask.

'Jim Watson? Yes, that's right. He's on tenterhooks right now.'

'Who, Jim or Francis?' I ask.

'Francis.'

'Isn't Jim meant to be the bawdy one?'

'Francis had a disagreement with Professor Bragg over his haemoglobin paper; he threatened to boot him out. He can be, *strong-minded*, as Maurice would say. Hadn't you heard? I thought you and Maurice took regular lunches together on the Strand.'

I haven't seen Maurice, who often prowls the corridors of the university with a copy of *The Times* in hand, since our trip to Cambridge. 'We haven't spoken since I told him to go back to his microscopes and leave DNA alone.'

Bruce splutters. 'Oh yes, he won't stop going on about that.'

'Is that what you men talk about in the common room?'

'Sports, mainly. Anyway, I'd better go and mingle,' he says, getting up from his chair.

I catch him talking to himself under his breath, between speaking with and smiling at his visitors.

'The three chains in your model are spaced equally apart,' I say, pulling him aside a few minutes later.

'Yes, and?'

'It contradicts the X-ray diffractions.'

'We have a bit of tweaking to do,' Bruce says, lifting his foot as though he is about to step away.

'Remember the tortoise and the hare?' I say.

'The tortoise exploited the fact that the hare sat on its laurels,' Bruce says.

I stare at him in disbelief.

A few weeks earlier, Bruce had begged me to assist his model-building exercise. He asked me how many chains of atoms knitted together to form a single molecule of DNA. This was the holy grail. It was the crucial key to understanding the structure. The water measurements suggested it had multiple chains, certainly more than one.

'How many to be exact?' Bruce asked.

I had learned while studying coal that some bits of fibre usually don't crystallise properly, which is why the edges of an X-ray photograph often look smudged. So I told him that this meant it made more sense to increase the number of chains in the molecule, rather than decrease them.

'What does that mean for my model?' Bruce asked.

It didn't make sense to build a model until we had enough data to be certain of the structure. The X-rays suggested the molecule was spiral-shaped, with more than one chain. I began to explain to Bruce that our diffraction diagrams indicated it was likely to have two chains, but that the images of the outer layer were unclear when he made the assumption.

'If you increase the number of chains to make allowances...' I started.

'I know. So there must be three,' he said, leaping to conclusions. I could see little point after this in continuing the conversation.

'Have you seen Mary?' I ask him as we sit in his office observing the model while his guests are milling around in the background.

'She's back at home today after finishing up late last night with the herrings.'

'Oh yes, I forgot you two are married.'

'And she's feeling a little gnarly,' Bruce says.

'Poor Mary, is she sick?' I ask.

'She's vomiting almost constantly.'

'What do you think caused it?'

'She's having our baby,' Bruce says, after a sigh.

'What? Really?' I lift both hands to my mouth.

'Just don't say anything, Rosy,' Bruce says while composing himself. His blue eyes are twinkling.

He disguises a smile, which is easier to do in front of Dr Price – who is looking in our direction – than hiding a pregnancy bump. Bruce's job is reaching new heights while Mary is stuck at home either unwell with morning sickness, or fatigue from working late, or both. Who knows if her job will be safe when her boss finds out?

'As long as you promise never again to call me Rosy,' I reply, before turning to Dr Price, who is walking in our direction.

'I see you've taken my advice on the stacked bases and how the hydrogen bonds might combine with them,' he says to Bruce with a satisfied smile.

'That's right,' Bruce says.

'I paired it with Maurice and Raymond's early work on the diameter of DNA, as well as Rosy here's canny insight that the phosphates are grouped on the outside.'

I dig my elbow into Bruce's waist, but he ignores me and continues to smile. He then puts his hand on Dr Price's forearm and together they waltz off to take a closer look at the model.

He hadn't dared correct his supervisor on the ill-advised hydrogen bonds. By suppressing that misinformation to preserve a man's pride, the credibility of all of our work could easily be erased.

| 20 |

Icarus

London and Cambridge, one week later, November 1951

Br-ring, br-ring.

The idle quiet in the lab is soon broken by the tinny ring of the office rotary dial.

'We're off to Cambridge,' Maurice says, uncoiling the wire from his hands and hanging up the phone.

'That was quick,' Raymond replies. 'I didn't think Jim was taking any notes at our lecture.'

The train to Cambridge is bumpy. Bruce is sitting on the far side of the carriage with Maurice and his student Bill, and they are talking animatedly.

'The thieving reprobates,' he says. 'Thank goodness I'm moving to Australia, away from this godforsaken playground.'

Maurice is strangely silent. He has as much to defend as any of us.

I have a sinking feeling. A call from Cambridge means the Cavendish lab has no doubt made progress. Has the past year been futile? Was I too cautious in abstaining from model-building?

'You can't rush science,' Adrienne always said.

I can still remember Professor Bragg introducing her as a

'student of Pierre Curie… and his wife Marie', and the way she calmly thanked him despite her grimace. She taught me that progress was never made in isolation. Scientists are much like bees in a hive, each with a role to play in the whole bee colony. Even if we have missed out on a discovery, we have taught the Cavendish scientists most of what they would have needed to know. I wonder then if I have unknowingly donated ideas to Cambridge's cause, much like I'd helped fund Adrienne's board. Yet no act of kindness, no matter how small, is ever wasted. My mother, who helped feed and clothe refugees during the war, knew as much. Similarly, no amount of progress, no matter how small, is ever worthless. Reflecting on this, I am able to transmute some of my despair.

When we get to Cambridge, Raymond and I wait at the bus stop. Across the road, Maurice and Bill get into a cab parked by the station.

'We'll have a pleasant walk at the other end when we get off the bus. The sun is shining,' I reassure Raymond.

'I trust you had a good journey,' Francis says when he opens the door to his office upstairs in the new Cavendish building.

The same broad smile creeps across his dimpled cheeks as I have seen on many a victorious tennis opponent.

'How was the bus? Glad you could join us finally,' Maurice says with a sardonic smile.

The desk in Jim and Francis's office is strewn with papers and books. On one side is a lopsided mechanical device propped against a whitewashed brick wall. The sculpture is made from rusty clamps, bolts and metal rods.

Francis, who is standing next to it, looks as if he is about to deliver a sermon. He speaks with the buoyancy of a schoolteacher on their first day in class, lifting his eyebrows to give full berth to the muscles around his lips. The corners of his almond-shaped eyes pinch together into optimistic creases as he talks.

'First I want to start by summing up the advantages of

a helical theory. Jim shares the same interest as myself. Afterwards, Jim and I will explain how we arrived at the proposed structure,' Francis says.

Francis is no older than Maurice, but his strawberry-blonde hair has receded to his ears, and he has wispy caterpillars for eyebrows. He is wearing an unironed, threadbare coat that matches his brown corduroy trousers and his woollen jumper is visibly bobbled. Sensing that he has lost our attention, Francis coughs.

'Afterwards, we'll go to the Eagle pub for a spot of lunch and discuss how to proceed with the final phase of the problem,' he says.

Still, nobody flinches.

'So. We have determined that Bessel functions give a clear answer to the problem.' Francis's unruly eyebrows rise and fall in crenulations as he talks.

Maurice crosses his arms. 'I'll stop you there, Francis,' he says. 'Alec has already had the idea to use Bessels to measure spots on the image. He worked it out on the train home. You can't tell us we've come all the way to wop-wop for that.'

Francis switches back to his dialectical analysis. 'Well, you can argue different points of view. You can say that DNA is likely to be a helix or is not a helix,' he says, 'But by looking at a few fundamental *qualia*...'

He canters in successive false starts, chasing the tail of a conclusion, as though his efforts were clipped, time and time again, in a correctional institution – a boarding school, perhaps.

'You're regurgitating a lot of theory here, Francis. Where's the proof?' I ask.

'Thank you, Rosy,' Francis replies. 'We will need to be answering such questions. If you look at Pauling's model, proteins are shaped like a helix. These are common shapes in nature, as they have been for millennia. A helix would make sense.'

'We're already well aware of these theories; everyone in Stockholm was talking about the alpha helix,' I say.

'Why don't we take a look at our model in that case, Rosy,' Francis says.

His eyebrows are raised hopefully, as though he realises he hasn't convinced his audience but thinks he will carry on regardless.

'The phosphates and the magnesium ions that hold our model together are on the inside of the structure, as you can see here,' Francis says, grinning.

'I'm afraid your model is inside out,' I say. 'The phosphates should be on the outside.'

Everyone in the room turns to Jim, who is slouching in his chair, willing himself not to be seen. He's wearing canvas shoes without laces and his shirt is loose. He obscures his gaunt face with his hands and caresses his bottom lip with his thumb.

'Your model couldn't possibly work,' I elaborate. 'The magnesium ions would be squeezed by tight shells of water molecules. The water content is about ten times larger than you've accounted for.'

It occurs to me that Jim must have misinterpreted my explanation at our annual lecture.

'Are you writing a book, Rosy?' Jim whines. 'Why all the accusations?'

Francis appeals to him for reassurance. 'Jim's done all the sums. We believe DNA has three chains,' he says, with Cheshire-cat glibness. 'The exact water content may not be necessary anyway. The water could fit into the empty spaces around the atoms.'

'No need to go nuts,' Jim says. 'Let's call time and grab some lunch.'

He stands and beckons for us to leave, extending his bony arm towards the door.

'After regurgitating my lecture, you could at least listen,' I say, tucking stray strands of hair behind my ears and getting my things to leave.

Jim freezes for a moment.

'Don't be a sap, Rosy,' he replies finally, smiling at the men before changing the subject. 'The food isn't exactly high table at the Eagle, but Francis eats there most days.'

Jim and Francis have made little real progress with model-building. Both theirs and Bruce's models have three chains, and both are wrong. Yet no one in the room seems ready to admit that.

'Lunch is just the ticket,' says Maurice, heading towards the door.

Jim, Francis and Bill walk out of the room, leaving Raymond and me trailing behind. They dawdle through the backstreets of Cambridge, crossing the River Cam and passing the sandstone chapel at the halls of King's College. The Cambridge college's full name, King's College of Our Lady and St Nicholas, has always seemed paradoxical to me as it is a male-only college.

'She won't let up with the biochemistry,' I overhear Jim say to Maurice. 'It's so pedantic.'

He is so careless with his words, and yet he cannot withstand the slightest criticism.

At the pub, the men order pints, and raise their voices above the hubbub. Everyone is shouting to be heard. The room smells of rancid beer, and the cacophony is deafening.

'It should only take a few weeks to know if the ions are of any relevance,' says Francis.

'With any luck, we'll be done by Christmas,' Jim adds.

'Our work won't be affected either way,' I say.

'Except maybe by giving us all a headache,' mutters Raymond.

'Don't be so negative, Rosy. Let's see what the experiments show before making conclusions,' Maurice says.

In the time it has taken to walk to the pub, he has altered his argument like a chameleon changes its skin. Bill nods in agreement.

'Shall we zigzag back to the lab?' Maurice suggests once we have finished eating.

'They didn't let fillies in in your day, did they, Rosy?' Jim bellows over his shoulder on our return.

I lean forward with a performative smile. 'Rosy, what am I, somebody's daughter?'

Raymond told me that they used the endearment ironically, as they didn't find me at all friendly. But I am not a girl. I am thirty-one years old and, unlike some of the other researchers, who are still completing their doctoral theses, this isn't my first postdoctoral fellowship.

Back at the Cavendish lab, Francis begins to discuss their model once more. His belligerence falls on deaf ears.

'I'm sure you'd like to know how we did it, and I can tell you,' he starts, stubbornly oblivious to the flaws in his theory.

Maurice checks his watch.

'If we move quickly, the bus might get us to the station in time for the three-forty train to Liverpool Street Station,' he says.

'Morning.'

My hands are slumped on the table in the women's tea room as Mary enters the next day. I put the kettle on and step aside, as she takes aim at a mug on the shelf. The cup lands on the tabletop with a bang.

'Did you hear about the Cambridge model?' I reply reflexively, straightening my blouse. 'How does Bruce feel about it?'

'Excellent, why?' Mary asks, articulating each syllable.

She seems to mask, rather than manifest, her feelings. Despite her smile, her jaw is clenched. Soon she will be leaving the plight of ordinary working women behind. The tradition, now she is with child, is that she will be dependent on her husband.

Our circumstances are as far apart as two comets hurtling

towards opposite ends of the galaxy. I do not envy Mary. The thought of asking for money to buy a comb, or groceries, makes me feel unwashed. The small degradations that housebound women must face, day in and day out, at the mercy of their husband's tempers, do not bear thinking of. Every time my mother smiled, it felt like she was closing a lid on her future. The long hours we had whiled away as children, waiting for our father to return home before we could eat, were mired in the hourly grind of the local buses. My parents have always had a traditional partnership; my father's wage was expected to pay for the family. My mother's smiles were a salve, when inside it felt like we were drowning.

I am better off living an independent life, earning my own money and choosing who I let in and when.

'Bruce wasn't upset then?' I ask.

There was once a time when Mary would regale the inside scoops from the men's common room to anyone who asked, but when there was the possibility of gunfire, she, like most women stayed well out of the firing line.

'I'm afraid I have to go, this calf DNA won't isolate itself,' she says, sauntering off with a mug of Earl Grey with a healthy dollop of cow's milk in it.

She swings her shapely hips leisurely from side to side as she walks. I gulp my coffee, black with no milk, as fast as possible and wait to feel the effect of the caffeine.

None of the women in the lab want to challenge the status quo. I marvel at how willingly they endure oppression. For me, it is a reminder of childhood days when my life was not my own.

V

NOW

| 21 |

Song of Songs

Paris, France, December 1951

The beating heart of Paris is alive with music. It is several days after the Festival of Lights, and the noise of children playing in the streets can be heard above the tooting of traffic in the square. The smell of freshly baked pastries emanates from the bistro on the corner. The air is infused with the woody, intoxicating scent of Gitanes from the couple crossing the road in matching overcoats.

Vittorio meets me outside the bistro, on the square nearest to Quai Henri. By now I am used to the Parisian air kiss. He leans forward and pecks me on each cheek.

'*Ciao*, Ros,' he says as he removes his felt hat and trench coat.

The air inside the bistro is pungent with the smell of coffee and the aroma of warm, flaky croissants. Circular tables are arranged on either side of the aisle, laden with fruit, crêpes served with Grand Marnier, and espressos. Waiters are flitting like insects from one side of the bistro to another in a blur.

'Tell me, how's it going? How far have you got?' Vittorio asks.

He stares into my eyes with laser focus.

Vittorio has the bare optimism of a man on stimulants – caffeine is his poison of choice – and his confidence is contagious. He is as fast as a hummingbird, as sharp as a bee, and as laser-focused as a predator. Some people find him confrontational, but I appreciate how he always casts his beam directly upon the shadows. He has gusto, Jacques would say. His direct manner means he often cuts to the heart of things. He can quickly identify problems, and something about his probing means he always elicits them out into the open.

'Well, our photographs are the clearest yet,' I say. 'Hexagonal nitrogenous bases run along the fibre. They are evidence for a spiral structure.'

'Go on,' Vittorio prompts, sweeping his hand in an imploring motion.

He leans back on to the burgundy upholstery in the booth and lights a cigarette. When the waiter comes, he orders croissants, orange juice, coffee and crêpes. He is commanding, much like my father, in a challenging rather than punitive way.

'There's an absence of reflections on the nucleus in the crystalline DNA. The non-hexagonal packing suggests there's a helix, with more than one chain,' I say.

'I see,' says Vittorio.

'We also observed a change when the DNA got wet. Only the equator shows a sharp reflection in that diagram.'

'What does that mean?' Vittorio lightly taps the bottom of his rolled cigarette paper on the table.

'It suggests the units are randomly displaced.'

'What have you got for me then, show me what you've got,' he says, while drumming all five fingers on his right hand against the table and taking a puff of his cigarette.

I pull my faded paper notes from my satchel.

'DNA appears to be a helix,' I say. 'And I have found that when the fibres get wet, the photos are much clearer.'

'But…?' he asks.

'Professor Randall handed that work to Maurice,' I say, resting my hands to one side of my crossed legs.

The café is busy and steam is coming out of the kitchen. I feel my cheeks flush.

'So, you have to work with this?' Vittorio says, pointing at the page on the dry DNA structure. 'You want to prove it's a helix?' he asks, leaning forward to examine it more closely.

'I need to know how many chains there are,' I say.

The question has escaped everyone so far.

'So, what's wrong?' Vittorio says.

'The Cavendish got the phosphates the wrong way around. They also got the water content wrong. Professor Randall was furious that they tried to use information from my lecture, it was just meant for internal staff; they couldn't even get that right as Jim didn't take notes,' I say.

'Huh,' Vittorio says, looking pensively at my notes while nodding to himself.

I stretch my legs over the soft burgundy leather, longing to be living here in Paris again, where conversations are flowing, not stunted, and people are helpful instead of critical.

'What do you think?' I ask.

'Amateurish,' Vittorio says.

'Well, I didn't claim it was ready,' I say, pulling my pencil skirt over my knees.

'The work at Cambridge, I mean,' he replies.

I recall Professor Bernal's lecture, where he said while you may think you have *a* solution, it doesn't mean it's *the* solution. That the difficulty is knowing how to distinguish between the two.

'Bruce's model doesn't match the X-rays either. The Cavendish lab sent their jigs, but the hasty model building hasn't got us very far.'

'What?' Vittorio asks. His eyes are wild.

'Raymond wasn't exactly enamoured by the idea of continuing to do calculations by hand,' I say.

'Doesn't Maurice want the jigs?' Vittorio asks.

'It seems not. I overheard him say Alec doesn't have

any interest in DNA now either. He's more concerned with theoretical problems.'

'And Bruce?' asks Vittorio.

'He's off to Australia. He and Mary have a baby on the way,' I say, sighing and looking down at my plate.

Vittorio does not let me sit with my uncomfortable feelings for long. It's a small kindness to save somebody from themselves, and I am always harder on myself than anyone else around me.

'So, you have few disturbances,' he says, then after the waiter delivers his espresso, 'tell me about Maurice.'

'Maurice tried to take back DNA. I told him to jolly well go back to his microscopes.' I pause for several seconds, unsure whether to explain the altercation with the professor. My conviction that he'd acted unfairly by giving away the wet DNA was strong, but I wasn't sure anyone would grasp enough of the problem to understand that. Randall's decision to separate and distribute the work between the dry and wet strands was admission enough that my discovery was significant. 'The professor handed the B DNA back to him.'

'So, he took the work from you?' Vittorio says.

'The B form, yes,' I reply.

'So, what can you do?' he asks, crossing his arms after stubbing his cigarette out and looking up at me.

'Come and work with you?' I say. 'If you need help investigating solutions, you will call me, won't you?'

I cup my chin in the palm of my hand and smile at Vittorio from across the table.

'I mean, what are you going to do about this situation?' Vittorio says, lifting his hands up in the air.

'I need a way of measuring the atoms, so we can work out their position. That would be indisputable proof of a helix, none of this model-building speculation,' I reply, gripping my coffee mug with both hands.

'Have you tried using the Patterson function? Try it. It

might yield something,' he says, clapping the leather folder with the bill together with both hands.

Arthur Patterson had once worked with William Henry Bragg, father of the head of Cambridge lab Professor William Lawrence Bragg. The father and son had together jointly won a Nobel prize. Before the war, Patterson began measuring the intensity of light to show how deeply a ray of it could penetrate an atom. His formula was able to produce a two-dimensional atomic image, but scientists had to use their imaginations to interpret the results. The method could plausibly show the depth of an atom within the molecule, to aid in drawing up an electron-density map. In the centre of each scattering of electrons, you could find the pearl: the atom.

'It's on me,' Vittorio says, discarding the change from his pocket onto the table when the waiter delivers the bill.

'Let me leave something,' I say, reaching for my purse.

'You're a visitor here in Paris, you are my guest,' he says, standing up and wrapping a cashmere scarf around his neck.

'They *are* paying me at King's, you know,' I say, tossing a couple of francs on the table.

'Yes, but how much?' Vittorio says.

My face is warm. I am too embarrassed to reply.

'I wasn't joking before when I said I would come and work with you. I miss Paris,' I say, as we exchange goodbyes outside the bistro.

'Paris misses you too, don't leave it so long next time,' Vittorio says, leaning in for an air kiss.

'I could always come and work with you on solutions.'

But Vittorio still does not believe that I am serious. 'Why don't you speak to Dorothy Hodgkin? She's the queen of the Patterson,' he says.

With those words, I part from my friend, with no idea when we will see each other again.

13 December 1951

Dear Maurice,

Just a brief note to thank you for the letters and to try to cheer you up. We think the best thing to get things straight is for us to send you a letter setting out in a mild manner our point of view. This will take a day or so to do, so we hope you'll excuse the delay. Please don't worry about it, because we've all agreed that we must come to an amicable arrangement...

So cheer up and take it from us that even if we kicked you in the pants it was between friends. We hope our burglary will at least produce a united front in your group!

Yours ever

Francis and Jim

| 22 |

Queen of the Patterson

Oxford, spring 1952

'The museum? What would you be wanting there now?'

The taxi driver unwinds his passenger window. The roads are the arteries of his city and passengers are its lifeblood.

'I'm just visiting a friend,' I say, getting into the back seat.

'What, a bunch of old dinosaurs?'

The driver's tweed cap bobs with the reverberations of the engine. He speaks in a mix of cockney and Midlands.

'A lady like you shouldn't be out at this time of night. Don't mind if I smoke, do you?'

With his left hand, he pulls out a Lucky Strike from a cigarette packet by the gearstick, while still holding the wheel. They're the new cigarette brand being imported from America.

'I wouldn't. Smoking causes cancer,' I say.

'Don't believe what you hear in the papers. Liars, the lot of them,' the cab driver replies.

'It's in the medical journals actually.'

He lights his cigarette anyway and then crosses several red lights. I am thrown from one side of the back seat to the other each time he grinds the pedal. I grab the handle above the door, after readjusting my cotton poplin shirt dress, and smudge dirt onto my gloves. As I wipe the soot off my glove against the handle, the bow is pressed out of shape.

In the glaucous mist, the Oxford museum resembles a cathedral.

'Glad you could make it. Good journey?' Dorothy's wide eyes are enquiring. She is standing by the ecclesiastical arched front door, under a neo-Gothic lantern and spire.

She was the first chemist to model the structure of penicillin, which she did while raising a young family. She'd also been a student of Professor Bernal, whom I heard speak in Stockholm. Their affair was widely known.

'Yes, aside from the driver wanting to tell me who I should and shouldn't visit at night,' I say.

'Indeed, why would anyone let a woman out into the world at all?' Dorothy says, creasing her eyes and sweeping back her ear-length hair.

Her bottom lip hangs loosely as she speaks. She has the languid voice of someone who has grown used to speaking with the older generation. During the war, she was brought up by her grandparents, after being sent back to England from Cairo, where her mother was a textile archaeologist.

'It's true, I don't get out of the lab much,' I confess.

The main hall inside the museum has high, intricately vaulted glass ceilings riveted together with iron bolts. The museum is filled with ancient relics, a colossal Tyrannosaurus rex, and other Mesozoic dinosaur bones and Pleistocene fossils. There are fossilised sauropods, ornithopods and theropods, and restored ichthyosaur, plesiosaur and crocodylomorph skeletons. Some of the fossils are recognisably from fish, the size of carp or larger, while others are from less recognisable vertebrates. As I cross the main hall, I accidentally walk into a table. A large stone fossil is still quivering in the glass display cabinet as we move on. Dorothy brushes off the accident, but her eyebrows are raised.

The floor of the museum is dusty. We walk through the

main atrium, past the display cabinets and down the corridor, which is lined with beech glass-fronted chests. Once we get to her workshop on the first floor, Dorothy spreads my photos out onto her desk. She curls her rangy body over them. Her loose-fitting shirt slides against the desk as she leans forward. She extends a stiff hand and traces the atoms in the photographs with her index finger. Her knuckles are taut and inflamed from an early affliction of rheumatoid arthritis.

'These pictures are beautiful, it ought to be possible from these to tell the space grouping,' she says.

My thoughts tumble into a series of rapid vignettes before my eyes. I cannot believe that one of the scientists who took the very first X-rays of protein crystals has given my photographs a sign of approval.

'I've reduced the space group to three possibilities,' I say enthusiastically. The words spill from my mouth.

'Which ones?'

'C2, CM, and C2 over M.'

Dorothy's face drops. She looks at me with retiring eyes. 'But Rosalind,' she says, reeling back slowly from the desk. 'Two of those don't conform to the theory. They're impossible.'

My heart runs cold. It had seemed a feat enough to reduce the possibilities down from hundreds. Matching thousands of scattered atoms in the X-rays to formations commonly found in organic materials was nothing but an art.

'My postdoctoral researcher could explain it to you,' Dorothy says. 'Explain it to her, Jack.' She calls over a researcher from the other side of the floor, a doctoral student in his twenties.

'Explain what?' he asks in a Scottish accent.

'Jack, what have I been saying about handed molecules?' Dorothy says.

'That no biological molecule exists in a mirror image?'

'Precisely,' she replies. 'So, which of the space groupings do you see here in these photographs?'

'It would be impossible to tell. There are hundreds to choose from,' Jack says.

'I've narrowed it down to three: C2, CM, and C2 over M,' I tell him.

'Well, then it has to be C2.'

This means that the atoms would be clustered together in rhombus formations, in tiny fragments that together made up the molecule. DNA is beginning to take shape.

'Thank you,' I say, taking a deep breath, relieved that there was a solution. 'I understand.'

'Most biological molecules exist in a handed form,' Dorothy explains. 'They're always found in the same handed structure. You'll never see a mirror image of the molecule.'

If the atoms had been arranged in either of the other two formations, the molecule would have no chirality. They were not a configuration ever seen in nature. While the underlying molecules in proteins usually veer to the left, sugars like the ribose in deoxyribose are always right-handed. Dorothy has given me a gift, another piece in the jigsaw puzzle that is DNA's structure.

The next morning on the journey home, hay bales flash past the train window at rapid speed. They remind me of Van Gogh's wheat fields, and long walks with the sun on my back through the fields in France. As they meld into one, my future begins to look less opaque. I have gained another piece of the puzzle, the space grouping of the atoms in DNA. All that is left to decide is whether the molecule has the same shape when it is wet. The new 'detector', as we fondly call it, allows the brass protractor to manoeuvre around the DNA specimen. The tilting camera stand will finally enable us to collect even more precise X-ray data than before.

I did not tell Dorothy about my job offer from Professor Bernal. There had been no right moment to mention it. I didn't want to upset Professor Randall, who'd had such trust in me when I first joined his lab. But it can't stay a secret for long.

| 23 |

On the Shoulders of Giants

Royal Society of Chemistry, Burlington House, Piccadilly, 1 May 1952

Sir Christopher Wren is standing on the precipice of the vast Georgian brick façade, next to Leonardo da Vinci. The Royal Society's founder is looming over the fountain in the centre of the courtyard. The water spray is lost among the torrents of rain pelting the cobbles outside. From the reception room on the first floor, it feels as though Wren and da Vinci are winking straight at me. They remain unflinchingly still. Lord Burlington's statue stands proudly in the fountain in the middle of the courtyard, overlooked by the two grand statesmen. The Georgian palace was, first and foremost, his home, before becoming a home for the Royal Society of Chemistry.

'Fancy seeing you here.' Francis intrudes on my thoughts.

Jim is standing behind him, fidgeting and reluctant to engage in conversation. I am trapped on the floral carpet, between the window and the ersatz Grecian columns that dot the circumference of the room. Avoiding Francis and Jim wasn't an option, though I would happily be swallowed up at that moment into a time vortex. Perhaps I would visit da Vinci and his flying machine if it were possible.

'Shame Pauling couldn't make it,' Francis says after an uncomfortably long silence.

'Do you mean he's not here?' I ask.

'Couldn't get a visa, the authorities think he has links with the Commies,' Francis replies.

'Again? I was hoping to ask him how he thinks his protein structure might relate to DNA,' I say.

'The alpha helix?' Jim addresses me for the first time this afternoon. 'What does that have to do with DNA?'

'That shouldn't worry you, Jim, now that you're working on RNA,' I say.

After they failed abysmally to create an accurate model of DNA, the head of the Cavendish lab banned them from working on the problem any longer. Jim, meanwhile, took an interest in the tobacco mosaic virus, a plague on tobacco crops, which by no coincidence was the first virus ever to be discovered. Wreaking such havoc on one of the most profitable global crops wouldn't do; and the reason had to be identified and eliminated. To many scientists, the virus offers a cheap and abundant material for studying ribonucleic acid, or RNA, a ubiquitous acidic compound found in all viruses that appears to mirror DNA.

'Was, Rosy, *was*,' says Jim with mock indignation. 'DNA is once again my *raison d'être*. Professor Bragg was foolish to stop us working on it.'

Jim hasn't shown any interest in anything besides ornithology and biology previously and now he is talking about X-ray diffraction and DNA. Something is awry.

Francis asks, more warmly, 'And how is the DNA work at King's?'

'It probably doesn't make sense to tell you if you're back on the problem.'

'Come on, Rosy, a problem shared is a problem halved,' he says.

Sometimes you make a mistake and get redirected quickly. At other times you get so lost that you begin to sink, and every step forwards feels impossible as you sink farther. In science, an unexpected result can be your fortune, it can put you on the path of a new discovery, or it can be your undoing.

Empirical evidence can never be ignored. This month, one of the DNA fibres did something unexpected. At first, it seemed like a fortunate accident. There was a chance that it could confirm the indexing scheme. The photograph was somewhere between a rotation photograph and an oscillation image. Half the atoms behaved the same as the wet fibres and the other half behaved like the dry ones.

Anomalies are sometimes clues. If Isaac Newton had ignored the apple landing on his head, then perhaps he wouldn't have stumbled on gravitational force. But they can also be just that: outliers or non-repeatable accidents without meaning.

'The latest X-ray of the crystalline form doesn't show any symmetry,' I say, not expecting the onslaught that follows.

'Well, you're wrong, of course,' says Jim, smugly. 'So, you don't believe DNA is a helix. It doesn't sound like you do, do you?'

'That's not necessarily true,' I say. 'It just appears from these findings that we can't rule out asymmetry—'

'Look, Rosy, it's clear you don't know the first thing about DNA, or biology.' Jim cuts me off before I have a chance to finish.

My throat and chest feel tight. I bury the anger and the tension in my arms until it becomes a blunt pain in my stomach.

He never speaks that way to either Francis or Maurice.

'Jim, Francis, I really am very hungry. Goodbye,' I say, and leave before I say something I will regret.

While browsing the food in the lunch hall, I hear Jim laughing. His howl is brazen. It echoes loudly above the noise of the crowd. I feel as though I am shrinking into the ground beneath me from where I am standing in the queue, by the soup kettle. I have seen older scientists in the lab expunge their bitterness on those around them. Competition and in-fighting had eroded what was left of their souls, and they slowly calcified as they became more embittered despite their mounting accolades. It was not a fate that I wanted.

But I have spent hours, days, months and weekends on the work and now it has been taken from me. What is left without it?

While sitting alone in the Royal Society dining hall, I decide not to waste any more time and to accept the job offer from Bernal.

| 24 |

Crystalline

King's College London, The Strand, 2 May 1952

That morning, the mahogany box where the tabulations for our calculations are stored ricochets off a table leg in the room next to my office and falls upside down on the floor. It's the era of automation, but still we aren't able to produce complex atomic vector maps at the click of a button. Bessel functions, which we can use to plot the atomic distances in a molecule, are only tabulated on the paper system up to forty microns. We must slowly and precisely do all the calculations by hand to determine the distance between the atoms.

The scores of paper Beevers-Lipson strips that are kept in the mahogany box are dispersed unevenly on the ground and are now lying face down in the puddle of water from the leaking roof, absorbing moisture from the leak like Litmus strips. The stagnant pool is gradually fading the printed trigonometric expressions on the paper pieces, which are essential to sine and cosine arithmetic. Without them, a day's sums will take a week.

Raymond is standing by the box with a concerned look on his face.

'That will put us back by at least a day,' he says, waving at the mess.

'Hurry and pick them up before the ink fades,' I urge him.

'The darn things are so fiddly,' he complains while getting down on his knees to help rescue the strips.

'Why don't you take the slides to the dark room, if it's still open, to develop the negatives?' I suggest once we've collected the limp paper pieces and spread them on the windowsill to dry.

He's delighted at any excuse to avoid my acrimony. When he's gone, I spread the existing list of calculations out onto the laboratory bench and peer at them to judge what is missing. They are the fruits of our attempts so far to plot out the position of the atoms in DNA.

Doing the calculations by hand isn't the fastest way to conclude a theory. We are working blind; starting from the numbers, and extrapolating outwards, with no map to guide us other than the X-rays themselves. But working backwards from a model would only leave room for error, it would be guesswork and we would have no proof that it was right.

However, little by little, with consistent effort, the truth is sure to reveal itself from the numbers. Numbers are firm and immutable. I trust them more than feelings. They don't bend or twist, like emotions. Emotions flit and curl and seep from the seams. They are fallible in ways that numbers aren't. Numbers hold their weight. They blend and subtract from others in a logical and hermetic world that's reassuringly predictable. Life's secrets are hidden in the data.

'Dr Franklin,' Raymond says minutes later.

'Can it wait?'

'It's the filament. It's burned.'

'What do you mean it's burned?'

'It's burned through, Dr Franklin.'

The X-ray filament had incinerated ten days ago during one long photographic exposure. The filaments have an average lifespan of just 250 hours, it turns out. We have been testing longer exposures to increase the resolution and clarity of our photographs. Our latest long exposure experiment has run for two days already but was interrupted. After a series of spoiled photographs, we have replaced the copper target and removed and put back the pinhole.

'Again? That's the second time in less than a fortnight.' I feel glad that I will soon be leaving the lab.

'What shall we do?' Raymond asks.

'We will continue,' I say.

'What's the point, if the image is overexposed?'

A recent oscillation photograph had cross-pollinated with a rotated image, throwing doubt into the mix about whether the DNA molecule was symmetrical or not. If DNA is not symmetrical when a fibre is viewed at its core, then it can't be shaped like a spiral, which all the other evidence has pointed to. The only way we can be sure that it was a true anomaly and not a testable difference is to produce even clearer images.

'We'll re-expose the photograph, this time using a different film,' I say after a few minutes.

'Got any second thoughts about building a model?' Raymond asks as we stand together reviewing the data, which is spread out on the workbench in front of us.

'Let's start with the evidence before making theories,' I say while scoring a line over the page with my finger. 'Any model would be guesswork.'

'Can we leave the calculations until after the bank holiday?' he pleads.

'We'll run the experiment overnight. That way we will start afresh tomorrow,' I say.

'But it's Friday tomorrow,' says Raymond.

My eyes don't drift from the calculations.

'Right, Dr Franklin.' Raymond has begun to take off his leather jacket, but hesitates, before putting it back on the door hook again.

'Let's re-expose the fibres at seventy-five per cent

humidity and check again in the morning,' I say. 'We'll run the experiment again, using two films over three days.'

'Yes, Dr Franklin.'

That night, to rescue the experiment, I tease the calf-thymus fibres into place on a glass slide before mounting it onto the X-ray apparatus, using a pipette needle, just as Jacques showed me how to fix specimens at the State Chemicals Lab. I imagine his steady arm and smooth voice as I carefully stretch one of the fibres into place. Setting the strands in place is a surgical operation on a microscopic scale. The fibre has to be placed directly over the copper target so that the X-ray beam slices through the centre of the molecule. Only by doing so can we determine if the molecule, when examined through the core, is symmetrical or not.

Each time we take a photograph it feels as though we are reaching at intangible gossamer threads, with solutions appearing before us briefly and then softly disintegrating, like spores in the wind or soap bubbles gently expiring. The structure of the molecule seems always to be just beyond our grasp. With every step forward it feels as though we are taking two steps back. It is only ever on reflection that the dots begin to join.

| 25 |

Secret Discovery

King's College London, The Strand, 2 May 1952

The next day the lab is as humid as Saigon at sunset. It's a national holiday, an inopportune day for Professor Pauling's colleague Dr Robert Corey to be visiting. Most of the students have already left for the bank holiday weekend. While just a few droplets of rain came in from the ceiling at first, now the roof next to my office is leaking stalactite formations. The walls in the basement absorb whatever conditions permeate from the outside, as if by osmosis. The leak and the mice infestation have made the building almost uninhabitable. There is still talk of restoring the crater in the quad, where a bomb hit a decade ago, just missing the grand marble columns in Bush House on the Aldwych by a few yards. But scientists are unlikely to be a priority for the government while emergency housing is still being built.

'We need a bucket,' I say to Raymond, trying desperately to save our workings for the vector map. 'We've got a visitor next week from Pauling's lab.'

'Surely not,' says Raymond, slapping his forehead.

Water droplets have begun to soften the edges of our

atomic map. I pass Raymond an empty cup to collect drips from the leak as he hesitates.

'How's last night's experiment moving along?'

'I completely forgot, Dr Franklin. Do you want me to develop the film?' he asks sheepishly.

'Yes, why don't you,' I say, putting the map into my top drawer to keep it dry.

I head upstairs to the main hall to get some fresh air. On returning to the basement, I see that the door of the darkroom is open. I go to shut it, to prevent overexposure. The clarity of the latest photograph depends entirely on how successfully we have saved the experiment. Developing the negatives has to be done quickly, as the chemical coating takes just minutes to dry, and it must be done in complete darkness so as not to overexpose the film.

'You left the door open,' I whisper as I walk in.

'Dr Franklin, see this,' Raymond says urgently.

A shimmering sheet of film in the chemical bath in front of him catches the light. The photograph is bobbing up and down in the solution. Tiny nodules of light, which look like speckled stars, have merged together into an amorphous constellation on the film. Raymond lifts the photograph from the chemical bath.

'X marks the spot,' he says, flapping the sheet of film to dry. A ghostly image rapidly appears. It is absolutely beautiful. The image is shaped like an hourglass, with two strands of atoms that intersect in the middle, like a figure of eight, or an infinity sign. Each of the molecular strands is flecked with dark spots.

'What was the humidity?'

'Seventy-five per cent, just as you asked,' Raymond says.

'Remarkable.' I inch forward to take a closer look. 'These dark spots here are the atoms.' I point to them. 'Follow the curves, here, and here. There are two overlapping strands.'

The image is perfectly symmetrical. The X-ray has sliced directly through the centre of the molecule. The calf-thymus fibres must have been aligned right over the copper target. The molecular chains overlap almost exactly in the centre of the film.

'It has all the hallmarks of a helix,' I say.

'How can you tell?' Raymond asks.

'Look, it has the same Maltese cross pattern, visible in the diffraction of light on the film, as when a torch is shone through a spring.'

That afternoon, instead of using the same waterlogged calf-thymus experiment, we try using a fresh specimen. We run the experiment for almost two hours from twenty past three that afternoon to 5 o'clock, but the specimen is poor. Experiment 50 is a dud. I cannot help wondering whether, together with the earlier anomalous 'double orientation' photograph, it suggests an oval or elliptical helix. In the evening, instead of drying the calf-thymus fibres from the last experiment that had shown a very good wet photograph, as usual, using a desiccant, we run the experiment for a second time using the same waterlogged calf-thymus fibres from the prior experiment, to try and replicate the last result. Whereas one accident is a mistake, two could indicate a fault. One result can be an anomaly, but two might just be proof. Before I leave the office that night, I put our photograph back in the top drawer of my desk, along with our atomic vector maps and X-rays of DNA and asbestos from earlier experiments, record the results of the experiments over the last few days. The filament burning through, far from ruining our work, has led to an unexpected breakthrough. By re-exposing the calf-thymus fibres and hydrating them to the perfect humidity, taking special care to align them precisely over the copper target, we have produced a clearer image of the molecule than ever before. It shows with little doubt that DNA is a helix, or spiral-shaped, at least when it is hydrated or in humid conditions, just as it would be in nature.

| 26 |

Drop by Drop

London, 6 May 1952

Storms rage over the rest of the weekend. I don't tell anyone about our findings. My family wouldn't be interested anyway, and neither would my neighbours. The only people who might be are Vittorio – but an ocean separates us – or Jacques. But the gulf between me and him is now so wide that we barely exist to one another. Love and friendship seem to easily coexist for everyone else; my brothers have both found wives and my sister seems taken with a student studying medicine at Cambridge. This has not proved the case for me.

My father once said that you need to do something in order to be loveable, that it was selfish to expect to be loved for not doing anything at all. Otherwise, it would be down to chance whether or not you were loved by the people you loved in return. And so I laboured every weekend with a soldering iron in the shed at the back of my parents' garden, determined to steal my father's affections away from my brothers. Despite that, now the only interaction I have with my parents is a brief call on Friday evening where we discuss synagogue, my aunts and their ailments, and the plight of the refugee centre.

I spend the rest of the bank holiday alone, cooking and reading, leaving the house only once to browse furniture lots at an auction house off the King's Road.

On the Tuesday, it is two degrees colder than before the weekend.

'You're in early,' Len says, jumping down every other step of the stairwell. He looks flustered.

'What's happened?'

'The generator had a blasted power cut. Rain probably got to it. The engineers are in.'

'Do you know when they'll fix it?'

'I don't know. Why do you need to know?' He stops and stares at me.

I struggle to answer his question. There is no time to explain.

'Even if I told you, you wouldn't understand,' I say, sighing.

The only light visible in the corridor is from the windows on the far side of the basement. They aren't typical as they are set several feet below ground and light is let in through a chute, with only a thin slice of the ground level visible. My cubicle is dark except for a few scant rays of morning sun that flood in from the chute. The only part of the quad visible through the windows in the early morning sunlight is a small sliver of the rooftops opposite.

'Don't worry, I've got matches somewhere.' Raymond is standing by the window holding a drawer up to the light, which he's tilted at an angle.

'Stop,' I insist.

'We need light to see the calculations,' he says, rifling through the drawer's contents to find a matchbox.

'Light a match and the hydrogen tanks could explode,' I warn.

'Surely that's the last of our worries if the photo's over-exposed?' He claws at a matchbox that's nestled underneath a sea of pens in my desk drawer before casting it aside, to my relief.

At that moment, the incandescent bulbs above us suddenly

come to life. As the lights glow, it becomes clear that Raymond has put the drawer back in the wrong way around. While sliding it back onto its rollers correctly, I suggest leaving the experiment to run for a little longer.

'Rosy, there you are,' the professor says as he barges into my office later that morning. 'Corey has been asking to meet you.'

I have no doubt that Dr Corey, a biochemist and an associate of Professor Pauling, will be shocked by the state of our lab. The California Institute of Technology where they work has all the latest equipment, without leaks, mould or mice.

It appears that Professor Randall has arrived early to make an impression on the moustachioed American scientist.

Dr Corey extends his arm to shake my hand. 'Pleasure,' he says, gripping it firmly.

'What do you make of this? It's from one of our latest experiments,' I ask, tentatively showing Professor Pauling's colleague a glimpse of our latest photograph from where I have put it away in the top drawer of my desk while the professor checks in on Raymond. 'If I put it on the projector, we will be able to see it more clearly.'

Dr Corey flaps the image, moving it closer and farther from his eyes until the resolution is at its clearest under the lens of his glasses.

'Tell me about your work on protein,' I ask as he examines it.

'Oh yes,' he says. 'The alpha helix. It's been quite a ride.'

'The alpha what?' Professor Randall exclaims from the other side of the office where he is continuing to flex his intellectual muscle to my assistant.

'Protein is a spiral,' says Dr Corey.

'Not one. We think it's made up of many single helices.'

'You must have made a mistake there,' says the professor, coming over to join us. 'Protein's far too complex to be a single strand.'

'Herman's been busy with that mainly, anyway,' Dr Corey

says, smiling at Randall. 'You probably recognise the name from our papers.'

'Herman Branson, yes, I think I met him,' he replies.

I had not had the chance to meet him, or Erwin Chargaff, in person.

The associate, who has the same name as Professor Pauling's father, has been working in the professor's lab in California for the past year.

'Pauling wants me to review his sums,' Dr Corey says. 'It's all math. Hard to believe. Herman's going back to Howard University, to work on sickle-cell, now.'

'Were there any objections?' I ask.

The professor is peering up at the ceiling. 'We must get that leak looked at,' he says.

'No,' Dr Corey answers, checking the time shortly afterwards before leaving to catch a flight back to California.

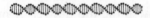

'The power was out for thirty-two hours, there or thereabouts.'

I check my watch when Len delivers the news that afternoon.

'That's sixty-two hours,' I mumble.

'I said thirty-two hours, Dr Franklin, you must not have heard me,' Len says as he walks off down the corridor.

'It's been going for sixty-two hours,' I call after him.

'What, the power cut?'

'The time since we started the experiment, minus the interruption.'

We had left the experiment running for nearly four days over the bank holiday weekend, from Friday evening at half past seven to five o'clock this afternoon, the Tuesday. The power was out for more than a whole day, so I estimate in my notes that the actual exposure of the film lasted for sixty-two hours.

Raymond returns from the darkroom in half the usual time it takes to develop the film.

'Dr Franklin,' he says, gasping for air.

'What is it?' I turn to face him.

'It's the photograph,' he says, catching his breath like a fish out of water. 'It was instant.'

'Spit it out. What's new?'

'Just look, Dr Franklin,' he says.

I sift through my drawer for a torch to examine the image more closely.

'Isn't this the photograph from experiment forty-nine?'

'No, I took it straight out of the camera,' Raymond says.

'Are you sure you didn't get them mixed up, like those Beevers-Lipson strips?'

'No. This is from fifty-one.'

'It's a perfect replica,' I say, holding the photograph up towards the light.

'Almost, this one's slightly askew,' Raymond says. 'Do you know what it means?'

'What's the water content of a human heart and brain?' I ask him.

Water is crucial to life, so much so that we cannot live without it for more than three days. Humans can survive for up to three weeks with no food, but not without hydration. Almost two-thirds of the entire human body is made of it, including seventy-three per cent of our hearts and brains.

Water had been abundant that May bank holiday. Humidity is a crucial variable in our experiment, as any change could affect crystallisation. If the air is too dry, the calf-thymus fibres will dry out, but if it is too humid they dissolve into thin air. In an earlier experiment, we saw the fibres decompose before our eyes. They reached a point of no return, where it was impossible to restore them to a crystal structure. When they metamorphosed, irreversibly, from crystalline to saturated, shortly before they expired they produced better photographs than ever before.

'Two-thirds or thereabouts,' he says eventually.

'There's more water in the heart and brain, and even more again in the lungs,' I say, before adding, 'I guess it's not surprising really.'

Perhaps it is the torrential rain that bank holiday, which has got me so focused on water and its significance in our experiments. While there is a point at which too much water oversaturates the DNA fibres, before that comes an optimal point at which its atoms can be viewed with exceptional clarity. It seems no coincidence that this is when the water saturation is at the same ratio typically seen in nature; in human organs nearly three-quarters of the cells are made up of water. When crystallised calf-thymus fibres are hydrated to a similar amount, so they are roughly three-quarters saturated at seventy-five per cent humidity, the atoms appear to stand proud and are visible in our atomic photographs like never before.

'What isn't?' he asks.

'That the photos are clearest in those same conditions. DNA is in its natural habitat.'

'You could have fooled me,' says Raymond.

| 27 |

Pluto

Strand Campus, King's College London, England, 27 June 1952

'We've been forced to live like moles,' Maurice mutters. 'It's complete chaos.'

A man in a baker-boy cap is clearing the last of the rubble from around the edges of the courtyard. Builders have spent the summer excavating it from the bomb crater into vast cast-iron tankards. They have been building new labs in the underground vaults beneath the quad to meet the height restrictions for buildings close to the naval base. The surrounding buildings can't be too tall, or the naval squad won't be able to spot an enemy approach.

The entire university is standing in the quad for today's opening of the new network of underground labs. Some of the students and academics have lined up around the fringes of the courtyard, while others have piled on to the stone staircase. Red tape is preventing anyone from getting a closer look.

'We haven't suffered in the least from our subterranean location.' Maurice starts his speech with a quip.

That was not what he'd been saying all summer when he'd been moaning about the lack of light. Rather than stay to listen more, I scale the steps and unhook a rope to get inside the main building. Bags of cement are blocking the way of the swing doors. The professor is standing inside the foyer talking to Lord Cherwell, who has the tight-lipped look of repugnance that many people mistake for gravitas. Cherwell, who once advised Churchill on bombs during the war, is heralding the restoration of the bomb site at the university. The irony is lost on the crowd, who are cheering his imminent speech.

Downstairs in the basement, the walls of the new labs are brightly coloured with fresh paint and an intoxicating vapour of solvents saturates the air. The old incandescent light bulbs have been replaced by new fluorescent tubes. I feel a lump in my throat on seeing them. A local optician in Kensington said that he'd been stockpiling the old bulbs. He said he had seen far too many cases of macular degeneration to trust the newfangled tubes.

'The builders have left cement outside,' I tell the technician on duty.

'It's for concrete technology,' Len replies. 'Soil mechanics is on the other side. They've got a drawing office; it's a bit fancy really, for soil boffins. All paid for by the Americans.'

A discovery with no financial backing is like a bird with its wings clipped. It has nowhere to fly. A sum of more than 5,000 times the average wage – of £3.90 – has been ploughed into the new laboratories under the bomb crater and the funders are preoccupied with finding the genes that determine sex drives. I do not understand why most scientists in the field are obsessed with the differences between people and not the essence of what makes us human: our DNA.

'Do you know where they've put us?' I ask.

'The animals make a right hullabaloo in the night; it's pandemonium in here,' Len says as we pass the animal enclosure. 'At the weekend I pop by to check on them.'

He walks on, forgetting my question.

'Biophysics, is it?' he asks.

'The physics department,' I say.

'Oh yes, it's only Dr Wilkins who calls it that. He likes to talk like he's with the Medical Research Council, doesn't he?'

'I can look in on the animals for you if you like. I often work Saturdays,' I offer.

'What, the rabbits? Darwin would miss me, wouldn't you, Dar?'

'He looks scared,' I say.

'He's jumpy, that's all. We don't want them getting used to us.' He tickles the rabbit's nose with a blade of hay.

'Do you know where mine is?'

'A few of them make it out of here, but they don't usually last long,' he says.

'Sorry, Len, I mean my office?'

'Of course, Dr Franklin, you could take one home with you if you like but I don't want you grieving over a sick rabbit. Your office is over there by the basement wall. I'll show you.'

'I hope he goes to a good home,' I tell him, stroking the skittish rabbit through the wires of its cage.

The walls on the other side of the basement are cold to the touch, almost as cold as blocks of ice, despite it being early autumn.

It's been nearly two years since I first arrived at the lab after leaving Paris.

'Five hundred and seventy,' I mumble as I stuff my hands into my blazer pocket to keep them warm.

'You like your numbers, don't you, Dr Franklin?'

'It's how many days I've been here.'

'You say that as though you're leaving us,' he says.

I stay silent… not knowing what to say. He has guessed correctly, something that no one else in the lab knows.

'Don't tell anyone. Please, not yet.'

'Right-o, Dr Franklin,' Len says with a knowing wink.

The fellowship committee said they will allow me to transfer my fellowship to Professor Bernal's lab at Birkbeck, but I still haven't told the professor that I am going, in case he treats me differently for it.

All of a sudden, I feel an inexplicable sadness standing alone here in the new office. In the two years that I've been working at the university, I have often stayed so late that I haven't been able to remember the last time I ate. Usually, I didn't pass a delicatessen or patisserie without looking inside. Food is fuel for the brain, as I discovered at university. It was the Roman poet Juvenal who wrote *'mens sana in corpore sano'* – a healthy body is necessary for a healthy mind. Some of my best work in Paris was done between meals out.

'Collaboration with physicists…' I hear Maurice say through the open window as I shut the door behind me, '… is desirable when, and some say only when, the information is physical in nature.'

I take a deep breath, relieved that in just a few months I will no longer be seen simply as an assistant to Maurice, or a part of his scheme to take any glory for the lab's work on DNA for himself.

| 28 |

In Memoriam

It is with great regret that we have to announce the death of D.N.A. Helix (crystalline) on Friday 18th July 1952. Death followed a protracted illness, which an intensive course of besselised injections has failed to relieve. A memorial service will be held next Monday or Tuesday. It is hoped that Dr M H F Wilkins will speak in memory of the late helix.

R E Franklin, R Gosling

'Let's post it.'

Raymond's peals of laughter echo in the stairwell.

'It was a joke,' I sigh.

'It was you who wrote the words, Dr Franklin,' Raymond says. 'We have a funeral to attend, remember? It's death to the helix.'

If it were the end of the world, you could be sure that Dr Wilkins would be delivering the sermon, along with the roaches.

'Really, it shouldn't go any further than us,' I say.

'Relax a little. I can't wait to see the look on Maurice's face.'

'I'd rather not,' I say, trying to rid my mind of the image.

Raymond holds our note, which is written in thick black ink, out ahead of him. His overly bitten fingernails are tightly squeezed around the black-edged card. As I chase him down the corridor, glimpsing behind us every now and again to see if we are being followed or might be heard, the sound of my heels against the floor betrays my effort to be discreet.

'I'll take it to the post office,' Raymond says when he gets to the gates towards the Strand.

The post office is opposite the Strand campus, less than two minutes away on the other side of the ring road.

'Who will you send it to?' I rest my hands on my knees in exhaustion.

'All the other scientists working on the DNA problem,' he says through the gaps in the iron gate.

I cover my mouth to prevent myself from screaming. That is more than half a dozen people. There are Jim and Francis at the Cavendish lab in Cambridge. There are the three Americans in California, Herman Branson, Robert Corey and Professor Pauling, whose lectures make the am-dram productions at Cambridge seem diffident. Then there is Maurice – and us – in London.

My court shoes begin to rub against my sock-less heels. Rather than running after him, I give up and go back to the lab.

Our note is light relief from Bessel functions. It won't fool anyone, I tell myself. But it can't hurt to blow a little smoke behind us – for others to think we know less than we do. The helix is no more moribund than bacteria on a cadaver. In humidity, its crystals splay into independent spirals, each coiling around the same axis. The only question left is does the molecule behave the same when it is dry? Since the Professor has insisted that we pivot to the tightly packed dry structure, the question is impossible to ignore.

| 29 |

Diamond Fire

'We'll never finish this vector map,' Raymond says one chilly afternoon in October.

His face is drained of colour from a lack of sleep; he has been having a recurring nightmare. If still alive, Sigmund Freud would have called the dream wish fulfilment. Each time Raymond has it, he says it ends the same way.

Just before he realises he is dreaming, he drops a box of paper Beevers-Lipson strips and searches for them interminably on the floor.

No matter how hard he looks, he can't find all of them – more strips appear, as if by magic, and the task never ends. He wakes suddenly with a start, and a hollow feeling in the pit of his stomach.

'Have faith,' I tell him.

'But the reflections are causing distortions,' he says.

'A diamond cannot sparkle without light.'

When light refracts from the surface of a diamond, it shoots a rainbow of colours in all directions. Without it, there would be no diamond fire.

'The same effect is distorting our photographs,' I explain. 'How can we measure the position of the atoms if the photos are warped?' Raymond has deep purple shadows below both of his eyes.

'Have you finished yet?' I ask him.

'But how...' he begins again.

'Good, could you pick up some oranges from the shop? Make sure you get the pebble-skinned variety,' I say, continuing to ignore his incessant questions.

'How on earth can oranges help us get to the bottom of DNA?' he asks, his shoulders slumped.

'You'll have to trust me.'

On his return, minutes later, Raymond tips the box of oranges too far and spills them across the carpet. His eyes are glassy, and it is almost as though they are protruding slightly from their sockets. At least he resists the urge to roll them. He remains suspended in the position for a few seconds, before hanging his head in despair.

'Peel back the pith to reveal the fruit, like this,' I say, handing him an orange I have already started. 'There you have it, reciprocal space.' We spend the day peeling the rest of the oranges and using them to measure how the shell of a molecule might affect the diffraction of light from the outer layer of atoms. In X-ray diffraction, the Fourier calculation for the movement of a wave of light involves some estimation, and grasping the reciprocal space that this creates can help give us a more precise picture of where the atoms really sit from our electron maps.

Later that afternoon, Raymond scoops up a bruised fruit that's rolling down the uneven floor and surveys the piles of peel around the room. 'Anyone would think we've been eating them,' he says, before adding, 'Have you heard about Professor Pauling?' He rests his chin on his palm while sitting cross-legged on the threadbare carpet.

'That his son's joined the Cavendish. Yes, why?'

'Not that. Guess again.'

'Well, I doubt he is very happy about it. I don't know, tell me,' I say.

We are surrounded up to our knees in fruit peeled at varying degrees. Raymond tosses an orange in the air and catches it.

'Francis is publishing his own theory of keratin,' he says.

'What, like the one Pauling has been working on?' I ask.

'Yes. And he wants to send it to *Nature* before Professor Pauling gets the chance.'

The news is a blow to the stomach. It suggests they might come after us too. Keratin, the protein in hair and nails, is an obvious target for anyone who has an interest in genes. Some scientists believe complex proteins hold the code to life itself. Unravelling the make-up of such protein, which DNA is found alongside, could be key to unlocking one of life's secrets.

'We must write a paper.' I stand up, wiping orange residue from my hands.

'On keratin?' Raymond asks.

'No. DNA.'

'Now?'

'Yes. We must write our findings and submit them independently. But don't tell anyone, not a soul. Promise?'

'If you say so, Dr Franklin, but I'm sure the Cavendish lab hasn't come up with anything on DNA since their lousy replica of Bruce's model a year ago.'

'That may be true but we can't be sure, or rest on our laurels,' I say.

Raymond scrambles to his feet, using one arm to push himself up from the ground to standing.

Before I can say any more, we are interrupted by a knock.

'Someone's here for you, Dr Franklin.' Len curls his head around the door. 'I said you were busy, but he's most insistent.'

'I must go,' I tell Raymond.

His trousers are stained with juice from a stray orange. 'What about the paper?'

'It'll have to wait.'

I go to my desk and search frantically through the discarded pens, pennies and farthings in my top drawer. It's the place where the mess goes. In it, everything is orderly. The drawer is for the forgotten things, the things that can be put aside for later. My pearl necklace has got in a tangle at the bottom of it and is wrapped around a ballpoint pen. In the evening light, the pearls are opalescent. They have kept their iridescence in the moist air and are glowing in a misty haze of reds, greens and blues. The navy evening sky, green carpet and my vermilion dress are all reflected in the glossy sheen. The necklace is in symphony with everything around it, with multifarious colours reflecting from its beaded surface. I reach back into the drawer for my Clarins lipstick and draw two slanted lines on my philtrum before smudging my lips together, ready for a night at the opera. A violinist from the Royal Opera House has invited me to a performance. I have visited the opera many times since leaving school, with Jean and when entertaining scientists for work, and he said he remembers seeing me in the distant crowd more than once.

In the university foyer, Raymond is standing at the bottom of the stairs wearing goggles and a motorcycle helmet. The thought of the violinist talking to anyone from the lab is blanching. I have swapped my lab coat for a bolero that I smuggled into work this morning in a paper Jaeger shopping bag, though I tell myself that it isn't a date and that we are just friends.

'Dr Franklin, you look...' Raymond stumbles on his words.

'Am I right in thinking it's a seven-minute walk to the Royal Opera House?' I say, noticing the violinist's silhouette outside the revolving doors and saving both of us from the chagrin of him finishing the sentence.

| 30 |

THE GREAT SMOG

The Strand, London, 15 December 1952

By winter, the Great Smog of London has engulfed the city. All the shelves at the Smithfield meat market in Farringdon are bare; the cattle have been asphyxiated by the smog, my local butcher in Kensington said when I visited at the weekend. The city is grey with noxious particles and the air is sulphurous, as though the content of the chimneys has been emptied straight on to the streets. Nobody knows what has caused it, though petrol cars are a likely culprit and the weather has mocked our intentions for the best part of the year. It snowed in March, then rained in May, and by the middle of December, snow seems to be a permanent fixture.

The smog hasn't yet reached Cambridge, Dr Perutz says, smiling urbanely as he greets Professor Randall outside my office.

'Tell me about this new evidence,' he says.

I overhear him explaining to the professor that he is here in his capacity as director of the Medical Research Council, which oversees the molecular biology research at the university.

As he wipes back his gelled hair, which looks as though it is wet from the rain, he insists, he jokes, that he is not here as Francis Crick's thesis supervisor.

'It's no business of anybody outside the Biophysics Committee, of course,' Professor Randall replies – in a bid to guard our lab's latest finding, while scanning Dr Perutz's face. Although Dr Perutz claims he is there solely in an official capacity, I sense that Professor Randall has doubts. I watch them spar from my desk.

I consider faking an emergency to get the professor's attention, but cannot will my legs to move. He does not yet know about Francis's plan to undercut the work of the California lab.

'Professor Bragg regrets there isn't more... open... collaboration,' says Dr Perutz.

'We'll let the council make up their minds about who is leading the DNA work based on the evidence,' says Professor Randall, standing on his tiptoes momentarily before planting his heels back down on the floor with a thud.

'So, what do you have for me?' Dr Perutz says. The professor's comment hasn't punctured his glib façade.

'You mean our research report for the committee?' the professor asks him, extracting a document from his pocket.

Here at King's College London, the professor has carte blanche over the physics department day to day, but ultimately he defers to the Medical Research Council's executive committee. In his Rickmansworth home, the professor has salt-of-the-earth aspirations. He plants vegetables and flowers in the meadow gardens, just like his father, a nurseryman, did years before him. Although he will never be a seedsman, like his father, he dabbles in his vegetable patch now and again too. The research council similarly has a hold over his work in the lab. They organise much of the funding for the university's work on DNA. So although he may be sceptical of the committee in private, there would be little point in not complying.

'There you go, Perutz, I trust the council will be impressed. Our work is confidential, but I'm sure they'll take care of that at HQ.' I watch as the professor hands over our latest workings on DNA, including a compilation of my workings on the atomic structure, and my latest X-ray images. It includes the crucial knowledge I have deciphered about the water content of the DNA molecule, the space grouping of the atoms and other information about the axial repeat or rotation of the pattern. He sounds hopeful that the higher-ups at the research council will honour the confidentiality of our work at King's College.

I desperately want to say something but cannot find the words.

'Marvellous,' says Dr Perutz, who is wide-eyed as he scans the cover page.

Professor Randall must know that Dr Perutz could not overlook my data. If he understands it, he will not forget it. And as Francis Crick's thesis supervisor, he may be tempted to tell his colleagues at Cambridge about our latest work.

'Professor,' I say, getting up from my desk.

'Yes, what is it, Rosalind?' The tone of the professor's voice is strained and indignant.

'Nothing, Professor, it can wait,' I say, defeated, sitting back down.

It is not worth jeopardising a reference for my new job by causing a scene.

Dr Perutz deflects the pushback with a smile. 'It's a summary of our data and recent lectures,' Professor Randall says as he shows Dr Perutz the door. 'I trust that Bragg and the council bosses will take care of the administrative work around our report, such as compiling a record for the Medical Research Council's latest anthology in the strictest confidence,' he adds, with a nod that is Dr Perutz's cue to leave.

Again, I think about faking an illness or staging a protest, though I would risk permanently embarrassing myself in front of a key member of the research committee, and possibly get fired on the spot. A few minutes of discomfort may seem in theory to be better than biting my tongue to spare Dr Perutz's feelings, but I cannot risk losing my job and spoiling my reputation so soon before joining Professor Bernal's lab at Birkbeck. After eventually giving up on the idea of protesting,

I realise I have no choice but to lay low for the rest of the month so as not to draw the ire of the professor in my final weeks. My only, and safer, option is to ensure we publish our paper as soon as feasibly possible.

Chanukah and Christmas pass and no telegrams alert us to another Cavendish model. The silence is unsettling, like the slow dance of a cobra hypnotising its prey. I feel the same sense of purgatory as I did when sitting in the Anderson shelters that my father built at the bottom of the garden during the Blitz.

'I have something to tell you,' I say shortly after returning to the office following the holidays, while pushing open the heavy door to Maurice's office.

He is sitting inside on a mahogany swivel chair, with one knee cocked as he ties his shoelace. His bureau is inlaid with green leather, which matches the colour of the glass on his brass desk lamp. It is far grander than my office. On seeing me, he gives a half-smile. Tension has forced his shoulders and spine into a hunch.

'What is it, Rosy?' he asks, tetchily, without even looking me in the eye.

'Can't we at least be civil?' I say.

'What is it that cannot wait?'

It was too cold to cycle to work this morning, and it took every ounce of my energy to rehearse my words on the crowded train. Now is the moment to deliver those words out loud.

'I'm leaving to join Professor Bernal's lab,' I say, letting the news of my departure sink in for a moment.

'Bernal, well, he's very desirable to work with,' Maurice says with surprising equanimity.

'Of course, he and Professor Randall are good friends,' he adds, equally sangfroid.

He speaks with the same unnerving tone of an emeritus

professor, who is sitting at the top of a hill and casting an eye over all that he has built. The intonation of his voice, and the way he rolls his consonants more than the usual staccato, is oddly unmoved. He continues tying his shoelaces.

His words throw doubt into my mind once more about the nature of Professor Bernal's approach. I begin to wonder whether Randall had gone behind my back to arrange for me to leave – indeed, he did not seem too surprised when I told him about my departure – and judging by Maurice's tone maybe he too had been in on it.

'Will you be finishing up the DNA work before you leave?' he then asks, as though my leaving is no surprise.

'Naturally,' I say, steeling myself for an imminent bruising. 'But since I'm leaving, I wanted to tell you where I have got to with the data,' I continue, checking that the buttons on my blouse are done up properly as his eyes glance at my chest, still averting them from my gaze, as he does so often.

'I thought we went through this already, and you made it clear that your view was anti-helical,' Maurice says.

'That's one possible interpretation,' I say. 'It's my duty, responsibility even, not to overstate the facts.'

'There you go again.' Maurice flares his nostrils. 'It seems plain to me, Rosy, that your position is anti-helical, and if it's not, then, well, it's all so convoluted.'

I feel a strong urge to leave. How dare he change the rules of the game like this? I have offered a perfectly good explanation of how DNA is likely helical, or shaped like a helix, warning that we can't be sure the same is true in all conditions, at least not without more evidence. Now he pretends not to hear me, as if I am speaking in tongues. He has insulted me again, this time blaming the complexity of the DNA problem on my explanation, and not his inability to understand it. I take a deep breath while pulling my photograph from the May experiment out of a brown paper envelope in my satchel. With steady eyes, I press it onto his desk. He gulps when he sees it.

'Where have you been keeping this?' he asks, with a similar calmness to the stillness that precedes a storm.

'It's the B form,' I say, taking a step backwards. 'It's evidently a helix.'

In my latest sketches, I envisage that DNA is made of two chains that run back-to-back, like two snakes entwined or infinitely woven figures of eight.

'How long have you had this?' Maurice asks me, in rising decibels.

'Since May, and now I'm leaving I plan to prepare a model based on all of the data Raymond and I have compiled.'

'What data? What do you mean?' Maurice asks tetchily.

'The atomic data is consistent with the B form, and most likely the A form too, being helical, but we must be certain,' I say.

Maurice's desk is empty except for a pile of books and an open letter. From where I'm standing, reading upside down, it appears to be addressed to Francis. It is written in Maurice's handwriting. A cluster of words leaps to my eyes, as readily as if a magnifying glass was on the letters.

I hope the smoke of witchcraft will soon be getting out of our eyes.

I make a logical deduction as to what the words mean. The mixed metaphor is an insufficient balm to the injury. The words deal a necrotic blow, decaying any shred of decent feeling I had left towards Maurice. Madonna or whore, witch or wench, it's the same wolf in different clothing. He may as well have spat the words right onto the page. *Let's have some talks afterwards when the air is a little clearer*, the letter reads, above the word *witchcraft*. I wonder for a second whether Maurice wasn't the first person to use the term *witch*, and whether instead he was simply parroting the term back to his friends in Cambridge.

'I shall be… getting out of your hair soon,' I stutter, leaving the room.

I pull the door to his office closed behind me, before

leaning up against the back of it, breathing heavily. Pride prevents Maurice from following me.

I go to the only place where I can be alone: the university chapel. In its cool atrium, the unbidden words, 'witch' and 'witchcraft', play over in my mind. The fluttering sensation of my beating heart makes me wonder if a ghost has passed straight through me.

Each time I projected our photographs of DNA onto the screen of my mind, the structure became even more unknowable. Back, eight, back, the molecular chains looked like figures of eight, or the infinity sign, the lemniscate. And if Chargaff's rule were correct, then it would seem there could be an infinite number of nucleotide combinations to choose from. Conjuring the image of my X-ray photographs to mind now, I wipe the tears from my eyes. Even in the deepest hole of a crisis, like a moon is to the night, a guiding light can be found through it and out on to the other side. Dawn is on the horizon.

My brother Roland catches sight of my tear-drenched cheeks that weekend and asks me if I am besotted with Maurice. I brush off the comment. Nothing could be further from the truth. But his question continues to spin on its axis in my head. It makes me wonder if perhaps love and hate are entwined, like the two hemispheres of the figure of eight, or the symmetry in the lemniscate. In our X-rays, the coupled nucleotides seem to be like yin and yang. Just which nucleotide is which cannot be gleaned from a photograph alone, at least not at any resolution conceivably possible, and with each chemical component destined to be present in equal measure under Chargaff's law, their interchangeability would appear to allow for endless possibilities. While mulling over this possibility it occurs to me suddenly that perhaps by averting my gaze whenever I looked at him, Maurice may have intended to disguise not just words, but feelings, of uneasiness or embarrassment, or maybe even misplaced affection.

My mind is overcome by clarity in the way that rain clears the glass. That's it. The dyads, there is symmetry in our photographs; the molecule has two faces.

The only way to solve a problem is to invert it, to flip it on its head. Our studies of oranges showed that the flecks in the outer peel were just noise, they were pith.

If the wet or hydrated form of DNA is helical, then it follows that the dehydrated or dry form must be too.

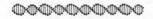

Fri (23rd January 1953)

Francis,

… There is… a silly muddle over Franklin's talk here. I got a big notice saying it was internal only — just a discussion between colleagues who work in the same lab. Then a lot of notices went round about the Colloquium & I took it for granted all had had the other note. Hence [Pauline] Cowan's remark to you.

I think that as the intention was to have it a private fight it would be best to keep it entirely so, as I said to Jim. It should be either public or private. Let's have some talks afterwards when the air is a little clearer. I hope the smoke of witchcraft will soon be out of our eyes.

PS. Tell Jim the answer to his question ["When did you last speak to her?"] is this morning. The entire conversation consisted of one word from me.
Maurice

| 31 |

Cerberus

'You look distracted,' Raymond says as we enter the sparse lecture hall and pull a couple of chairs from their dense stacks.

'I was just thinking about whether the dry DNA could be a helix after all,' I say.

There is little time to talk as Professor Randall and Maurice arrive a minute later, just after the hour. They each take chairs and sit a yard or so away from the projector, where I place my X-rays. Alec arrives minutes later. Their chatter is rousing.

'The latest photo of the dry form showed a double orientation,' I begin to explain when they finally settle.

'Double orientation?' Maurice, who is sitting nearest to the projector, repeats the words. The professor is scratching his head. The top buttons of the three other men's shirt collars are undone.

'That's a sign of lopsidedness, it would rule out symmetry,' Maurice says.

'That's right,' I agree.

'This helix needs to be sound as a pound,' Professor Randall says as he leans forward, digging his elbows into his knees. 'There's no room for error. If these X-rays of the crystallised form are asymmetrical, as you say, we can't then be sure of a helix.'

'You did ask me to look only at the dry DNA, Professor,' I say.

It doesn't seem relevant at this stage to bring up my photographs of the B form, my experiments at different humidity, given the professor had curtailed that aspect of my work.

Maurice mouths something to Alec, momentarily looking like a frustrated ventriloquist: 'We should check her data.'

Alec's eyes are fixed in my direction. He is making a strange noise, which sounds both like a laugh and a sigh, as if he is unsure whether to believe what he's hearing.

'It's not possible to have both a helix and not have a helix,' Professor Randall says sternly, hushing the other two.

'That might not be the case,' I say. 'Studies have shown that when it's stretched, protein behaves like a coil that has been pulled out of shape. The atoms are laid flat.'

'So that's that then, the A form isn't a helix,' says Maurice. He uncrosses his arms and puts his hands on his knees, briefly, before throwing them in the air.

'There's more if you'll stay to hear it,' I say.

'I think that's all we need to know,' Maurice says.

Alec also excuses himself to leave. 'There's an optical problem I need to attend to,' he mumbles, apologetically.

'Disappointing, Dr Franklin. I expected more from you,' says Professor Randall.

'Will you hear what I have to say about the B form, the wet DNA? Our findings really were very interesting,' I say.

'You have told us all we need to know,' says the professor. 'You made that quite clear in your note.'

I stand there speechless.

It has been trial enough to get this far in working out the structure of DNA, but it appears the real challenge is getting anybody to listen. Professor Randall doesn't want to hear what I have to say; it's as though it has no value, as though I am worthless. It is such indifference, not hate, that is the opposite of love.

'Do you mean the joke we posted?'

'Is that what you call it, Rosalind? A joke? A year's work, a joke?'

'No, Professor. Please, hear me out. The B form is a helix and I've observed a figure-of-eight pattern in my X-rays.'

The professor gets up from his chair, saying, sparsely and disparagingly, 'Maurice is working on the B form.'

That's the problem, I think to myself, but it's too late to tell him.

The professor shuts the door behind him before I can explain my X-ray photographs and the evidence for a helix with two strands.

My mother told me what she had heard, at the refugee centre, about the soldiers who had been dehumanised during the war. They had done anything to maintain their positions, to avoid the most unbearable punishment of all: ostracisation. No one in the room had questioned the professor; and in pulling rank today, he has missed one of the biggest subtleties of the discovery, that DNA behaves differently when it is wet.

'A total leg pull, with an undercurrent of steel,' Raymond says, reclining backwards in his chair after the other three leave. 'Did you hear Pauline invited Francis to your lecture?'

'Why would she? They'd use all our data, again.'

'Maurice didn't see the notice that the meeting was internal, hence her remark,' he replies. 'He had to go back and un-invite Crick, after all the other messages that went round about it.'

Professor Randall would doubtless have disagreed to our rivals at the Cavendish lab accessing our data in this way, after his reaction the last time Jim and Francis made a model so soon after seeing my lecture. It was a consequence of his ensuing fury that the head of the Cavendish lab, Professor Bragg, ordered them to stop working on DNA. Randall had similarly written to Professor Pauling's lab in California to say that, on no uncertain terms, his lab could not access our precious DNA data.

'She's just joined us from Dorothy Hodgkin's tutelage to work on collagen, hasn't she?' I ask him.

'Yes, and I expect Maurice tried to bend her arm to get her to invite Francis,' Raymond says. 'Perutz, Francis's supervisor, would already know half of it anyway so there's no point in him coming.'

For the past month, I have wondered whether Perutz could resist mining our findings after he visited our office in December to collect the report containing our latest data. That report was meant to be sent straight to the Medical Research Council's headquarters and only be shared with council members. As Francis's thesis supervisor, Perutz was evidently conflicted. After narrowly avoiding such an intrusion from Francis on my last lecture before being due to leave in March, I resolve to hasten my analysis of my X-ray photographs before it is too late.

| 32 |

Janus

King's College London, The Strand, 30 January 1953

'Uninvited guests usually knock.'

Jim is standing in the doorway of my office.

I do not know why he is here. His presence is ominous, much like a crow or any other harbinger of an unlucky event.

I am bent double over the light box, where I've been measuring the spaces between the atomic dots on an X-ray. I can feel the heat of the light on my chest. It is rising slowly up towards my neck.

'Maurice was busy,' Jim says.

He checks behind his shoulder briefly, then peers at the light box in front of me. His mouth falls open, dumbfounded.

I smooth my hair behind my ears and step in front of the projector to block his view of my X-ray photograph.

'I have Pauling's manuscript,' Jim starts.

My heart is beating loudly.

'Professor Pauling? But how?'

Whenever my brothers cheated at puzzles growing up, their wins were instantly reduced to losses. It was then that I could claim a victory. There was no glory in a shortcut. But Jim doesn't seem to be satisfied in degrading his own integrity by stealing; instead, he wants to take all of us with him.

'Trading secrets again, are you?'

He coughs as though he hasn't heard me and takes a step forward towards the light box.

'Just look at it, Rosy, and see if you can see what's wrong with it,' he says of his contraband, thrusting a white folder out into the space between us.

From where I am standing, I can see the title.

'Where did you get it?' I say, unwavering.

'Peter,' Jim says.

He waves the stolen work in front of my face.

'Does his father know you have it?'

'It's the phosphates, Rosy.'

Whenever I am within breathing distance of a finish line, it seems that the old rules change. Outside of academia, the old infrastructure of externally marked exam grades and accuracy don't seem to matter any more if they are inconvenient to the people in power. They could be changed at the last minute, without any discussion, and without a fair arbiter. Beyond education, meritocracy seems to be just an illusion.

'I've already said all I will. They're on the outside of the molecule,' I say, silently wishing for him to leave.

'Read this and tell me how the chains could hold together if the phosphate groups aren't ionised,' he says.

I look him straight in the eye and walk towards the door. He stiffens as I reach for the handle, raising his shoulders and arms above his head. It looks as though he is miming an escape from an invisible box. Perhaps his subconscious has calculated a retribution.

'Please, just leave,' I say.

He remains in front of the door, unmoved, least of all by the words of a woman.

Maurice appears minutes later, and it is only then that Jim

finally shrinks away from the door frame. They pat each other on the back and shake hands.

Jim's eyes are bulging in oscillations, partly out of relief and partly as if he cannot believe what he's got away with.

'There you are. We'd better get on before the pubs close,' Maurice says.

I shut the door before he has a chance to say anything else and rest the crown of my head against the back of it. I wait for them to leave. They do not ask if I would like to join them, much to my relief.

With a fast-beating heart, I collect my things to leave the lab for the weekend. I sense that I have just had a narrow escape. I switch off the laboratory light, walk down the corridor and push open the heavy swing doors, mulling over what just happened.

How dare Jim intrude like that, I think to myself. As I reach the ground level of the university building, closing the swing doors in the basement corridor behind me, I spot him speaking to Maurice. I hold back for a few moments so they don't see me. Their voices are loud and brash. Jim is laughing and Maurice is slapping him on the back of his shoddy grey blazer. I overhear that they are planning to drink in the pub on the corner of the Aldwych. So I walk in haste in the other direction towards Temple station.

On returning to my flat later that evening, I slowly pour myself a glass of water and sit down for the first time since this afternoon. But as my glass hits the table, I take a deep breath: my photographs. I couldn't be sure whether I had left them in full view on the light box or put them in my top drawer as usual for safe-keeping. Had Jim seen where I left them? I half suspected Maurice knew where they were kept.

7 March 1953

My dear Francis,

...I think you will be interested to know that our dark lady leaves us next week and much of the 3-dimensional data is already in our hands. I am now reasonably clear of other commitments and have started up a general offensive on Nature's secret strongholds on all fronts; models, theoretical chemistry and interpretation of data crystalline and comparative...

At last the decks are clear and we can put all hands to the pumps! It won't be long now.

Regards to all.

Yours ever

M

P.S. may be in Cambridge next week!

| 33 |

Informant

The Strand, London, March 1953

A newspaper catches in the spokes of my bike on my morning cycle ride to the lab by the River Thames.

I tear it from where it has adhered to the tyre, taking out my anger on the sheets of paper by ripping them from the spokes. The short headline emblazoned across the crumpled and now dirty page reads *Stalin is Dead.* I expire a brief sigh of relief; the tight grip with which he squeezed the Soviet must now loosen, even though his web of spies and enforced labour camps will take many more years to untangle. I begin to wonder then what motivates an informant. Is their biggest seductress an idea or the person they supply information to? It has been little over a month since Jim's visit and just a fortnight since Valentine's Day. Professor Pauling's son Peter has been releasing his father's secrets to the Cavendish lab all year, as fast as the barrel of a gun sheds bullets. Talking about his father's theory will undoubtedly be of no credit to him, though. He'll probably be cast aside like any other vessel.

Because each heavy thought begets another, I consider then whether Jacques's confidants were accomplices in his affairs. My relationship with Jacques eclipsed all other love from my life. It was not that I never thought of his wife. Yet the desires of my own heart had equal force. But if she ever saw my letters... he promised when he wrote to me last, that he would destroy them if anything ever happened to me.

Just a week after Jim's intrusion this January, storms sank the *Princess Victoria* boat in the North Channel, taking with it more than a hundred innocent lives. By mid-February, I had begun to document my evidence for the two-chain helix. Valentine's Day was overshadowed only by the hole it left in my diary. I longed to be one of the couples laughing outside my flat, without a care in the world, overjoyed and in love.

When I finally reach the lab, Raymond asks, 'Did you hear the news?' while holding up a day-old copy of *Nature*.

'About Stalin?'

Communism has polarised England. My friends in Cambridge have total conviction in it, glossing over the deaths of political dissidents, while my father's friends rant and rave about Russian spies coming to Britain. Stalin's end is unlikely to stop the Gulag camps. Nikita Khrushchev, whom the papers predict will replace him, murdered hundreds of political rebels in the camps when he was a chief in Ukraine.

'Pauling went for three chains.'

I pause.

Raymond is talking about the paper that Jim tried to thrust on me weeks ago.

'But that doesn't fit with the data,' I say, matter-of-factly.

'We could have told them it was rubbish; they would have known it if they'd seen our photographs,' Raymond says.

Professor Randall had refused to give Professor Pauling any of our data, writing to him to reject access when the Americans heard we had no further use for it.

'Randall wouldn't have let them see it,' I try to reassure Raymond.

'Things have moved beyond the data now, Ros,' he replies, scratching his head. 'The rumour, from Bill Seeds, is that

Francis went into the Eagle pub at the weekend declaring they'd found the secret of life; like they were gods.'

My belly swells with laughter at picturing Jim and Francis's giddy blaspheming. Bubbles of air rise up to my nose, making me sneeze. The patrons in the pub must have thought they were mad but would have probably joined them for a toast anyway, especially if it was on them. They aren't the first scientists to make such assailable claims and given Jim had been trying to fish for information just weeks before, I discern that they must have little evidence to back them up.

'They've made another model, this time using cardboard cut-outs for the sugar bases,' Raymond says. He forces a perplexed smile. 'You don't seem concerned?'

'Why would I be? They have no evidence,' I reply.

I gather our notes and start to check the sums are right and that there are no spelling mistakes. There are just weeks left before I will leave the lab for Birkbeck and it would be wise to ensure our paper is finished before I go. The truth, which I try to hide from Raymond, is that beneath it I am more than a little wary of the news. Maurice had gone for lunch with Jim and Francis while staying at the Cricks's house at Portugal Place in Cambridge a week before Valentine's Day. The revelation that they have made a model within weeks of his visit to Cambridge has come too soon after that to be coincidence.

'Maurice will help you, won't he, when I leave?' I ask Raymond, who is looking withdrawn.

'I don't know about that,' he says.

Maurice has been scarce all week. He took leave last minute, with no explanation. He seems disinterested in the DNA work now that I am going and, while I didn't expect him to throw a party for me, he could at least take the time to bid me farewell.

Later in the morning, Raymond heads to the photographic room to ensure there are no X-rays missing from our final paper outlining the probability of a two-strand helix. He freezes at the door to my office.

Maurice is blocking his path. His arm is outstretched.

'I think it's best that you both hear this,' he says, speaking rapidly and insistent that we should stop everything and listen to him. He seems to have little regard for anyone else's schedules. 'Jim and Francis have built a new model. I went up to Cambridge last night and it seems very, well, aligned.'

'Did you know about this?' It is the only question I can force myself to ask him.

'They asked me if I wanted to co-author their paper. I declined,' Maurice says. 'I'll be doing my own thing. They're a couple of rogues but they might have something. Bruce will publish his three-chain model, which is a darn sight better than Pauling's.'

I stand there speechless, unable to make a single utterance. There are no words to describe the shock and anger that I feel. It appears to be nothing but a foregone certainty that Maurice has colluded with and possibly even – somehow, though I am unsure of the details – leaked my data to Jim and Francis. Almost every plot and coordinate to DNA's structure, the two-chain helix outlined in my latest findings, was included in my fellowship report and the folio Professor Randall so freely handed to Francis's supervisor, Dr Perutz. It was all there, the water content of the molecule that had been misunderstood and warped by Francis in their earlier model, the clue to the pattern of the atoms, the rhomboid formation I had discussed with Dorothy Hodgkin – nobody was privy to that meeting but her student – and how that configuration repeated itself along the vertical axis of the structure. Indeed, it was all pictured in my data: the helix.

'We want to publish as well,' Raymond says eventually, in defiance.

Maurice smirks. 'I'm sorry, what?' He smooths a cowlick back from his forehead with the palm of his hand.

'We've drafted a paper, it's on my analysis of DNA,' I stutter. I reach into my top drawer and take out my typed lab notes. They are half an inch thick.

Maurice swallows audibly. His face is now pale. 'I'm not sure about that,' he says, reticently.

'It's our data,' I say. 'It's all there, two years of work. We will make sure it aligns.'

He spends a few minutes flicking through the pages. 'Perhaps there's room for it, at the back of the journal,' he says, disappointingly, after some thought.

'But it has all the proof,' I say. 'It shows DNA has two chains. Nobody else has any evidence.'

'Hmm,' Maurice says. 'Very well.'

He takes a second glance at our paper.

'Jim and Francis also went for two chains, funny really,' he says.

Raymond looks as though he is about to speak. I put my hand on his, urging him to pause before he erupts in anger.

'How's that possible?' he demands anyway, pushing my hand away. 'Randall wouldn't have let anyone see our data.'

Maurice smirks as though he's witnessing a toddler's outburst.

The irony in his smile is telling, and for a moment a flicker of a memory bursts into my consciousness. I picture Professor Randall squaring up to Dr Perutz as he eyeballed him while delivering our annual summary for the Biophysics Committee at the research council.

'How is anything ever possible?' Maurice says, perplexingly, before insisting that he must immediately inform Bruce, who had wrongly assumed, like Pauling, that DNA had three chains. That he should see any urgency in informing our old colleague seems odd, almost as much as his comment. Bruce is starting a new life with Mary and their baby in Australia. Lab politics is the least of his concerns. It takes all of the force I have to quell my suspicions that Maurice is colluding with the Cambridge scientists at the Cavendish lab, and that Dr Perutz could have leaked my findings – so much so that my eyes, rather than my ears, feels like they are burning. After all, as Professor Randall said, those annual reports to the Medical

Research Council are intended to be confidential, everybody knows that. Surely, that is a time-honoured tradition, or no lab worth their salt would sign up. As Professor Randall had told me when I first joined King's, there was money at stake in DNA; not least the money put towards my research by my fellowship sponsors, as well as the lot given by the financiers who funded our equipment.

After some wrangling with Raymond, by the end of the working day Maurice begrudgingly agrees that he will share our paper on the double helices with the lab in Cambridge in return for a byline. Raymond is still reluctant to share our data on DNA with the Cavendish lab as much of it will contribute to his thesis. It is not an easy decision for me either; while I'm his supervisor and, like him, question why we should give up our data, I also do not want to miss out on the opportunity to have our work published. My mind is now firmly fixed on the new horizons at Birkbeck and, to some extent, our work at King's already belongs to my past. Professor Randall might have previously declined to share any of our data, not least with Linus Pauling, but it now seems he has done a deal with Professor Bragg at the University of Cambridge, though he hasn't had the courtesy to mention it to us. From what I understand, the gentlemen's agreement will go some way towards concealing the fact that Francis and Jim have, somewhat mysteriously, suddenly come to many of the same conclusions about DNA as us, despite everything that they have said before.

VI

NOW

| 34 |

Schrödinger's Equation

Birkbeck, University of London, Bloomsbury, March 1953

Torrington Square is set back from the main street and built around a Georgian courtyard. The surrounding brick town houses are aged in soot, which hides the smart arched fanlights and elaborately moulded balconies. The houses were bombed on either side, leaving just a cluster of dilapidated surviving buildings. They are bordered by iron railings, which are still upright despite many being melted for munitions during the war. The square escaped the same wartime rule that robbed many other London streets of ornamental railings, perhaps due to its proximity to Westminster and the wealthy status of Bloomsbury residents, or at least because the rails protected a light well, until such time that the country had too much dismantled iron to know what to do with. The Birkbeck Laboratory is nestled between the School of Oriental and African Studies and the Royal Academy of Dramatic Arts, hidden behind tree-lined walkways. Blossom from the trees that line the Regency squares of Bloomsbury carpets the pavements below. The white, yellow and pink stained petals curl at the edges like day-old confetti.

I wheel my bicycle up the stone steps by number 21 Torrington Square and lean it against the ebony gates. Inside, the fanlight above the open door floods the nail-ridden floorboards in natural light. I climb the stairs hesitatingly. The landing on the first floor has worn carpet that is ragged around the edges.

'You must be Rosalind.'

I look up to see a tall man with glasses and black hair – peppered with white strands, betraying the youth of his smooth skin.

'I'm new here,' I say.

'I'm Aaron,' he says in a nasal voice, scratching his head. 'I think we're going to be working on the tobacco mosaic virus together. You'll recognise your office by the taps and drawers.'

The doors on every floor of the building are closed. It is only when I reach the top of the staircase that I finally see there is one open. The sink inside is carved into a wooden worktop, which is underlined by several drawers. Above it is an exposed boiler. A glass water dispenser sits on the shelf above the sink and empty jars are stacked on the rung below. The room is filled with more desks than any scientist could ever need. Natural light streams in from the vast window and fills every corner of the room except for the insides of the cupboards. I arrange my notebook on the desk next to the window, resting both hands on it, and stare outside to the courtyard below.

'Dr Franklin, excuse me for barging in.' Aaron is at the door. 'I know there's lots to do to get settled in, but the post came. This is for you.'

'I haven't even announced my move yet,' I say, surprised that anyone has written to me at this address so fast.

He hands me an A4 envelope, which is ink-stamped *Aldwych*.

'I expect they're sorry at King's to have lost their first-class analyst,' he says.

'Maybe,' I reply under my breath as I thumb open the letter.

I half expect it to be from Maurice, who, struggling with

the crystallised-to-wet DNA transition again, is probably asking for my help.

Instead, the letter is from Raymond.

This comes with regards from the Cavendish; it concurs well with our data. Francis's wife Odile has drawn a sketch, it reads.

There isn't any clue in the words about the intonation of his voice when he wrote the note. Enclosed with it is an updated draft copy of the Cavendish lab's article for *Nature* journal, based on the manuscript Maurice showed me the day after I presented my paper in March. It's entitled, *A Structure for Deoxyribose Nucleic Acid.*

There it is, the double helix, pictured on the first page of the paper. This time it isn't just in my imagination, but drawn in pencil for all to see. The sugar bases and phosphates are in the right position. The space grouping also matches. It fits my data, exactly. It is almost too good to be true.

When I reach the end of the draft, I check whether any pages are left in the envelope, as it finishes abruptly without including any data to support the theory. It should really be the addendum or the explanation, I think to myself.

'Working late?' Aaron hangs his lab coat on the back of my office door later that afternoon.

I didn't notice the creaks of his feet on the stairs.

'Indeed,' I reply. 'I would tell you about it, but I'm sure you wouldn't want to know.'

'Oh yeah? Try me,' he says.

'I had it,' I say, slapping the envelope back down on the desk.

'That bad, is it? Had what?'

'The two-chain helix. Randall has asked me to stop working on it.'

'What's this then?' Aaron says, picking up and scanning the first page of the Cavendish draft. 'Hmm, it looks like young Jim has a lot to say on the topic.'

'You know him?' I ask Aaron.

'We speak about the TMV work now and again. Isn't he in Paris?'

'Yes, that's right. He's gone to ask a biochemist there about Chargaff's bases. Chemistry isn't his strong point,' I say.

'Lucky Jim,' Aaron says with a belly laugh.

'I could kick myself, you know. For not seeing it.'

We had been so close to obtaining the structure of DNA. I had mapped the two-chain helix almost in its entirety. The only outstanding piece of the puzzle was identifying the configuration of its chemical elements.

My heart begins to ache with regret on seeing that Francis and Jim have used Austrian scientist Erwin Chargaff's ideas in the Cavendish paper. They weren't the first people to suggest that his theory could go some way in filling in the gaps in DNA.

'Not seeing what?'

'The ratios; how the sugars fit together. Adenine and thymine, guanine and cytosine, pyrimidine and purine. They're always present in equal ratios. It's all there in Chargaff's work. If only I'd had the chance to meet him,' I say.

'What are your plans for TMV?' Aaron asks, refocusing my mind on the task at Birkbeck.

'The tobacco mosaic virus?' I clear the envelope from the desk. 'Well, nobody knows how it infects the tobacco plant. Not yet, at least. Now, what's the use of doing all this work if we don't have some fun?'

By leaving a problem alone and distancing from it, so often you find that things fall into place. You stumble on or realise the answers you were looking for, or notice what was there quietly sitting in front of you all along.

'All calculus and no play is no good for any day,' Aaron agrees. 'We could grab a coffee at Bar Italia in Soho. They do spaghetti.'

Frith Street, a short walk from Bloomsbury, is manifestly European. Gone are the vacant faces of England's provinces. Inside, everything from the tiles on the floor to the leather-bound stools, and the granite worktop and enamel cups, has the gloss of newness.

We sit together outside the café, on slender bar stools, and order Americanos.

'Where do you sit in relation to the Party?' Aaron says unguardedly as we sit down.

The question seems strange. Being loyal to a party doesn't interest my generation. I vowed never to discuss my vote, which was always Labour, with anybody.

It only occurs to me after a few minutes more that, by the Party, he means the Communist Party.

Professor Bernal, from the way Aaron is speaking, is, unlike my father, buoyantly optimistic about the new Khrushchev regime in Russia.

'Churchill would have a hard time arguing with Khrushchev,' Aaron says. 'It is he himself who has been the architect of the Cold War.'

That evening, while watching the sun fade beneath the clouds from the courtyard in Torrington Square, I pull out the Cambridge team's paper once again, checking disbelievingly that little needs changing. I seal it and post it in a nearby postbox on my ride home.

| 35 |

Occam's Razor

Cavendish Laboratory, Cambridge University, spring 1953

After writing to ask whether I can visit, I go to the Cavendish lab to see Jim and Francis mainly out of curiosity. That, and Francis said he had a few questions for me. He keeps writing to me with much enthusiasm about my DNA data, which I thought I had already left behind. Cambridge's model stretches up from the floor to the ceiling. It resembles a giant school project. Metal rods are jutting clumsily from its unwieldy clamps, which are arranged in rudimentary hexagons to represent the nucleobases. It looks like an instrument of war. The assemblage is a world apart from the hermetic and smooth maquettes that my students are making at Birkbeck. I follow the curvature of the rods. Between each chain on the model, I see the invisible spaces from our electron-density map. In those spaces are the numbers from my report. In short, I see my data. Each repetition of the molecule is a fractal branching outwards from its kin; with subtle, but infinite possibilities.

Then I notice that something is missing. The chains, by our calculations, shouldn't be equally spaced apart.

'Elegant simplicity: the Greek test,' Raymond says, standing back to look at the model.

He's referring to the notion that the simplest of ideas are often the truest. Greek philosopher Aristotle and later Islamic astronomers such as Ibn al-Haytham chose between competing theories by asking which idea was the simplest.

In Britain, the same concept – despite its ubiquity – is called Occam's Razor, named after friar William of Ockham. He and Aquinas before him used the idea to argue the likelihood of God's existence. The Latin, *numquam ponenda est pluralitas sine necessitate*, the notion that unnecessary duplications only add confusion, was common among theologians arguing in favour of monotheism, a single God.

Its more useful application, however, was in Islamic science, which absorbed and assimilated the Aristotelian concept (the idea that the more compelling demonstrations use 'fewer postulates or hypotheses').

My worry is that without evidence, any theory about DNA risks being an oversimplification. While it may have looked compelling, the evidence proved their first model to be wrong.

'It's pretty, but how do they prove it?' I say.

The truth about Jim and Francis's model, which is a visual demonstration of what the DNA molecule might look like, is that it must ultimately rely on evidence. Otherwise, it is merely intuition. The model pieces together what little they already knew about the structure of DNA, and anything beyond that would simply be guesswork, unless it was proven otherwise either by our data or some other means.

We are interrupted by Francis, who has made himself scarce until now.

'Rosy, there you are. You must excuse me, I've been showing around our fifth visitor of the day. Dorothy loves the model,' he adds magnanimously as he sees me examining the detail.

'Hodgkin?'

'Yes, a bunch from Oxford made the drive up. So, pray tell, how can we be sure about the atoms lining up in a rhomboid formation?'

'I got your letter asking about the space grouping,' I reply. 'I narrowed the options down to three possibilities, out of two hundred and thirty. Of those, it had to be C2. Dorothy pointed out that organic molecules usually have chirality; they are "handed".'

'Well, that's fascinating, Rosy. You see, if that's the case, it would mean that the chains run in opposite directions.'

As every tiler knows, you can't stack rhomboid tiles vertically without inverting every other tile. When done right, the tiles fit together in a geometric jigsaw. If done incorrectly, the tiler is left with an overhang. To apply the same logic to DNA means inverting a chain. The arrangement of the atoms in each turn of the molecule most closely corresponds in shape to a parallelogram prism similar to a rhomboid; that, known technically in crystallography as the C2 grouping, is the only atomic pattern that is chiral, or handed, that can be determined from an exhaustive analysis of my X-ray photographs. This idea that the chains would thus be inverse to each other is only an afterthought – dessert to the main course, if you like.

It couldn't be called a discovery in its own right, yet Francis sounds more pleased with himself about this point alone than he seems with his entire model.

'We should be ready to send our paper on Thursday,' he says. 'We've put Maurice's paper after ours, then yours and Raymond's.'

'We'll send our article separately to the editor,' I say. 'I'll post it directly.'

Drayton Gardens, Fulham, London, 25 April 1953

The day the findings are published, my phone doesn't ring once. My paper on the molecular configuration of DNA, compiled with Raymond during my fellowship and his doctorate, was due to be published alongside Jim and Francis's explanation on the very same day. This had been arranged by Professor Randall over a handshake with the head of the Cavendish lab, Professor Bragg. We used the proper chemical name for crystallised DNA, sodium thymonucleate, the descriptive term for sodium salts of nucleic acid extracted from calf-thymus glands. I had deliberated over the headline, favouring the specific description over more general headline terms. A punchy header may have been more likely to catch the attention of the masses, but we chose the more accurate and precise definition to describe our experiments; which any scientist should appreciate, if they understood it. Now I am anxious to see where the editors at *Nature* journal have placed our paper, 'A Note on Molecular Configuration in Sodium Thymonucleate', and what significance they have given it – pride of place or peripheral mention. That day, my parents are too busy being grandparents to pick up the phone. My mother helps my brothers with childcare one or more days a week, while my father dotes on his grandchildren by lavishing them with expensive gifts.

Outside my apartment block that evening, in gardens set back from the art deco Fulham Road cinema, I am fumbling for my keys when I hear an Antipodean voice.

'G'day,' he says.

Startled, while trying to unlock the main front door, I mistake his voice for Maurice's.

It's a relief to turn around and see that it's not him.

The stranger is toying with a set of keys and smiling at me as though he wants something. Despite trying my hardest to squeeze my bicycle through the door into the hallway for several minutes, it won't budge. The front door of the block will only partially open and even after applying considerable force, it remains still just slightly ajar.

'There's something in the way,' I say, yanking my front wheel out from the open crevice.

As I force the wheel backwards towards me, it releases

suddenly from the doorway. A torn envelope has got caught between the underside of it and the bristly doormat.

I nudge the envelope with my foot, but it doesn't move from where it is wedged underneath the door. It must be my copy of *Nature* journal.

'Let me hold it for you,' the stranger says as he gestures at my bike, before trying to wrestle it from my hands.

'I'm fine, thank you,' I reply, holding on to the frame tightly.

'I won't steal it, I live here,' the man says, waving his keys as proof. They have the same keyholder as mine, which is specific to the building. If the man does indeed turn out to be a burglar, he could easily be found out.

Inside, a second envelope of nearly equal weight is stamped from Cambridge. It must be the Newnham round robin. Every year they send it to me, but they never post an apology. The women's decrees have long since been vindicated with degree status and while such an apology won't change the past for those of us who came before, it might persuade the professors to swallow their pride and do the same.

The man follows me into the lift. We reach for the buttons at the same time, before he asks me which floor I live on and presses the number for me.

'Would you like to come in for a drink?' he asks as the bell sounds to signal his floor.

The lift jolts into a stationary position.

'I'm fine, thank you,' I reply to the stranger, looking firmly at the floor. Just because I am a single woman, living alone, does not mean I want to go for a drink with any man who asks.

The passage of time has taught me that bottling up my feelings is fruitless. Evi, who moved to Chicago but has now returned, is persisting in trying to match me on a date with her sociologist friend Ralph Miliband. She is all but by blood my little sister. As handsome as she protests he is, I feel sure he wouldn't understand either my work or me. She doesn't know about Jacques. Nobody does. But maybe if I tell her about the meeting with the stranger, she might stop asking questions about my love life, at least while I process my feelings for a little longer.

I still haven't told anyone about my meetings with Jacques. He sometimes comes to visit me at my flat, as he did after attending a recent physics conference in London. I see Jean and her whole family who come to stay in my tiny flat more often than I do him. I wish that the visits were more regular.

| 36 |

Creatures of the Night

21 Torrington Square, Bloomsbury, 25 July 1955

The sound of footsteps galloping down the stairs in the building next door can be heard from within the town house on Torrington Square. Everyone knows what the noise means. Shortly after getting into the lab one Friday morning in July, from the spyhole in the front door of the building, I see the outline of a woman leaving the house and crossing the square outside. She must be one of Professor Bernal's mistresses, or perhaps a lady of the night from the dens of iniquity in nearby Soho. Once I found a pair of fishnet stockings outside the front door. Another time, his missing car was found parked outside one of the walk-ups in Soho's red-light district. Professor Bernal had married young – he was still a student when he wed – and he adopted a laissez-faire, *tout-le-monde* approach to everything, including love and marriage. It was well known that his was an open marriage and he had fathered two children by other women. Like politics and science, the opposite sex were equal opportunities to him; whether they were married, single or otherwise.

Soon after I joined Birkbeck, Professor Randall wrote to me to ask me to discontinue the work on DNA. It came as a hurtful shock. My fellowship from the building company Turner & Newall had been granted to investigate the structure of DNA, at least ever since Professor Randall had switched my study from solutions. After Professor Bernal's initial job offer, much wrangling had to be done with the fellowship committee in order for me to transfer the sponsored research programme to the University of London's Birkbeck college.

With his help, I was able to convince the committee to allow me to study the role and structure of ribonucleic acid in the tobacco mosaic virus under my fellowship. It was a bitter salve. The virus had interested many scientists who were otherwise preoccupied with DNA and the gene, not least James Watson, as the mysteries of ribonucleic acid, or RNA – a component of all living organisms most active in viruses – and its interaction with genes, had yet to be uncovered.

This morning I got to the lab early. My stomach is bursting with butterflies. It is the final week of July, which means it is nearly payday, and, more pertinently, the day of my pay increase. With the extra money from the raise, I may even be able to afford a ticket to Paris. I collect my wage envelope from the mantelpiece in the hallway. Then, on reading the slip, I notice that the committee has made an awful mistake. My pay has not gone up as I had expected, but has been cut from £1,100 to £1,080 per year without any explanation. There is no ombudsman I can call on the telephone. I cannot imagine this happening to a man. My insides are screaming.

After hearing voices through the walls, with the envelope still in my hand, I walk to the house next door and rap twice at the brass knocker.

The door opens and Professor Bernal stands there wearing only a flannel dressing gown. He looks unwashed and his hair is uncombed. I cannot imagine what attracts his lovers.

His ear-length hair is incongruous for a middle-aged man and he's carrying extra pounds. He makes a suggestive smile, as though he's read my thoughts.

'John, I must take something up with you.' I articulate each consonant to communicate to him that he cannot get his way with me, as he has done with these other women.

'It's seven o'clock in the morning. Now's not a good time,' he replies.

'The thing is, professor, my pay has been cut, and most other women are now being paid more. Did you put in the request for my pay rise to the Agricultural Research Council?'

'Let's talk about it when I get into the office,' Professor Bernal says, tying his dressing gown tightly around his waist. He shuts the door, mouthing, 'Goodbye.'

I stare at the closed door in frustration.

Back next door in the building where my office is, I make my way up the stairs to draft a letter, something he won't be able to close the door on. As I walk up the staircase, I hear yawning, followed by expletives, coming from next door.

Later that morning, a man walks into my office wearing a pressed shirt tucked into pinstripe trousers. His eyes are as wide as a deer's and his face blushes a deep shade of rose.

'Dr Franklin?' he asks.

'This is Ken Holmes,' Aaron says a second later, resting his elbow on the door frame of my office.

The young man nods.

'Ken's our new research fellow, he's your assistant,' Aaron says.

'Don't tease, Aaron,' I say while standing up to greet the newcomer.

'You usually reserve your comebacks for my maths,' Aaron says, winking.

'Ken, you'll be joining John Finch, our visiting fellow. He's not in today as he's off sick,' I say. 'It's all rather ramshackle here, I'm afraid, but soon we'll be moving into a new building.'

Behind Aaron, a third man wearing a suit and tie is carrying a satchel so full he has clamped his arm tightly around it to stop its contents from falling onto the floor.

'And this is James, James Watt,' Aaron says, adding, 'Dr Franklin is leading the lab's work on the tobacco mosaic virus.'

'Any relation to the James Watt?' I ask.

'If only,' he replies, adjusting his glasses nervously. 'I'm your new doctoral student.'

Later that morning, I catch Holmes observing the underside of the Beaudouin camera I'd brought back from Paris and looking puzzled.

'How do you think you should proceed with setting up this experiment?' I ask him.

We have been having trouble using the latest X-ray apparatus from Beaudouin, a manufacturer in France, due to a problem with the transformers. I went to Paris directly to confront the manufacturer about the problem and brought back with me the newest equipment. Just as I was with DNA, I am tasked with taking microscopic X-ray images of RNA from the tobacco mosaic virus to map its structure. The apparatus has to be set up by hand, and includes many moving parts.

'We should measure the vacuum,' he says, tentatively, referring to the vacuum effect in the X-ray tube. The intensity of the X-rays and their wavelength depends on these measurements, with the beam being at its strongest when interfering gases from a dirty tube are kept at a minimum.

I challenge Holmes to set up and adjust the X-ray apparatus himself, including the vacuum seals, something a novice couldn't possibly know how to do without extensive training.

'Go ahead, or else you might miss the finding.'

In X-ray diffraction, a scientist is only as good as her apparatus, and the skill with which she assembles it. Failing to properly assemble the equipment would ruin the experiment. And yet focusing too intently on the parts without being mindful of the wider experiment would only waste time. This is my new assistant's first test.

Later that morning, one of the technicians is hovering around my desk in the cramped top-floor office with unusually straight-backed deportment. He looks down at his shoes and coughs before saying, 'I want to take a week off, to study for an O level.'

I cannot believe what I am hearing. Even though I have practised science for more than a decade since gaining my doctorate, I am not even allowed in the same parts of the building as permanent staffers such as him. Temporary staff are restricted to eating lunch outside the building, as the faculty dining room is exclusively for full-time staff members.

'There are research assistants who are more qualified than you. How would you like to be an assistant and not a technician?' I say, then immediately regret my sharpness.

'Are you demoting me, Dr Franklin?' The lab falls silent.

Before I have a chance to respond to the technician or explain my outburst, Professor Bernal's booming voice echoes through the room.

'Rosalind, you wanted to speak to me?' he says, from where he is standing at the door, pulling his fingers through his hair.

In single file we walk down the stairs, which complain as we descend. The staircase is narrow and dusty, with many broken floorboards beneath the carpet which creak underfoot and are littered with rusty nails.

'Do you have any dependants, Franklin?' Professor Bernal asks me when we get to his temporary office on the third floor. He slumps his large frame into the cushioned armchair and sits with his legs spread apart. With each elbow leaning on the arms of his plush chair, he impatiently taps and rubs together his two index fingers.

'I don't feel that has any relevance to my pay,' I say.

'Then what makes you entitled to an increase?' he asks.

The professor's love of women, I realise at that moment, does not extend equally to respect.

'I may not cook for and look after a family, Professor Bernal, but I do have rent to account for like the head of any other household,' I say.

'Look,' he replies, turning his chair to face me while putting his elbows on his knees. 'I have every confidence that you can break new ground here. I fought hard for your fellowship to be extended so you could join us to work on viruses.'

'Did you ask for my pay rise?' I say.

'The Agricultural Research Committee refused the request for £1,250 a year.'

'Why would they refuse it, after the reform said working women should be paid more?'

'It's your age,' Professor Bernal says shortly.

'But I'm thirty-five.'

'You're still better paid here than you would be as a teacher or even in the civil service,' he replies.

By thirty-five years of age, my female cousins had already had children. So had my brothers, who apart from Roland are older than me. They also worked. David had joined my father in the family business, Keyser Bank, and they were talking about Roland doing the same. My cousins, Irene and Catherine, stayed at home to look after their babies, and my mother had done the same, volunteering to help refugees, and sitting on several school committees. She rarely has time to ring nowadays.

My situation within our family is unique. My brothers are still happily settled, having been promoted to directors at the newly merged Keyser Ullman bank, and my sister Jenifer has started dating an academic called Ian Galinsky. Evi is now married. Mamie Bentwich and Uncle Norman have no children, but their nieces and nephews are grown adults and so Mamie is free to pursue her political career as a Member of Parliament.

Now, my boss is telling me, from where he is sitting in his spoiled ivory tower, that by not marrying, and instead choosing to work – possibly sacrificing my chances of ever having a family of my own because of my age – I am too young to qualify for a pay rise. I am more aggrieved on hearing his response than I ever was about my grandpa's will, which forbade me to marry anyone who was not Jewish or else sacrifice any hope of a share of the family inheritance.

| 37 |

Life's Code

The Georgian town house in Bloomsbury is more than a century old. Its only insulation is the decaying Flemish-bond brickwork. In August the heat rises all the way to the top, where my office is. Most evenings, in the last of the summer heat, I can hear groaning noises from the house next door. By now Professor Bernal and his wife, who have two sons together, have all but separated except by the letter of the law. Our office in Bloomsbury is less than a mile away from Soho, where ladies of the night entice lone men wandering the streets on warm summer nights, by asking for a cigarette lighter. Such temptation is too great for the libidinous professor, who has all the self-control of a wild and tempestuous horse.

Now, as I walk downstairs to catch some air, voices are echoing through the floorboards.

'My car has been stolen.' Professor Bernal is gesticulating wildly in the hallway.

'Where did you park it?' I ask him.

'Soho,' he says as he tosses his leather jacket onto the end of the balustrade and storms into his office.

From behind him, Vittorio steps forward.

'What happened?' he whispers.

'Vittorio. You made it!'

I did not expect my friend would be able to get to the seminar on antimicrobial resistance in London all the way from Paris, but, loyal as he is, he has travelled to catch my talk.

'*Si*, I wouldn't miss the London conference. Tell me, how did Bernal lose his car?'

I reply to him in French, which is better than my Italian, though I do not know the French word for prostitute, so I make my best guess.

With Professor Bernal busy in his office, we make our way to Portland Place for the seminar.

'Is it always like that?' Vittorio asks me on our stroll to Marylebone.

'It's a slum, but a better one than the last.'

'I see.'

'Trouble is the Agricultural Research Council is refusing to change my pay, despite the law, and they're also ignoring my requests for new instruments.'

'*Cazzata*,' he tuts with disapproval.

Patting down my coat pocket, I realise I've left my purse in the office.

'You go on, I'll see you there,' I tell Vittorio, before hurrying back to Torrington Square.

Outside the building, Aaron is leaning against the iron railings, next to the new research fellow who is crouching on the front steps.

'We can't do anything until the new transformer arrives,' Ken is saying.

Seconds later, while I am still trying to reassure Ken over the X-ray equipment, someone calls my name from behind where I am standing.

'You must be Ros.'

The voluble New York drawl of the stranger reminds me of my friend Anne. She always says she would know another New Yorker instantly, not by intonation but by their gliding vowels no matter the rapidity of their words. All I can see of the person who spoke to me is a silhouette in the relief of the bright sun, which has cast a rainbow against the smattering of raindrops. His outline suggests he has a square jaw and moustache.

'Who do I have the pleasure of…?' I start, but before I am able to finish I'm interrupted by the thundering gallop of Professor Bernal pounding down the staircase.

'Don!' he hollers through the open door from the hallway. 'You made it. I'll cancel my meeting.'

'A don?' I ask, looking back in the direction of the man.

He looks too young to be a university professor, despite the enthusiastic reception from Professor Bernal.

'Don's my name, actually. It always confuses the British,' says the man, looking up in Professor Bernal's direction. The sun lights his angular brow line. 'Don Casper.'

'Don's going to tell me all about life on the other side of the pond,' Professor Bernal says as he puts his umbrella back in the stand by the door.

'Care to join us?' Don asks. 'I've heard a lot about you.'

'Really? Good things, I hope,' I reply.

'Don's an old friend of Jim and Maurice's, aren't you, Don? We go way back,' Professor Bernal says as he rushes back indoors to cancel his meeting.

'That dreadful lot,' I say, unapologetically.

'Yes, that dastardly pair,' says Don.

I try not to laugh, but that makes it even more boisterous when I eventually erupt. Suddenly, desperate to use the loo, I take a few steps up the stairs towards the door, while trying to disguise my need for bodily functions.

'I'm afraid I can't, I have to return to a conference in Marylebone. I've just come back for my purse. How is Jim nowadays anyway?' I ask.

'He's the same old Jim. Even now he's showing me the way around the tobacco mosaic virus.'

Jim is once again working on the structure of the virus after losing interest in DNA. He left Cambridge to join the California Institute of Technology, just a year after publishing in *Nature* journal, and is working alongside Don making electron-density maps of its RNA. Once again, he needs me to tell him if he has got his sums right. This time, he wants to know about the structure of the RNA protein, to fill in the gaps in their wrong-footed paper.

'Jim hasn't changed, surely not?'

I put one hand up to my mouth to feign surprise. At that exact moment, the sky begins to pour.

'I must fetch my umbrella too,' I say.

'Let me help you,' Don replies, following me up the steps.

'I'll just be a minute, honest,' I say, rushing up the stairs without pausing.

'I couldn't wait to meet you,' he says softly while trailing behind me nonetheless. 'Whenever Jim speaks about you, I sense that the opposite must be true.'

That is more what I would have expected from Jim. He is like a proud and hungry leopard who will never change its spots.

'But I don't think it's Jim you need to worry about,' says Don. 'That old colleague of yours, Maurice, advertised that you'd be appearing at the Christmas party as a clairvoyant; *Madame Raymonde Frankline*, the poster said. I thought, who is this woman?'

'So they weren't sorry to see me go at King's then,' I say, stopping for a moment with my foot still hovering over the step.

Until this point, I hadn't really been following what Don has been saying. Now my mind is racing, flooded with the words I had seen on the letter on Maurice's desk before leaving Professor Randall's lab. Some of my worst fears have been realised. My chest feels tight. I pause on the step for a second.

Professor Bernal calls up the stairs to say he has to take an important phone call with a funder.

When we get to my office, Don wails in surprise. 'What's that for?'

'Oh, the umbrella?' I reply. 'To keep my notebook dry. The roof leaks.'

I point at the pitched ceiling. The paintwork is discoloured from condensation from the pipes. The attic roof has been tested all week. I have opened an umbrella over my desk to prevent water from spoiling my notes. Underneath the parasol it is womb-like.

'Is that right?'

'I bet it's not like this in California.' I grab my purse from the desk.

As I rush out of the front door of Torrington Square to make my speaking slot, Don insists that we should continue our conversation over dinner that evening. By the time I get to the conference, the audience is clapping at the end of the main debate and I am due on stage. The ordeal passes in a blur. All I can think about are our dinner plans for later that night.

When I arrive at the restaurant, Don has the appearance of a mating pigeon with its chest puffed out and feathers on display.

'Is everything all right?' I ask when we bump into each other by the bar.

'I was wondering, will I see you again after tonight?' he asks.

| 38 |

Prophets

International Union of Crystallography Symposium, Madrid, April 1956

The air inside the fan-cooled building is stale. The distressed yellow wash brightens the orange-peel-textured walls of the villa. It is the first time I have seen Don since we met in London last summer. He is wearing dark glasses indoors and a V-neck jumper tucked into his trousers and looks like an airline pilot.

'Why the jumper?'

'It's eighty degrees Fahrenheit right now in Colorado, as you English would say. In here it feels about eight,' he says, kissing me on the cheek. His stubble grazes against my chin. 'Have you seen the price of a bagel here?'

'The price is only as good as the taste,' I reply.

'Listen, how would you like to get out of here?'

No sooner has he said the words than Francis and his wife Odile walk up to us. Odile and I are wearing matching pencil skirts, which fall just below the knee, and are the uniform for the scientific circuit.

'Here you are, all the way from England,' says Francis, nodding to greet us.

Don and I make several starts to leave, but each time we are interrupted. I confide in him that Maurice – who is still entrenched in trying to prove the double helix by repeating our experiments rather than trusting my data – is avoiding me.

'Maybe you shouldn't be so hard on him; after all, he was right, you know,' Don says.

'Right about what? He'd all but given up on DNA when I joined King's.'

'Well, you did predict the double helix,' Don says with a smile. 'And Madame Raymonde Frankline, clairvoyant, has a ring to it, doesn't it?'

We briefly step away from the group. Jim is waxing on about his impending visit to Cairo. Seeing that I am anxious to leave, Don pulls me aside. He asks what my plans are for the summer, while nervously pushing his dark glasses back onto his head. After the speed at which we worked to find the double helix and the pace at which I have had to get up to speed with the tobacco mosaic virus, I am ready to take a leisurely break in Paris or to stay with my friend in New York.

'Come to the States,' Don insists, gently gripping my arm.

I begin to make my excuses about how the work on the tobacco mosaic virus is taking off.

'We can work on it together,' he says.

I explain that my friend Anne lives all the way on the East Coast, and there is no one I could visit on the West Coast. 'Where would I stay?'

'With me in Colorado Springs.'

'That's miles from the lab,' I say.

'All right, then what about Berkeley? I know one of the professors at the University of California, Dr Heinz Fraenkel-Conrat. His wife loves having guests.'

'Well…' I hesitate.

'Well, that's it. It's done. You're coming.'

Suddenly, a voice on the tannoy ushers everyone out of the Spanish villa. The attendees are leaving the building in droves to stand outside for a photograph. As Don and I hold back from the throng, Jim and Francis walk past us.

'I feel sorry for Lord Rothschild at the agricultural council for having to deal with such an *obsessive woman*,' Jim is saying.

I swallow but my throat is dry.

Don looks angrily in Jim's direction and I rest my hand on his arm.

Jim hasn't changed at all. Lord Rothschild has been reconsidering my pay packet since my wage was mistakenly cut last summer. He is ignoring my requests to the agricultural council for more equipment. If I do go to visit Don, I would want to stay as far away from Jim as decently possible. I am far happier for an ocean and continents to separate us.

| 38 |

Atomic Constellation

Berkeley Hills, near San Francisco Bay, California, 25 July 1956

The sky in Northern California is a vast azure dome. It is as clear as a crystal and as ubiquitous as if it has melted into the ocean. The vast expanse gives a dwarfing sense of what it means to live in the universe. As the trees clear, the bay is peppered with large shards of shingle. The beach resembles the coves in Cornwall but on an enormous scale. Echoes of the Jurassic age are everywhere in its arid landscape. The dry climate is profligate with ancient trees and wildlife. Fireflies larger than my fist, in shades of turquoise, red and blue, are buzzing in the air. Nature is in full flight, without a single vehicle in sight. I peel off my outer layers and navigate the sand-logged grass next to the coastal path. The shingle is hot underfoot. I catch my balance using my arms, pulling them towards me as if I am snatching at invisible ropes.

The water is ten degrees colder here than in Venice Beach. After a few aborted attempts at dipping my toes into it, I venture in up to my waist, then shoulders.

When I surface for air, the full pelt of the sunlight hits my back. My eyes cloud over in luminescent halos and the land and sky transform into a wash of blue, red and yellow.

I loll in the sea for what seems hours, treading water with the rhythm of the tide. The only audible sound is the crashing of the waves. This precious moment of solitude is the first time I have released myself to the experience since arriving in California.

After time spent soaking in the salty sea, the skin on my shoulders is prickling in the midday sun. I scramble out of the water, and my feet sink into the pebbly silt below with each step. The sun is forbiddingly fierce. It takes several minutes to crawl over the piping hot shingle to the bayside, where I grab my cotton towel and change out of my wet swimsuit. It is impossible to withstand for more than a few minutes without shade. So I hopscotch my way to get my shoes from the waterside and edge back to the main road using only my towel for cover.

Dr Fraenkel-Conrat and his wife Bea, who let me stay after a rough encounter at a second-rate hotel, live a short walk from the marine reserve. Their wood-panelled house is surrounded by a well-trimmed lawn and trees.

As I open the gate, Bea is standing at the door wearing a flowery blouse and pearl necklace.

'Happy birthday, Ros,' she says.

'Just coming,' I reply, wringing the water out of my hair.

'Won't you come in and get dry?' she says.

'You're right, I wouldn't want anybody to see me looking like this,' I say, making my way up the wooden stairs to their spare bedroom. I change into dry clothes and listen keenly for the murmurs from below. Instead, I hear only the thrum of the boiler.

Back downstairs, sunlight is streaming through French doors, which open out into the garden from the dining area next to the kitchen. The table is laid with a sponge cake and three blue-and-white china bowls arranged pristinely on a crisp white tablecloth.

'Shouldn't there be four bowls, not three?' I ask Bea. 'Since Don's coming.'

'Sorry, Rosalind, his father had a heart attack. He can't

make it, as he's travelling back to Cold Springs,' she says, walking out of the kitchen holding an oven glove. 'This afternoon we're going to celebrate you being thirty-six and the world being your oyster,' she adds while laying spoons on the garden table. 'You must have the world at your feet.'

'You must excuse me, Bea, I've been having these awful stomach pains,' I say, running up to the bedroom before weeping in both pain and disappointment. Learning that Don will not be coming after all has made my entire visit seem unbearably pointless.

The pains had begun at a party in Los Angeles earlier this summer. California was a tale of two cities. On the day in question, on Santa Monica Boulevard at sundown, I came across an unshaven man in stained clothes doing an unusual dance. Each time my head was turned, he raided the bins for food, but whenever I tried to catch a glimpse of him, he stood as still as a statue. When he finally disappeared behind a bin lorry, another younger man, with livelier eyes and a shaved crew cut, did the same duck-and-flee manoeuvre. I turned to give him what dollars I had in my purse, but he retreated in the other direction, pretending not to see me.

According to the United States government, I was an 'alien' here in America, though even the president's family had lived here for less than ten generations. Without a safety net like the welfare state, people slipped through the cracks, like the men on the streets that day. I wondered how many of the women here too – even married ones with smart clothing but no time to work – lived a hand-to-mouth existence. Worse still it must be for the women in unhappy marriages who could not afford to leave.

'Can I buy you something to eat?' I asked the man, but he continued to hover in the other direction. My heart sank.

Rather than admitting to needing anything, the men were ashamed; they were as unaccepting of their circumstances as my father would have been in their position. No man was free in a country where green notes were the only currency. What was freedom anyway when men remained slaves to money? There was just a bank cheque separating those men from my father. I wondered what misfortune they had hit upon. What ill health had bankrupted them?

The Prof's house at the end of the boulevard was surrounded by white iron gates. From the roadside, the estate looked like a fortress city, impenetrable, with Arcadia within its walls. Behind a tropical Capability Brown-esque oasis was a sprawling, purpose-built residence. The palatial building overlooked the sea, and palm trees were planted in a line of artificial exactitude.

Professor Sam Wildman was known around the world as 'the Prof' and his reputation as a partygoer preceded him. He'd been studying the tobacco mosaic virus – one of the biggest threats to tobacco crops globally – in California since the war. We'd met during my visit to the Los Angeles campus of the University of California, and the Prof had coaxed me to come to the party.

As I entered the plaster archway at the front of the house, a waiter greeted me with a Martini on a silver tray.

'Let my butler take your coat,' the Prof said through the open door, letting out a blast of music. 'I'm only kidding, I just hired them for the night. Welcome to the party.'

'Professor Wildman, thank you for inviting me. Your residence is astonishing,' I said.

'My pleasure, Rosy. How were the roads? It can be Antsville out there at this time,' he replied.

'It was a pleasant enough walk,' I told him. 'I think the men scavenging the bins were suffering more from the heat than me.'

'You walked, in this heat?' He was shocked. 'The boulevard is always full of hobos. They're edging in from Skid Row.'

Inside his concrete Californian bungalow were two leather sofas in an open-plan living area teeming with drunk, coarse and beautiful guests. Outside, a man with red hair was juggling plastic balls and couples were kissing in the pool. Startled, I retreated back through the crowd into the hallway.

'Rosy, leaving so early?' The Prof stopped me as I tried to make a discreet exit half an hour later.

I forced a smile. The murmur of the guests' voices seemed to be getting louder. I didn't recognise anyone in the crowd and would rather have left than end up hovering in the corner alone without anyone to talk to.

Suddenly, I felt a sharp, prodding sensation in my stomach.

'I'd really better go,' I said, moving towards the door where the Prof was greeting more guests.

'But you've barely arrived,' he insisted. 'We can talk about work, if you'd prefer. What's the latest you're seeing with TMV?'

I had been working with strains of the virus taken from cowpea samples. The X-rays suggested it was hollow except for a single thread of RNA.

'The RNA is free to sew another pattern,' I said, desperate to leave.

'Very interesting,' the Prof replied. 'Don't let Jim Watson catch wind of it.'

'Surely it's better to share too much than too little,' I said, still trying to ignore the throbbing pain in my abdomen.

'With Jim of all people?'

I laughed. I had spent the trip worrying that I should be telling the scientists at the universities there more.

'Then why haven't you?' he asked.

'I forgot. I did tell Jim all about microsomes though,' I said.

'I see, Rosy, very smart,' the Prof replied. 'Did I hear you're working with Jim's colleague Don?'

'Yes, that's right, at Berkeley. Is he coming tonight?' It had been months since we'd agreed to work together that summer.

'Eh, what?' the Professor said, deliberately dodging my question.

'Professor Wildman, is Don here?' I asked again, straining to make my voice heard.

In England, my accent singled me out as having a wealthy family. The best thing about being abroad was the anonymity. In Italy or the Alps, my accent didn't label me as someone who might have been a debutante if only they had worn more lipstick or added more sparkle. As a woman, my family's money wasn't my money anyway; and I now earned less than before, despite a bid to pay women a fairer wage, because my age didn't qualify me for a rise. The Prof clearly found my accent amusing, but at least it bonded me with millions of other people: as a generic Briton.

'What?' he said again, mockingly, before eventually conceding. 'Don and Jim didn't show up. Why don't you come and meet my friends?'

I panicked. I didn't know anyone at the party and was not taken with the idea of making small talk with strangers. But he seemed oblivious to my desire to leave.

'This is Rosy, from England,' he said, presenting me to the group in the living area.

Inside I was reeling from being forced on the crowd. Despite wanting to leave – and being bewildered, like a deer in headlights – I tried to think on my feet and misfired in an attempt to distract my newfound but unadoring audience.

'How long do you think it's taken me to study American culture?' I asked.

'Days?' replied a man who was standing near the back of the huddle, with his tie loose.

I recognised him from the University of California's agriculture college, he had sent me some new viral strains. I began to wade through the crowd to speak to him, relieved to have found someone I knew at last.

'Are things better in England?' the Prof jested, and everyone turned to face me again.

'The education is,' I said.

'How, exactly?' asked the Prof.

'Really, I can't…' I said, but he insisted.

'Well, one of the questions on the eleven-plus says, continue the series: O, T, T, F, F, S, S.'

'O! It's a sandwich,' someone said.

'It must be E, E, since S comes before T,' the University of California's Albert Siegel joined in.

'The answer is E, N, T, for eight, nine, ten, and that's just entry-level mathematics.'

The crowd was baffled. It was my chance to leave. The throbbing in my stomach had worsened.

'The States have their own class system. You either have money, or you don't,' I said to the Prof, before making my excuses to go.

'At least we're honest about it. We don't hide behind wax jackets and wellingtons,' he said.

'No, just limousines and expensive art.' I nodded towards the pop-art landscape on his walls.

'Not Dior?' he said, looking at my dress and slowly taking a sip of champagne before walking off to join a group of women whose multicoloured stilettos clashed with his paisley shirt.

I chose to spend what money I had left after rent, bills and food on nice clothes. I wanted people to like me.

The week before the party in Los Angeles, my stay in New Hampshire had been a baleful reminder of my previous visit to the United States. On that trip to the Gordon Research Conference to see Jim Watson two years before, shortly after he left Cambridge, a hurricane had hit Cape Cod. It was as if the simmering tension between us was manifest in the weather. Water flooded the sea walls and tropical winds pounded the coastline. Scientists from around the world made a pilgrimage to the fertile soils of New Hampton in New Hampshire for the event each year. This year was no different, although the specialist subject this time was nucleic acid, as well as proteins. The beaches nearby smelled of seaweed, so I took a detour sailing in the lakes once it was over.

Before staying with the Fraenkel-Conrats and going to work at Berkeley, I returned to Woods Hole, where I stayed with Mamie Bentwich's niece, Rachel. The weather was once again unsettled. Seconds after jumping into the cool ultramarine water of a nearby fishing port, the blue sky above was suddenly eclipsed by clouds.

'Ros, there's a telegram for you.' Rachel, who we called Rae, sauntered down the jetty in shorts, board shoes and a jumper.

'Just a minute,' I replied from the lake where I was treading water.

'It looks like a storm's brewing,' she said.

'Won't be long.' I ducked under before paddling towards the jetty and lifting myself out of the water.

'The telegram is from someone called Bragg,' said Rae, surprised the word could also be a name.

As I uncrumpled the page, water rolled down my cheek and spilled onto the thin paper. The ink bled and the paper turned translucent.

'It's another model,' I said, wiping my eyes.

'Has Cambridge built a third?' asked Rae.

'This time they want one of mine.'

The telegram said the head of Cambridge's physics department wanted to exhibit a model of my work on viruses in the International Science Hall at the upcoming Brussels World Fair. It would mean that it would be seen by scientists from all over Europe. For a moment, I forgot that my pay cheque had been docked.

'Wait till Don finds out I'm going to be an internationally exhibited scientist,' I said.

As Rae pushed the boat off the jetty, an ominous storm cloud loomed over the lake. We stood on the wooden planks of the jetty trying to pull the boat back in and tie it to one of the masts. By the time we reached the port, the rain was torrential. Branches were scattered across the road. It seemed as though a hurricane was coming, just like on my earlier trip to the state to see Jim.

After the Prof's party, a guest of his drove me to the California Institute of Technology where Don worked. Don was travelling in Colorado, and it was still weeks before we were due to meet up in Berkeley. As I walked by the university's calm infinity ponds, I wondered whether he had walked under those same arches.

With time on my hands to spare, I agreed to join a group from the party who were going camping in the Sierra Nevada mountain range. After hiking up the Jostedal with my brothers before the war, climbing up Mount Whitney seemed like a cinch and so, with little else better to do, I threw my bag into the trunk of a rusty blue Chevy. Once we were past the crags and rocks on the side of the snow-capped mountain, from the high vantage point in the evening light, the desert glowed a deep shade of umber. The group unrolled sleeping bags on a grassy plateau and lit a log fire, keeping it alight after dark by surrounding it with stones assembled in a dome.

As I lay awake that night in below-freezing temperatures, I felt my ovaries ache. When I pressed my stomach, it was swollen, even though I had hardly eaten all day. Minutes seemed like hours as I stayed awake thinking, too uncomfortable to sleep.

Then when the sun finally rose, a thin coral-coloured ray of morning light broke the long shadow that was cast across the desert by the rocky mountains. The beauty of the scenery, with a red setting sun casting an orange hue on the sweeping desert, was overshadowed by the feeling in my abdomen.

I could no longer ignore the pain and decided to go and see the doctor on duty when we got back to the university. He advised me to take painkillers, though the pain did not fully disappear.

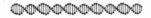

'Can I use your phone?' I ask Bea, after half an hour of rest. I go downstairs and ring one of Don's friends, a phage geneticist working at Berkeley, from the phone on the sideboard, which is right next to a tall, noisy grandfather clock.

'Is it true that Don's father is dead?' I ask her.

It takes two days for us to get to Colorado where Don is grieving. We drive through Salt Lake City in the back of their friend's car. As we attempt to sleep on a sandy mesa near the Rockies that night, I hold my stomach up from the ground, to keep the pains at bay. The desert floor is hard and uncomfortable by the dusty roadside. When we finally get past the salt flats to where Don is staying, I have just a few days before I must leave for New York to catch my flight back to London. When we are reunited, at last, he is aberrantly distant. He tells me the doctor has prescribed him sleeping tablets; we are both, it seems, haunted at night, me by my stomach pains and he by his loss. He describes eerily sensing his father's presence, especially in the evenings. I postpone my departure for two weeks.

VII

NOW/THEN

| 40 |

Figure of Eight

Hampstead, London, August 1956

'Are you pregnant?' Dr Livingstone asks, after taking one look at my stomach.

Her office is bare except for a leather chair. I have been struggling to zip up my skirt since New York. The diners there served fatty breakfasts, pancakes with a choice of maple syrup or jam, and cheese omelettes, in quadruple the usual quantity. The doctor beckons for me to sit down after seeing me hover in the entrance to her office. I pause. My hands are sweaty and my heart is pounding. She flicks through my notes, which are kept in a brown envelope, waiting for a response.

'I wish I was,' I say, betraying my fears of spinsterhood.

It makes me nervous when doctors ask such personal questions. I don't know how many of my parents' friends attend this same surgery in Hampstead. Dr Livingstone isn't my nearest general practitioner, but my family has known hers for a while. Even if I was pregnant, would I tell a person sitting behind a desk? Although, as my doctor, she's in a position of authority to elicit my most vulnerable secrets.

What would she think of me, if I tell her that I could be pregnant? Would she think I am a harlot?

'Are you trying?' the doctor asks, checking my notes once more.

'I'm not married.' The sound of my voice conveys my disappointment.

She does not react. Then, instead, she says, 'The doctors at University College Hospital are very good,' referring me to see a specialist.

'What will you say on the referral?'

'Patient notes are private, Ms Franklin.'

'Even so, please don't use the word pregnant. I don't want people to talk.'

'Do you think you might be?'

'No, I mean, I came about stomach pains, not pregnancy.'

'I'm referring you to see a specialist for your bloating and gastralgia. There's not much more I can do for you unless there's anything more you want to tell me.'

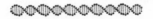

It is several weeks before I receive a letter with a date to see a doctor. In the interim, the gel specimens of the tobacco mosaic virus are keeping me busy most nights. I need to find a way to reconstitute specimens of the virus and prepare them to be X-rayed. Before my trip abroad we had struggled to get good specimens, as the slides were sticky with RNA. By treating the build-up, we are now able to get clearer X-rays.

At the appointment, the specialist Professor Nixon examines my stomach and immediately advises surgery. He says University College Hospital will operate for free under the National Health Service, which is less than a decade old.

'Is it really necessary?' I ask.

'I believe it is. We won't know what's causing your symptoms without investigating further.'

Before the operation, the nurse at the hospital clasps her arms around my shoulders and tells me not to worry. The next few minutes pass in a haze.

'Have you had a surgery before?' she says as she takes my blood pressure.

Her velvety accent sounds Caribbean.

'The only serious illness I've ever had is jaundice, except for a cold now and then.'

'When was that?'

'I was twenty-two.'

'You'll be fine,' she says. 'Don't you worry.'

She says it in the way that adults comfort children, with both benevolence and pity. In her palm, she is holding a small mountain of drugs.

'Three painkillers, one penicillin. Take them.'

The doctor returns shortly afterwards with a form for me to sign.

'It's for consent,' he says.

The form says that if one of my organs is damaged during the operation, the surgeon has permission to repair it.

'How often does that happen?' I ask him.

'Rarely,' he says.

Another box asks me to consent to my ovaries being removed if necessary. The form also says there is a chance of death from the operation.

'This is only meant to be exploratory,' I say.

The nurse puts her hand on mine and looks at the paperwork with me.

'They only do what's needed,' the doctor says.

He registers my details and explains the procedure. Then he hands me a pillow and sends me to wait outside in a cemented stairway. I feel as though I am holding my block for the gallows, as though I have signed my life away and am now waiting for the inevitable. My whole body, from my toes to my shoulders, is trembling.

'So, you're a physicist? What are you working on?' the anaesthetist asks.

'Polio,' I say.

We have made considerable progress with our maps of the radial density distribution of the tobacco mosaic virus, so much so that I'm considering submitting my fellowship work to *Acta Crystallographica* after the operation is over. Last year, I determined that the virus was regular, and that all the virus particles were the same length. Biochemist Norman Pirie, Bill for short, was so outraged at the suggestion that he stopped supplying samples of the virus to our lab. However, he remains on the Agricultural Research Committee that approves our funding. Due to the cessation, we had to start growing tobacco plants in the lab to culture our own specimens of the virus. From our latest experiments I am now sure that RNA is coiled like a helix inside the hollow virus.

Yet my mind is firmly fixed on what our research can tell us about other, more insidious, 'animal' viruses affecting humans; polio being chief among them. The scientists in America were convinced that my work on RNA could be relevant.

The anaesthetist asks me to lie down and count backwards from ten while he injects the drugs into my veins. As I say the numbers out loud, the summer sunshine begins to fade away on the horizon.

The grant that I'm applying for to fund my investigations into the structure of polio is the very last thing that goes through my mind when the anaesthetic starts to take effect. If we can map the structure of the virus, as Dorothy Hodgkin has done with penicillin, it may be possible to make a synthetic vaccine. It hasn't been done before. A denatured polio specimen is available, but an artificial vaccine would be cheaper. The more people who are immunised, the more effective any vaccine would be. Perhaps one day vaccination will entirely eradicate this disease, the most paralysing killer of the age.

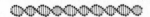

The next thing I know, I am being propped up on a hospital bed by two nursing staff.

'Did they find anything?' I ask.

Their silence is palpable. From the corner of my eye, I see the nurses turn to each other while they are adjusting the bedding underneath me. There is an almost equal chance of good or bad news, but their reticence is foreboding.

I go to the bathroom, where I am sick. As I push open the door, I see a yellow ghoulish face staring back at me. I barely recognise my own reflection. As I put my hand to my face, I see a shimmering reflection of an arm in the mirror and it is only then that it dawns on me that the person looking back at me is me. My eyes are tired and bloodshot. Recoiling in horror, I hobble back to my hospital bed.

Within a few minutes, one of the nurses comes over and examines the notes at the bottom of my bed.

'How do you feel?' she asks.

'Sick,' I reply.

She reaches deep into the pocket of her apron and pulls out more drugs. As I lie there, ward staff walk past the end of my bed and smile empathetically. Eventually, the pharmaceutical-induced inertia wears off and noisy thoughts begin to chug through my mind like a steam train.

After what seems like an interminable wait, I am escorted downstairs to meet with the surgeon.

'The findings are… unfortunate,' he begins.

I wonder if I have heard him correctly. The drugs were sedatives and so I can't be sure that what I am hearing is entirely true. I pause for a moment to process what he has just said.

'We found two tumours,' he continues. 'The lump in the

right ovary was the size of a croquet ball. Another on the left was the size of a tennis ball. We managed to remove them both and recover one of your ovaries.'

The doctor's nearest eye comes into sharp focus. Suddenly, it is all that I can see of him. The space around him blurs and recedes into the distance. His eyeball is large and round and appears to be just inches away from mine, staring at me, urgently. It feels as though a curtain is closing around me at that moment, casting a shadow over all my dreams.

'How did it happen?' I ask.

'We can't say. I'm afraid it's mad, bad and sad.'

I see a glimpse of his white coat and his grey hair, but his eyeball is still pointed unnervingly in my direction.

'Be honest with me doctor, am I going to die?'

'I know it's a lot to take in,' he replies.

Blood has all but drained from the doctor's face. The objects behind him shrink farther into the background and everything in the room becomes grey. The scene before me clouds into a halo of onyx.

My world is shrinking. I am consumed by an eerie sense of desertion. My body is still sitting on a seat in a hospital consulting room, but it feels as though my spirit is away somewhere else. The residual colours in the doctor's face, microscopic flecks of red and pink, are vivid but all around him is swallowed up in greyness. My life stretches out before me like a desert devoid of sustenance, wide and empty.

David collects me from the hospital. We walk in unbroken silence, until I see my mother, and can no longer hold back the tears.

| 41 |

Lamentations

University College Hospital, London, October 1956

A cramp seizes my abdomen. I fling my hip against the wall to quash the pain. It is just weeks after the surgery and I have been readmitted to the hospital with symptoms of an infection. The antibiotics seemed to have done little good and I have returned to the same hospital as before, but as a paying patient. My father insisted I should ask the doctor for a referral under the family health insurance. He was mistrustful of the new National Health Service and hoped a private referral would expedite my treatment. Ultimately, though, both the conditions of my treatment, and the staff, are the same.

My tunic falls open as I stand in the hospital corridor, with one side of my body pressed against the wall. My whole pelvis is still numb. The shooting pains in my stomach have briefly eased, but the gnawing sensation from my wounds comes and goes in waves. I lean my hip harder into the wall and use it to edge my body upwards, squeezing my hips in a repetitive motion. The hospital wall has become my crutch.

With the left side of my body still propped against it, I reach for the telephone receiver mounted to the wall in the corridor outside the ward. Almost as soon as it is in my grasp, it slips from my hand. The cool wire bounces up and down, hanging from the cushioned part of my ring finger.

'Ros, are you OK?' Jean's voice is distant and distorted.

'They just did another little operation,' I say, clutching the receiver and holding it against my lower lip. 'You can stay in my flat. Was everything in order when you got there? I won't be back for a while. My aunt Alice has the key.'

'What did the hospital say?' she asks.

'They can't say for certain.'

It's not the whole truth. I awoke from the second operation to be told the surgeon had performed a full hysterectomy. This time he had removed what was left of my remaining ovary. The tumours were gone, but so too were the same dreams that were impressed on all young girls about what their destiny held for them: motherhood.

My heart feels a heaviness that it never had before. Nothing can prepare you for being told you will never have children. I am godmother to my cousin Catherine's children, but it doesn't feel the same to me as creating new life from your own flesh and blood. The part of my biology that is fundamentally female is now gone. Yet I am no less a woman.

'Did anyone ring?'

'I haven't heard anything,' says Jean.

'Why did he have to do this now?'

I wrap my tunic more tightly around me while holding on to the receiver.

'I'm sure Don will contact you, Ros,' Jean says.

'Not him. Jacques.'

'Jacques, from Paris? What did he do?'

'He rang while I was last in hospital.'

Tears are streaming down my face. For the first time, I do not wipe them. I let them flood me.

'What about Don?' Jean asks, after a long pause.

'He wants us to go to the Alps together,' I say.

'Please go, Ros,' she urges. 'I want you to tell me that you'll go.'

But I do not reply; my mind is back on Jacques. He and I have seen each other – mainly in secret – every year since Paris. I still haven't been able to confide in anyone else; they would have told me the whole thing was fantasy. Though Anne has some idea of what happened.

Last month, after the first operation, she stayed in my flat while I was convalescing at my parents' house on a visit to England. She had relayed details of my condition to Jacques.

'I couldn't explain what had happened to you without mentioning the operation,' she told me on the phone. 'Jacques was in tears.'

'You told him about it?' I was distraught.

'He's only concerned for your health, Ros.'

I had grown tired of battling other people's expectations. I wondered what impression Jacques would have of me now.

'You don't understand Anne. I was in *love*,' I cried.

At that moment, suffused with emotion, all roads seemed to lead to nowhere. It might have started with a simple conversation but my heart had never looked back and, from the moment I met Jacques, the rest of my world had been devoid of colour. Everything was silent except for the chords playing on repeat in my heart. I couldn't feel the warmth of any other embrace. It made me wonder if the true definition of love is the hours of dedication spent by a person's side, or the single sentence that cuts like a bullet straight to the heart, and makes someone feel truly seen.

What I do know is that when a heart stops beating, no patient can survive. Mountains fade and canyons collapse. No brain or other organ will ever replace one. Our hearts are all that any of us truly depend on in this world. When they are all that we have left, shouldn't we follow them? Since the diagnosis, I can no longer rest in my faith in nature, and fear love as I do not want to lose more than I have lost already. I think it is our love of others that keeps us here. Like many others, I too had wanted a love so deep that it would dive into my soul and sit beside my heart. Yet cutting the thread with Jacques may be the kindest thing to do. No good can come from it.

| 42 |

The Cutter Incident

Portugal Place, Cambridge, summer 1957

'How did you get the poliovirus past immigration?' Francis asks from the hallway.

'With a bit of ingenuity,' I say, putting my book down.

I am secretly proud of the fact that, with the help of a virologist friend's wife, we have smuggled live strains of the virus past America's border control back into England for my experiments.

Patricia, the wife of virologist Dr Carlton Schwerdt – whom I had met on my ill-fated trip to Berkeley's labs where Don had not shown up, through no fault of his own – was stopped by customs in California with a live specimen of polio. Her husband had worked on trials of the recent live vaccine in Berkeley. When she was accosted by the guard she managed to assuage him by explaining that, under strict instruction, the virus was completely safe as it was crystallised and inert. This was most likely true. However, the first live polio vaccine two years ago had not been the resounding success that scientists in America had hoped it would be. The deadly vaccine had caused thousands of citizens, including children, to contract the disease and die within the first few months of it being introduced. The crisis, known as the Cutter Incident because it had originated in the Cutter Laboratories of Berkeley, would mar our collective recent memory in the scientific community. Dr Schwerdt had been inconsolable. The hope that one day an artificial vaccine could provide a safer alternative to injecting people with a live but deactivated virus was more than ample fuel for my work.

Francis, however, remains doubtful.

'You will tell me if you put it in the fridge, won't you, Rosy?' he says, knowing that I had stored the specimen in a thermos at my parents' house and anxious to ensure I do not infect their food with the lethal virus. 'You're sure you won't be joining us at the Eagle tonight?' he adds with some trepidation.

'Not tonight, Francis, Odile and I have catching up to do,' I reply.

Odile laughs.

'*Ne t'inquiète pas pour eux,*' she says after Francis has gone. 'Don't worry about them.'

Odile grew up in Norfolk, but her French mother wanted her to be bilingual and she honoured her wish each time she spoke the language. Marie-Therese Josephine Jaeger was something of a mystery and although Odile knew very little about her family, the time-honoured traditions of her mother's lineage were evident in her cooking. Her food spoke a thousand words, of women's histories, of the lives of her mother, and her mother's mother, and so on. She has given me the recipe for her mother's French onion soup, which prescribes a long-simmered stock for that singular umami flavour. For breakfast, we have coffee with croissants and cheese, another of her mother's legacies.

Odile's accent is crisp, like glass. If anything, it is more of a Parisian accent, rather than textbook French. It is perhaps almost Germanic, a hangover from her time cracking enemy code during the war, something few people know about even now. She speaks fluent German, which was gold dust for the intelligence services. They enlisted her to serve as a code breaker and she ended up working as a translator for the Admiralty, which is where she met Francis. Her team were known internally as 'Parisian Dressers'. She once told me they'd read thousands upon thousands of telegrams, all in German. She doesn't speak about it much now. Those memories are best left forgotten, or buried. She has since lived a life, had a son and a daughter and become a practising artist.

'I don't like how they speak about you behind your back,' she says once Francis has left. 'They don't know you like I do.'

'Scientists are in the business of being critical, and questioning things,' I say, adjusting the red patterned scarf around my head in the mirror over the fireplace.

Although the cancer has gone into remission, I still cover my head with a scarf. It's just until my hair grows back.

Odile pours us coffee from the cafetière.

I came to stay with the Cricks when Don moved to Cambridge for work so that we would have a chance of seeing each other again. From up high in the mountains during our trip to the Alps, the wings of my imagination could finally spread unencumbered. At that moment, I didn't need God. I just needed myself. So I travelled here to live in the town house in Portugal Place. It has been a year since my diagnosis and even though my womb is gone, my mother still cannot accept the idea of me sharing a room with a man out of wedlock. 'When you're not married? Come on, Rosalind, please!'

I packed my bags, promising not to stay with my parents for a moment longer than was necessary, and travelled to Cambridge, where I have the freedom to pursue a life of my own.

'Scientists do indeed ask a lot of questions. It's like that time Francis and Jim asked Dr Perutz if they could see your data,' Odile says.

'What?'

'Didn't they tell you?'

'Tell me what?' I ask.

'Well, I don't like to interfere,' Odile says, putting down her coffee cup before continuing somewhat hesitantly. 'Jim tried to describe your photograph to Francis, but you know what he's like.'

'It would be impossible to interpret my photo with any certainty without any data to support it. What photograph do you mean?'

'You know, the one Maurice showed him. The one that was in the Medical Research Council report,' Odile says.

'What, along with the data I had submitted in my fellowship report? Those reports are meant to be confidential.'

It was only after the event that I had discovered new information that led me to suspect that Maurice had been an interloper, going between our two labs, and agreeing to share our paper on DNA with the Cambridge team perhaps in return for a byline in *Nature* journal. He'd frequently shared sketches of our data with Francis. Jim, Maurice later told Raymond, had begged Dr Perutz for access to our data, saying it was critical to prove the double helix theory. It all of a sudden made sense to me why Professor Randall had eventually come to a 'gentleman's agreement' with Bragg, ensuring our paper was published alongside theirs in *Nature* that year. Now it seems that Perutz had shared our data with them well in advance. In short – Raymond and I did the work and everyone else took the credit.

'They asked me to draw what it would look like,' she says after a few seconds. 'Francis was so excited, he drew his own sketch in a letter to our son Michael.'

Michael must have been just twelve when Francis sent him a sketch of the double helix.

'The phosphates were on the outside – Francis said that was highly important,' Odile says. 'After seeing the report, which Francis's thesis supervisor showed them, they asked me to change the spacing.'

'Do you mean they asked you to sketch the double helix? From my lab notes? Did they say anything else?' I ask.

'Only to think of DNA as a prism,' she replies.

I slump on the sofa and wrap my arms around my knees.

'Francis asked me to think of each vertical slant as the edge of an elongated rhombus,' she adds.

I'd been suspicious of Francis's persistent questions about the space group of the atoms. Now I realise that he must have seen my report before asking me about it when we submitted our findings to *Nature* journal. Perhaps he wanted to find out more details, or maybe he was double-checking the facts. It wouldn't be the first time Jim and Francis had relied on me to spot their mistakes or tell them what they had got wrong. My annual report had given the water content, atomic spacing, and phosphate positions, all the crucial ingredients for a model. Their entry to the journal had so closely resembled that data, it had seemed more than a coincidence, but I had no evidence beyond a slither of suspicion at the time.

'It's really important, Odile, for me to know. Was this before or after Jim saw Pauling's manuscript?' I ask her.

'Before, I think. It was around Christmas. Jim had spent days in a muddle over the hydrogen bonds,' Odile says. 'Francis said they were lucky really, especially since Jerry Donohue, a student who'd been seconded to their office for six months, corrected their mistake. He saw Jim was using the wrong hydrogen bonds, or something like that…'

I gather from what Odile is saying that Jim had made another mistake from which he was lucky to be saved, this time by a junior in his own lab. It sounds as though he had mistaken the position of the hydrogen atoms in the nitrogen bases, unsurprising given his lack of skills in chemistry. It seems unbelievable that he had come up with anything testable at all. I wonder if it could have been possible for him to have come up with an accurate model without the use of my data and my photographs.

'Is that what they called it, luck?' I say.

'Please don't be too angry with Francis. He never let Jim forget his hydrogen bond mistake,' Odile says.

The room feels cold, and I feel cheated.

'I told Francis not to wear his tweed jacket when he met Erwin, you know, the one that makes him look like a fading racing tout,' Odile continues blithely.

'Erwin Chargaff?' I ask her.

'He and Jim asked Erwin to help them fit DNA to a helix. Bragg introduced them,' she says. 'Francis took his advice and tweaked their model while Jim was outside playing tennis. Francis was mightily impressed by the Henry Cavendish room where they met. It was one of the nicer rooms in Peterhouse College, apparently, full of Georgian panels and antiques. He promised to take me there one day.'

'I didn't think Francis or Jim knew anything about chemistry,' I say.

I hadn't had the chance to meet the enigmatic Austrian chemist Erwin Chargaff, who had given samples of DNA to our lab. It was only after leaving King's that I had a chance to travel more widely for my work.

'It was a small miracle that the candles on the mantel had never set light to the paintings,' Odile says.

Preoccupied with piecing it all together, I have lost track of what she's talking about.

'When Francis came home that night I thought he was delusional, saying he'd found the secret of life. He asked me to draw it; I mean I was used to drawing curves from doing nudes, but this was altogether different...'

She pauses, though doesn't appear to hear me sighing in exasperation.

'You don't let any resentment show, Ros,' she says, as she puts her cup back on the saucer.

Part of me is tempted to go to the Eagle immediately and give Francis and Jim a piece of my mind. But instead, I stay put in Portugal Place. What good would it do, to confront them about it now? I went blue in the face from trying to convince Professor Randall and Maurice, after they'd reached a 'gentleman's agreement' with the Cavendish lab, to include my paper in the submission to *Nature* journal. It had all the proof anyone needed.

That much is true. I have always believed that scientists stand on one another's shoulders and learn from each other. Isaac Newton said as much, philosophising that, 'If I have seen further it is by standing on the shoulders of Giants.'

Recent life events have changed my perspective. My vantage is broader than it was five years ago, when I was in the midst of mapping the structure of DNA. Though, if I had known then what I know now, perhaps I would have behaved differently, fought harder for recognition.

'We all influence one another. We're all connected,' I say, as I take another sip of coffee.

My data was published alongside Jim and Francis's and surely anyone could tell, if they looked hard enough, that it had all the proof. Indeed, this is why Jim insisted to Francis's thesis supervisor Perutz – who led the molecular biology working group at the Medical Research Council – that he needed our data, in order to prove the double helix theory.

Yet accolades seem so fleeting when you don't know how much longer you have left to spend in this world. You cherish every day and every soul you meet. I do not want to spend the rest of my days wishing I had done things differently, or that things had been different. As long as my work can be put to good use in some way, for the betterment of humankind or this world, then there is not any more I can ask for than that.

The truth of things always reveals itself in time. Maybe not in my lifetime, but the truth will out itself, eventually. It always does.

| 43 |

Chronicles

Royal Marsden Hospital, Fulham Road, London, November 1957

A woman passes through my ward in the Royal Marsden wearing a white coat and carrying an unopened parcel. She pushes the door open and reviews the notes at the end of my bed. Expecting she's in the wrong room, I wait for her to leave. I was admitted to the hospital a few days ago, for radiotherapy treatment. The dreaded cancer has returned only months after it first went into remission. Luckily, the tumours were found in time to treat.

'Ros,' the woman exclaims, still holding the door open with one arm.

'Yes?' I reply. My voice is slurred from the drugs. I've heard about doctors practising a more familiar bedside manner with patients, and wonder if this is it.

'It's Gertie,' she says as she walks in.

'What drugs will you be giving me today?' I ask her.

'I'm not here to give you drugs, Ros. It's Gertie, from Newnham. Do you remember me?' she replies.

'Gertie? I don't understand.'

I wonder whether I am hallucinating and check my hands to make sure they are real; they are solid to the touch. I lost contact with my friend from Newnham's Old Hall when I

moved to Paris. The government-run postal service in France was unreliable and I didn't have her parents' address; it had either been lost or forgotten amid the whirl of end-of-year exams. I can't remember which.

'I'm working here at the hospital and recognised your name: I had to see if it was you, and here you are! What an incredible surprise. I brought this parcel with me. It's addressed to you.'

She lays a densely wrapped package on the table by my bed.

'It's freezing in here, is there a draught?' I say, pulling my wine-coloured gown over the thin crepe tunic the nurses have put me in.

'It must be this November weather,' Gertie says, closing the curtain.

'I apologise, I'm not at my best,' I say.

I try to force a smile, and examine the parcel.

'What are you doing here?' I ask while heaving it onto my lap.

'I'm working next door in radiotherapy. I'm a medical physicist now,' Gertie says. 'It looks like you're a doctor too,' she adds, glancing at the label on my parcel.

'Only in the academic sense; I'm studying viruses at Birkbeck. We're looking to map the structure of polio,' I say.

'Polio, awful disease. At least for cancer, there's radiotherapy,' she says, hesitating. 'I hope they're looking after you in here.'

'The doctors are completely useless,' I confess. 'Perhaps I could come and see your radioisotopes one day?'

Radiotherapy treatment uses the same source of electrons as the beams in crystallography, but instead of being targeted towards an isolated specimen, the beams are directed at human flesh, penetrating the skin to destroy rogue cells.

'Of course you can, any time,' she says. 'Who's Roland?'

Gertie is looking at the notes at the end of my bed, which list my male relatives. The card describes my occupation as: *Spinster, and daughter of Ellis Arthur Franklin, a banker.*

More than a decade of scientific research seems, in sickness, to have counted for nothing.

'Roly? Surely you must remember him. Have you seen what else they've written on there?' I say. 'I can't even bear to look at it.'

Gertie gives a sympathetic smile. 'What are he and your other brothers doing now?'

'Roly's married to a woman called Nina. They had a baby and have a house in East Finchley. He's at Keyser Bank, with my father and David,' I say. 'Colin works in publishing. I've called him in the middle of the night every single day since I've been here. He always listens.'

A few days after the surprise visit, a nurse brings me a cup of tea. My hospital bed is bare except for a thin white sheet. The nurse leaves the strongly brewed tea in a polystyrene cup on the small table next to my bed. Steam is swirling from the surface of the liquid, which is covered with a thin translucent film. As I try to lift my arm to reach for the drink, it doesn't move, and it feels heavy and numb.

I remember the eyes of the border guard in the United States as he was inspecting the flask I'd used to carry the poliovirus back to England. The more that I sift through my memories, the less certain I am. Did I come into direct contact with the virus? Was the lid of the flask screwed on tightly enough? Did I expose passengers to the virus? Did the border guard open the flask?

'Help, please,' I call the nurse from my hospital bed.

Gertie is in the hospital corridor. She rushes in while on a break from measuring radiation in the next-door radio-therapy ward.

'My arm is numb,' I say. 'I have a fever, a headache, back pain and fatigue. It must be polio.'

'Polio? No, I don't think so, Ros. You're trembling; it's probably the drugs,' she says.

I scan her voice for clues that she might be lying. Anyone could catch polio if they are exposed to the virus, anywhere in the world. The initial stages of the disease are insidious. It starts off innocuously, like any other virus, with flu-like symptoms. Then, slowly, damage to the nerves triggers paralysis. There's one theory that the virus can lie dormant for many months after initial exposure and I fear that this is what has happened to me.

'The doctor is prescribing you more heroin, to take the edge off,' Gertie says.

I begin to fear for my life, just as I had during an air raid more than a decade before, another time when I had felt most alone.

5 Pembridge Place, Notting Hill, London, August 1942

Life inside my parents' house in Pembridge Place is comprehensible; everything has a place, including people. Outside, however, it is chaos. But soon the safety net of home is also torn down. When I returned to college for my final summer term in 1941, my parents wrote to say they were moving temporarily, renting a house in Hertfordshire because of the Blitz. The windows in Pembridge Place were blown out during one vicious air attack. By the time I left Cambridge the following year, after being excluded from war science and forced to sacrifice my fellowship on polymerisation in Norrish's lab, they had returned to Notting Hill and I moved back in with them. Shortly afterwards, I got the job at the Coal Board where I spend my days measuring the porosity of coal. Despite this being vital to improving gas masks, my father would still have preferred me to have got a job in agriculture.

'The Bolshies are at it again. Stalin's got Hitler cornered this time,' Father says, tossing his newspaper on the table.

The maid dishes food onto his plate using the family silver, which clinks against the china as the wind howls through the upstairs study. A door slams. Billowing bags have been taped to the upper windows to conceal the broken glass that was shattered in a raid in my parents' absence.

'Shh,' my mother says, looking at Evi consolingly and back at my father again.

'Cecil was mouthing off again this morning. He's schlepped back to Chartridge, even though the Blitz is over,' Father says loudly, filling the awkward silence.

'What about Irene? Where will she live?' I ask.

My cousin Irene has just graduated from Bristol University. She isn't the type to flee to the countryside with her family, especially now the Blitz is over. She wants to put her chemistry degree to good use and is far more likely to stay put in their family home so she can do so; London is where most of the jobs are. Suddenly, moving in with her seems like a perfect solution.

'Putney's much closer to Kingston,' I say. 'I could walk to the Coal Board from there.'

Father puts his knife and fork down suddenly. My shoulders are tense in anticipation of what his response will be. He turns to my mother and then looks back at me.

'I suppose Putney is farther from the epicentre,' he says, surprisingly, after a pause.

'It would save lots of money on train fares,' I reply enthusiastically, throwing my cutlery down on the table and going to pack my things before he can change his mind.

Putney is just a short bus ride away from the gardens at Kew. The Oxford–Cambridge boat race passed along the nearby river every year before the war. The last race was four years ago. The neat rows of the nearby terraced houses are unspoiled by the Blitz. Uncle Cecil's house has not one, but two gardens, one in the front and another at the back of the property. It is much more pleasant than anywhere I could have afforded to rent while working in industry.

Putney, London, November 1943

It is a cool and wet Sunday night in November when the foghorns ring.

'Ros, we must go,' Irene cries from the hallway of her family home.

She is volunteering in the underground stations. Instead of working underground, I have volunteered at the parks. When the sirens sound, it is my duty to patrol Putney Common and direct civilians to safety.

I haven't told Irene the real reason why I haven't joined her in the subways. Each time I walk past an underground station, an urgency grabs me, calling me to get as far into the open space as possible. There is no possibility that I could face the conditions below ground: the coal dust and narrow train shafts. I am paralysed by fear at the thought of the crowded platforms.

As soon as the foghorns sound that night, I put on my metal hat, which is embossed with the letter W, and dust off my Raleigh bicycle, which is parked in the hallway and beginning to rust. I wheel it out into the front garden. It is starting to rain.

'Stay safe out there,' says Irene, knocking on my hard hat.

I pedal the rusty Raleigh down the road, where a couple is waiting at the bus stop.

'This isn't a drill, you must get to the underground,' I say, but the pair, who are intent on getting their bus, don't move.

Putney Common at night resembles the fens outside Cambridge. The pastoral scene is inked in midnight blue and deep evergreen. The light from the streetlamps dances on the grass in front of me, while the middle of the common is completely overcast. We have been taught, as wardens, that we must guide citizens away from the centre of the park because a bomb could drop on the open terrain.

The downpour is so heavy that it has drenched my socks, but there is no time to stop and discard them. The rain is pelting down hard all around me, obscuring the beam from my cycle lamp, which is the type issued to all air-raid wardens in the city.

Suddenly, a wild animal runs at my spokes and my bicycle swerves. My flashlight crashes to the ground and flickers as the sound of sirens in the distance grows increasingly remote.

'Dastardly cat!' I catch a glimpse of the hairy animal's patchy coat under the flickering lamplight while searching for the nearest path. It seems that Irene's black and white house cat has darted out into the space before me and is now winding itself around my legs. As I lie there on the muddy ground, the sound of fireworks echoes across the night sky. I rest for a second and look up at the stars. It is two days past Guy Fawkes Night, though no one has seen fireworks or a bonfire in London for at least four years. They have been strictly prohibited since the war began, to avoid being spotted by enemy aircraft.

As fireworks are an impossibility, I realise that the noise must be gunfire. I am in complete darkness and behind every shadow lurks a possible threat. With trepidation, I shake the cat off my legs and attempt to cycle on the muddy grass with the torch between my teeth to search for people who might be hiding for cover.

Within minutes there is an awful sound, the chilling chorus betraying its deadly source. Aerial bombers have been assaulting the city all autumn. The din is amplified by the sirens in the background. It feels as though at any moment the sky could fall in, and then it does. Large fragments of shrapnel wallop the floor in the explosion. After several minutes, everything is silent, at least for a millisecond. Then, there is a whoosh as a shock wave tears through the atmosphere. The force of the blast pushes me back to the ground.

Lights are flashing in the distance. They cast whirling shadows on the grass. The shadow puppets look as though they are embracing one another in a grisly dance. They shapeshift into battalions, there to punish me for every unholy thought my brain has ever conjured.

'Who's there?' I cry, grabbing hold of my bike's steel frame. The metal is wet with acrid rain. 'Daddy!' I shriek, scrambling to my feet and sobbing.

I hobble until I am back on the bike and pedal as fast as I can.

'Get to shelter,' I cry out into the open space to any people who may have been left hiding on the common.

The path to the shelter is well trodden, but the trail is lost in the rain. There is nothing but darkness and mud below my wheels, except for the thin blades of grass that are glimmering under my faltering flashlight.

Suddenly, my bike skids on the wet turf. The front wheel has hit the root of a tree. My flashlight flickers again before expiring like a candle. There isn't a single other soul on the common that night. Late-night revellers, such as customers of the local picture house and dance hall, must have gone home or hidden for safety in the underground. I am utterly alone. It is too dangerous to get back on my bike while I am so close to the trees, so I drag the heavy machine behind me. Its metal frame is icy to the touch and I begin to shiver uncontrollably.

After several minutes of making my way between the trees, I stumble on a grassy mound. I feel around the sides for a handle, clawing open the squeaky door of the Anderson shelter and slamming it shut behind me. Hours pass as I sit under the tin roof of the small hole, which is devoid of light. I am too scared to move. My ears are alert for signs of life. The noises of the night are magnified. Every rustling leaf, every owl's hoot, sounds as loud as a bomb or infantry.

I wrap my damp scarf around my mouth and nose. The explosives have left a toxic plume. After several hours, I ride back to the house at the first signs of early morning light. I don't confide in anyone about what happened that night.

Several weeks after the air attack on Putney Common, the front door of my uncle's Edwardian terrace bangs open against the adjacent wall. I uncurl my legs from the armchair. It is Irene, who had gone to the cinema with the Czech doctor she is dating and wasn't expected back for several hours. They were going to see *The Great Dictator* at the Prince of Wales Theatre. Father disapproved, but I couldn't help thinking that if Charlie Chaplin was breaking his lifelong silence in film then it might have some virtue.

'I'm getting married,' Irene says gleefully, sinking her limbs into the middle of the red leather sofa.

The film must have been a pretext for a proposal.

'What, to the doctor?' I reply, closing my book and resting it on the arm of the chair.

'Yes, who else? He finally asked,' she says, moving her left hand towards me. She is wearing a sapphire ring, set amid a cluster of diamonds. 'It's his grandmother's.'

'Will you be moving to Czechoslovakia?' I ask.

'One day I want to live in a big house in the countryside,' she says, hauling her body onto the end of the sofa. She adjusts the needle on her parents' Columbia 100 portable record player.

'You'll be consigned to a life of drudgery, like my mother,' I reply.

'I can't imagine a life without marriage and a family,' says Irene.

She then turns to me with a conspiratorial eye.

'*Ros,* how are babies made?' she asks. I am put on the spot.

Frank Sinatra's track 'You'll Never Know' is playing in the background.

'Well, a couple must be married first,' I say, gulping. 'Then, the sperm must fertilise the egg.'

'So how does the sperm get to the egg?' Irene points to her stomach.

I resolve to ask a medical student. Our families don't even kiss each other on the cheek, let alone talk about sex, and physical studies were only a small part of the Natural Sciences Tripos.

'I'm not entirely certain,' I say. Irene bursts out laughing.

The thought that she will be marrying and moving away is not only hurtful, it makes me acutely aware of just how alone I am. Who do I have left? My eldest brother David has joined the parachute infantry and Colin is in the navy. My mother is overseeing a clothing bank for refugees as well as helping the army in her spare time. Father is volunteering to deliver home shelters when he isn't banking. It seems as though everybody leaves, in the end.

Chartridge Lodge, Chesham, Buckinghamshire, 1944

Irene soon learned how babies were born: a year after she married the doctor, Hanus Neuner, she promptly gave birth to a son called Thomas. Nowadays, all she talks of is nappies and feeding.

'The boys are fighting again,' I observe through the kitchen window as I watch family friends' cubs play rough and tumble on the lawn.

'Is Thomas safe?' Irene replies, rushing out of the kitchen to check on her baby, who is only a few months old. Only his mother can console him when he cries.

I stand there alone in the kitchen.

'Leave the parsley.' I can hear Aunt Alice scolding Uncle

Norman outside in the garden. Her voice is deep and hoarse, from many years of smoking. Her black hair is cut short, like a man's, and her body is sturdy. She approves of me because I attended college, something Grandpa had forbidden her to do.

As I step into the garden of my grandfather's old house overlooking the Chiltern Hills, she is berating him for eating the cucumber sandwiches. A cigarette is still hanging from her mouth. At weekends, Aunt Alice looks after the housekeeping at Chartridge Lodge. She whiles away the hours by embroidering elaborate coverings for the chairs. During the week she stays in London with her friend and lover, Mrs Gertrude Horton, from the Townswomen's Guild. I do not know what happened to Mrs Horton's husband, or whether he is even still alive.

During the Blitz the lodge provided shelter for many of our family members to escape London. The main house has since been sold, but the garden house is still in the family's possession.

The year that my grandfather died, 1938, was the year that I began to doubt the existence of free will. It happened on the second day of Chanukah, during my first term in college. He had continued to meddle in the family's affairs from beyond the grave and in his will he disallowed inheritance to any relative who married outside the faith. And so my family's expectations were set in stone, both in life and love. There was not only the expectation that I should marry, but that I should marry a man who was Jewish too.

At his burial, my overriding feeling was not sadness, but an indescribable feeling of anger that was just as painful. My arms, shoulders and jaw were tense. I quashed the sensation until it was just a dull pain in my stomach. It was easier to bury my feelings than to reveal them to others. There was never an answer about my love life that would please all the interested parties.

A fated life had seemed improbable before then, as much as the fact of God being a man when he could just as easily have been a woman. 'Why is God not a she?' I asked my mother when I was nine.

When Grandpa died, my father inherited a bank, his brother Cecil got a publishing company, but Aunt Alice was left without a penny. Each of us grandchildren received a small sum from the sale of the main house, but it was no substitute for our family get-togethers there.

Mother's maid interrupts my thoughts. 'This looks worth a bob or two,' she says.

She puts a dusty cardboard box containing an old lathe and microscope in a pile of things to take back to Pembridge Place.

'Put it over there,' says my mother, who's spied a place for it in our living room.

She and Mamie Bentwich, who is now the Member of Parliament for Bethnal Green North East, are sifting through the other boxes from the big house while my father and Cousin Norman eat outside. Strangers usually approach Aunt Mamie with hesitation. Men tip their caps and ask after Uncle Norman. He's involved in making laws, Father says. Before taking her seat in Bethnal Green, Mamie had tried for Parliament twice, but each time lost to a man. To us, it didn't matter, because she was always our Auntie Mamie, the one who brushed our knees when we fell and helped us get back on our feet.

As the maid lifts the box, two sky-blue badges fall to the floor. I scoop one of them up in my hand and see that it is sewn with a white star of Saint David and embossed with the letters *JLWS*.

'They must be your grandma's,' says Mamie Bentwich while dusting it off with her thumb and inspecting it more closely.

To mention my grandma in front of Aunt Alice is a sore topic. She was solely charged with her care after her mother had become ill. Often it's women who are lumbered with the care of relatives, elderly, children, or the sick, with no monetary compensation. Such domestic chores are expected of women, and that expectation is embedded into the very fabric of our society and the economy. Societies are oiled with the unpaid, unaccounted for, work of women. Much, such as Alice's, goes unrewarded. It is the very glue that binds us together, and yet we are blind to it; a woman's work remains invisible.

Next, Mamie pulls out a faded sepia photograph from the box.

'Oh look, this is your great-aunt Beatrice from Herbert's election campaign,' she says.

Much of my great-uncle Herbert's past remains a mystery to me, though Father had said he was the first Jewish Home Secretary. He didn't let us forget that.

My great-aunt Netta hobbles towards us in the living area. Her long necklace is chattering as the beads knock against each other like teeth when she walks. She sinks into the dusty embroidered chair by the cardboard boxes, discarding her walking stick.

'You found my emblems,' Netta croaks. 'Herbert never did listen, to me or Beatrice. He shocked everybody by proposing to let women into Parliament.'

She delights in telling us about how she ran the Jewish League for Women's Suffrage. Aunt Alice had also worked there. She and my grandma were members, but Beatrice – Herbert's wife – was the only sister who wasn't.

'Did someone mention Hugh?' says Alice as she walks into the room.

She repeats his name several times, like an echo, and then goes back out into the garden. No one speaks about Uncle Hugh except for Aunt Alice nowadays. The melodic way she says Uncle Hugh's name is as though she is teasing Grandpa's ghost.

Uncle Hugh joined the front line to fight for votes for women a generation before me, despite relentless teasing from his brothers, for which I am eternally indebted. When growing up, to say his name in the Franklin household left the room so bereft of sound you could hear a coin drop. While he was still alive, Grandpa wouldn't let anyone mention it. Hugh had married a gentile and not just any, but one of the suffragist rebels who'd set fire to the post office, where he subsequently lost the job that Grandpa had set him up with. My suffragette uncle was an embarrassment to the family, especially after his brother-in-law Herbert became the leader of the Liberal Party. It had been that way since school, Netta says. He'd had trouble with his heart and lungs, so had to sit out on games.

'Little Hughey hated dirt, always sat on Mother's skirt,' my father had sung to his younger brother Hugh in the playground.

In one suffragist protest, Hugh had set fire to a train and once whipped Churchill, whom he blamed for police brutality at the Black Friday suffrage march. 'Deeds, not words,' Christabel Pankhurst had said, but deeds alone did not make greatness. A man full of good intentions, but without people to recommend them, would fail to make a mark on the world in the same way as men with questionable intentions but single acts of boldness. It's the war heroes, not the peacemakers, who are remembered in the history books. History, like myth, relies on reliable narrators. Who would history make its hero, my uncle Hugh, a suffragette, or Churchill?

Hugh's fate was the same as many women's, with no endowment to speak of, other than the odd handout from my aunt.

'Your grandpa didn't tolerate radicals,' Mamie Bentwich says, turning to me.

She doesn't need to mention Hugh by name.

'Ellis is growing more like him with age,' my mother says.

'He always was pompous,' says Mamie Bentwich.

'But your grandpa viewed your father, in fact everyone apart from Cecil, to be a disappointment,' Mamie continues. 'Of course, death has not stopped him trying to rule from the grave.'

She is alluding to the way he had tried to take control of the family's future by carving up the finances.

'Life has always persisted despite death. Hugh wasn't

always the way he is now. I take it that's who you're talking about, and you're all too scared to mention him by name. They were calling it a medical holocaust,' says Netta.

'Oh, Netta, you shouldn't be worrying about such things,' Mamie says, patting her arm.

'Influenza means "influence of the stars" in Italian, it's an act of God,' Netta says as she stokes the embers in the fireplace with her walking stick. 'People were saying it was brought to Europe by soldiers.'

Europe had emerged from the Great War two decades ago only to be tested by an even deadlier adversary. Fifty million people died from the Spanish flu, twice as many as were infected by the bubonic plague in Europe.

'Hugh kept a ton-bag of oats in the pantry,' Netta says. 'He knew better than to go up to London on Armistice Day. Elsie had the same heat rash on her cheeks as he'd seen in his own reflection, mottled and crimson.'

'Who's Elsie?' I ask Netta, sitting on a cushion by her armchair to listen.

'Elsie Duval, sister of the head of the men's suffragist union, Hugh's wife.'

Hugh, who my aunts said had once dressed as a woman to flee the country and escape force-feeding, married Elsie in a synagogue a year after the first war began.

'Her lungs were weak, from the force-feeding,' Netta says.

'She was force-fed?' I ask.

'They put tubes down the throats of all the suffragists,' Netta says, sighing. She then starts to giggle, blinking, saying, 'It took several men to restrain them. Hugh took the tube more than a hundred times,' she adds. 'He covered his mouth with cloth, doused in water, whenever he left the flat, but it was too late.'

'We don't need to go through all this again now,' says Mamie, but Netta interrupts her.

'I want Rosalind to hear this,' she says before continuing. 'They gave us the first votes ten days after Armistice Day.'

Netta begins coughing and Mamie hands her a glass of water.

'Hugh was miserable. The consumption had got Elsie. That July, he finally picked up the phone. Ellis was glad that he had and said, "We're calling the new baby Rosalind. Rosalind Elsie Franklin, in Elsie's memory."'

My heart skips a beat as I realise that she's talking about me. I had never known before where my middle name had come from. I am overcome with sorrow as dew saturates the morning grass. Elsie, I had never got to meet, and Hugh had gone through so much, alone.

| 44 |

Breath of Life

The Royal Marsden Hospital, London, 1958

In the synagogue, we are taught that the soul is immortal. Ancient Hebrew teaches that celestial beings eat from the tree of life to live on forever. Like a breath, Neshamah transcends the fabric that connects the spirit to bony flesh, in one ephemeral expiration. It is the undying soul. Nishmat, the breath of God, breathes it into being.

In my mind's most lucid moments in the hospital, I am occupied less with the spirit and more with the world around me. I have secured the grant money to study the poliovirus, and am busy planning the experiments.

My brush with mortality was not polio but, as Gertie had suggested, a side effect of the drugs. It felt like an exorcism at the end of a long dark night of the soul, and made me realise how little time there is to waste on trivial concerns; I had wasted enough time on those already. There is no redemption in my illness, no martyrdom. On the other side of the sadness and the fear comes a realisation: that the onus is on every individual to create meaning in our own lives. When all is done, the worth of our lives is measured by the love we share, not the things we have.

I have been left alone for hours at a time, with little real connection to a human being since being readmitted to the hospital. But today, I have a special visitor.

'I'm so glad you're here,' I say to Aaron. 'We must get back to work. I… I haven't taken this much time away from the office since… seeing Don. We're going to travel together again, once radiotherapy is over.'

'There, there.' I feel a hand take mine in theirs.

'Aaron, I have to tell you something.'

The room is a blur.

'I'm leaving you my estate.'

'Oh, Ros,' the person sobs.

I can feel their arm across my chest, hugging me gently.

'It's not Aaron, darling, it's Gertie. Don't worry, you'll feel better soon.'

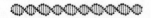

'I agree that faith is essential to success in life (success of any sort) but I do not accept your definition of faith i.e. belief in life after death. In my view, all that is necessary for faith, is the belief that by doing our best we shall come nearer to success and that success in our aims (the improvement of the lot of mankind, present and future) is worth attaining. Anyone able to believe in all that religion implies obviously must have such faith, but I maintain that faith in this world is perfectly possible without faith in another world. It has just occurred to me that you may raise the question of a creator. A creator of what? I see no reason that a creator of protoplasm or primaeval matter if such there be, has any reason to be interested in our insignificant race in a tiny corner of the universe, and still less in us, as still more insignificant individuals. Again, I see no reason why the belief that we are insignificant or fortuitous should lessen our faith.'

Rosalind Franklin

AFTERWORD

Stockholm, 10 December 1962

The auditorium was encased in concrete, which from a distance resembled ice. The Queen of Sweden wore diamonds. The dress code was white tie and the Nobel Prize winners' daughters, wives and girlfriends were wearing opulent gowns, while their partners wore tails.

Jim Watson took the podium on the garlanded stage and the Nobel awards fell silent.

From the pulpit in the middle of the auditorium, he was bellicose as he began his acceptance speech:

'Francis Crick and Maurice Wilkins have asked me to reply for all three of us. But as it is difficult to convey the personal feelings of others, I must speak for myself. This evening is certainly the second most wonderful moment in my life. The first was our discovery of the structure of DNA.'

He paused for the usual coughs and rustles in the audience.

'At that time, we knew that a new world had been opened and that an old world which seemed rather mystical was gone. The wisdom of these men in encouraging us was tremendously important in our success.

'Fortunately, we were working among wise and tolerant people who understood the spirit of scientific discovery and the conditions necessary for its generation. Good science as a way of life is sometimes difficult. It often is hard to have confidence that you really know where the future lies.'

He then alluded to the unspoken rivalries. In his inimitable, supercilious style, Jim called Francis 'difficult' and Maurice 'very strange'. But what of Rosalind Franklin? He did not mention her name. He continued: 'We must thus believe strongly in our ideas, often to the point where they may seem tiresome and bothersome and even arrogant to our colleagues.'

He spoke of the wise and tolerant people whose conditions – he said – were necessary for scientific discovery. Then he said something, just a faint breath, which sounded like her echo. She had often said that scientists stand on each other's shoulders.

'I feel that it is very important, especially for us so singularly honoured, to remember that science does not stand by itself, but is the creation of very human people.'

The discovery of the structure of DNA was a very human tale indeed, and one littered with the same hubris and folly that has gone hand in hand with mankind's forays into greatness for centuries.

Francis was under no illusions that the photographs of DNA taken at King's College London had inspired their Nobel-winning theory. The photographs were 'beautiful', he said in a homage in their draft paper for the scientific journal *Nature*.

Maurice Wilkins had started work on the DNA project before Rosalind Franklin came on board and crossed out the tribute with obstinate lines.

As they say in fencing: *En garde. Prêtes. Allez.* Laboratories in Cambridge, London and California competed to uncover the structure of DNA. Of all the possible commentators, the Nobel Committee asked Nobel Laureate Linus Pauling from the California Institute of Technology to opine on the 1960 award nominations.

Before Rosalind Franklin took her definitive series of photographs of DNA's double helix in May 1952, including the now infamous 'photograph 51', other laboratories working on the problem had theorised that deoxyribose nucleic acid had three atomic chains.

Despite later controversy over his own 1954 Nobel award, Professor Pauling said in his response that Jim and Francis 'may to some extent have been stimulated by this [his alpha Helix theory of protein] proposal to formulate their double-helix structure, as well as by the X-ray photographs of Maurice.'

His letter to the Nobel Committee made no mention of Rosalind Franklin, and instead notably attributed King's College London's X-ray photos to her colleague Maurice. Perhaps if Dorothy Crowfoot Hodgkin, who had helped Rosalind to determine the space-grouping of the DNA molecule and herself later won the Nobel Prize for Chemistry in 1964, had been asked for her opinion instead, then the outcome of the 1962 award may have been very different.

Professor Hodgkin was one of just eight women to have ever won the Nobel Prize for Chemistry. Only sixty-four women have won a Nobel prize in more than a century (from 1901 to 2023), out of approximately 965 individual Nobel Laureates excluding companies in that time.

As the clock ran down, Francis sought to clarify the matter. The New Year's Eve before the Nobel award ceremony, he wrote to Jacques Monod, a French biochemist who had nominated Jim and him for the Nobel Prize in Chemistry, and said quite plainly:

'The data which really helped us to obtain the structure was mainly obtained by Rosalind Franklin, who died a few years ago.'

It was an open secret that Rosalind, the woman with no name, had given so much in such a short space of time, not least to DNA. Maurice had admitted as much privately, calling her contributions 'very useful' in a letter to Leonard Hamilton, his supplier (of DNA). Very useful, indeed, they were.

Yet Monod's nomination would prove to hold no weight

with the Nobel committee. The reason was arbitrary: most of the nominations for the double helix theory – in what was often a coordinated effort on the part of nominating scientists – voted in favour of it winning the Physiology and Medicine, not Chemistry, prize.

Regardless, Jim was the one who had the main say on the stage on that bitterly cold day in December. Maurice mentioned Rosalind only briefly in the acknowledgements to his Nobel lecture. The rest was covered up, crossed out, and hushed away for some two-thirds of a century to come.

ACKNOWLEDGEMENTS

I am indebted to Jenifer Glynn, Rosalind's sister, for graciously and candidly responding to my queries, Colin Franklin for heartfelt correspondence about Rosalind's character, and Eric Franklin for correspondence around the life of Rosalind's uncle, Hugh Franklin.

I am also immensely grateful to Professor Jack Dunitz, one of the last surviving scientists who knew Rosalind Franklin professionally. I am indebted to him for giving an enthusiastic account of the DNA discovery, including what it was like to work with Dorothy Hodgkin. In conversation, he spoke of his relationships with Francis Crick, James Watson and Rosalind Franklin, explaining how he and Dorothy were able to help her to decipher the space grouping of the atoms in DNA. Sadly, I was not able to fulfil my promise of delivering him a final copy of the book before he passed away. I am also grateful to Professor Brian Sutton for lending his in-depth knowledge of crystallography, and insight into the history behind the double helix discovery at King's College London, as well as his familiarity with Franklin's colleague Raymond Gosling. Special thanks also go to Luke Nicholls for explaining some of the science behind the discovery, such as Fourier Transform, and for showing me Rosalind Franklin's office environs. I also owe thanks to archive staff at King's College London, the Churchill Archives Centre, and Oregon State

University Special Collections, including Chris Olver who helped curate the Maurice Wilkins collection, for insight into the collections and conversations. In addition, I would like to thank staff at the London School of Economics' Women's Library, particularly Indy Bhullar, for help and conversations. I also owe thanks to staff at Newnham College, Cambridge, and Birkbeck for answering my queries.

I would also like to acknowledge my editor Cari Rosen and Legend Press for believing in Rosalind's story (and me as a writer). Special thanks to Cari and Ditte Loekkegaard for gracefully tolerating my last-minute queries.

My mum Mandy, Fiona, Dan, Georgina, Heather and Nick were all invaluable in their generosity and time spent reading early drafts of the book. Special thanks especially to my husband, Matt, who also helped read drafts, for his unending encouragement and support throughout the late nights and years spent researching, writing and pitching the book.

I must also thank the Greenwich & Blackheath Writers' Group for their weekly meet-ups, encouragement and engagement on early drafts and scenes, where I received indispensable feedback.

My novel editing course leader Amita Murray is another person who I am indebted to, for her astute editing advice and reading recommendations, as well as to fellow course mates. I also owe author, coach and editor Niamh Mulvey special thanks for an early developmental edit, and author and coach Kate Worsley for helping to nurture the novel.

Rose Cooper also deserves thanks for producing lovely artwork for the UK edition, as does Marta Brinchi Giusti for early artwork and collaboration.

BIBLIOGRAPHY

With special thanks to Rosalind Franklin's sister, Professor Jenifer Glynn, relatives Colin Franklin (her late brother) and Eric Franklin. Also many thanks to the late Professor Jack Dunitz, who knew Rosalind and worked alongside Dorothy Hodgkin in Oxford.

Additional thanks to the King's College London Archives, the Churchill Archives Centre at the University of Cambridge, the Oregon State University Special Collection and Archives Research Center, the Cold Spring Harbor Laboratory Archive, and the Wellcome Library.

Thank you also to Professor Brian Sutton, Luke Nicholls and library archive staff at King's College London Archives, including the coordinator of the Maurice Wilkins collection at the archives, Chris Olver, for conversations. An additional thank you to Pauline Harrison (née Cowan), a colleague of Rosalind's, and her daughter Sheila Harrison.

Excerpts, quotations and text citations (with credits and permissions):

1. Crick, F. and Watson, J. (13 December 1951) 'Cheer up and take it from us that even if we kicked you in the pants, it was between friends. We hope our burglary...', Letter to Maurice Wilkins, Cold Spring Harbor Laboratory Archive, Sydney Brenner

Collection, SB/11/01/0177_005. Available at: Cold Spring Harbor Laboratory Archive (Accessed: December 2021). *Included with permission from CSHL archive.*

2. Crick, F. (1961) 'On the structure of DNA and the replication mechanism', Letter to Jacques Monod, Francis Harry Compton Crick Papers, Correspondence: Monod, Jacques, Crick, Francis, 1916-2004, PP/CRI/H/3/5/1. Available at: Wellcome Collection (Accessed: January 2022). *Quotation included with permission from the Wellcome Collection.*

3. Franklin, R. and Gosling, R. (c. July 1952) 'Copy of joke death notice for the DNA helix', Wilkins, Maurice Hugh Frederick Papers relating to scientific research, 1948-1976, chiefly in DNA, and the Francis Crick Papers, K/PP178/2/26 and PP/CRI/H/1/42/7. Available at: Wellcome Collection (Accessed: January 2022). *Text included with permission from KCL archives.*

4. Franklin, R. (1940) 'Science and everyday life cannot and should not be separated...', Letter to Ellis Arthur Franklin, The Papers of Rosalind Franklin, FRKN. Available at: Wellcome Collection (Accessed: December 2021). *Excerpt included with permission from Rosalind Franklin's sister Jenifer Glynn.*

5. Wilkins, M. (23 January 1953) 'There is also a silly muddle over Franklin's talk here. I got a big notice saying it was internal only...', Letter to Francis Crick, Cold Spring Harbor Laboratory Archive, Sydney Brenner Collection, SB/11/1/177. Available at: Cold Spring Harbor Laboratory Archive (Accessed: December 2021). *Text extract included with permission from CSHL archive.*

6. Wilkins, M. (7 March 1953) 'Our dark lady leaves us next week...', Letter to Francis Crick, Francis Crick (1916-2004) and Wilkins, Maurice Hugh Frederick

(1916-2004) Collections, PP/CRI/H/1/42/4 (4.) and K/PP1783/5/8. Available at: Wellcome Collection (Accessed: December 2021 and January 2022). *Text extract included with approval from KCL archive.*

Background research and wider reading

Journal and academic publications (reference only):

1. Finch, J.T. and Klug, A. (1959) 'Structure of Poliomyelitis Virus', Nature, [online] 183(4677), pp. 1709.

2. Fitzpatrick, M. (2006) 'The Cutter Incident: How America's First Polio Vaccine Led to a Growing Vaccine Crisis', Journal of the Royal Society of Medicine, 99(3), p. 156.

3. Franklin, R. and Gosling, R. (1953) 'Molecular Configuration in Sodium Thymonucleate', Nature, 171, pp. 740–741.

4. Franklin, R.E. and Gosling, R.G. (1953) 'Evidence for 2-chain helix in crystalline structure of sodium deoxyribonucleate', Nature, 25 July.

5. Gann, A. and Witkowski, J. (2010) 'The lost correspondence of Francis Crick', Nature, 467, pp. 519-524.

6. Gann, A. and Witkowski, J. (2013) 'DNA: Archives reveal Nobel nominations', Nature, 496, p. 434.

7. Klug, A. (1968) 'Rosalind Franklin and the Discovery of the Structure of DNA', Nature, 219(5156), pp. 808-810, 843-844.

8. Paterlini, M. (2003) 'History and science united to vindicate Perutz', Nature, [online] 424.

9. Pamphlet on the Opening ceremony by Lord Cherwell, (1952). King's College London Archives, K/PP178/4/3/2.

10. Pauling, L. and Corey, R. (1953) 'Structure of the Nucleic Acids.' *Nature* 171, 346. Available at: https://doi.org/10.1038/171346a0

11. Watson, J. and Crick, F. (1953) 'Molecular Structure of Nucleic Acids: A Structure for Deoxyribose Nucleic Acid', Nature, 171, pp. 737–738.

12. Wilkins, M. (1952) 'Engineering, Biophysics and Physics at King's College, London, New Building', Nature, 170, p. 261.

13. Wilson, H.R. (1988) 'The Double Helix and All That', Trends in Biochemical Sciences, 13(7), pp. 275-278.

Media articles (reference only):

1. 'Anne Sayre, 74, Whose Book Credited a DNA Scientist, Dies' (1998) The New York Times.

2. Daily Mail Reporter (2010) 'Naughty goings on at Newnham: Have the women of the all-women Cambridge college always been so raucous?', *Mail Online*. Available at: Mail Online (Accessed: 11 December 2023).

3. Hevesi, D. (2007) 'Odile Crick, Who Drew Iconic Double Helix, Dies at 86', *The New York Times*. Available at: The New York Times (Accessed: 11 December 2023).

4. Kirz, J., Miao, J. David Sayre *(1924–2012). Nature* 484, 38 (2012). https://doi.org/10.1038/484038a (Accessed: 11 December 2023).

5. Lawler, M. (2018) 'Rosalind Franklin still doesn't get the credit she deserves for her DNA discovery', *The Conversation*. Available at: The Conversation (Accessed: 11 December 2023).

6. Lloyd, R. (2010) 'Rosalind Franklin and DNA: How wronged was she?', *Scientific American*. Available at: Scientific American (Accessed: 11 December 2023).

7. Samakov, J. (2017) '11 women who did groundbreaking

things that men got the credit for', *Huffington Post*, 16 March. Available at: Huffington Post (Accessed: 11 December 2023).

8. Toksvig, S. (2018) 'The gender pay gap isn't the half of it: our economy runs on women's unpaid work', *The Guardian*, 9 April. Available at: The Guardian (Accessed: 11 December 2023).

Websites (reference only):

1. Gregersen, E. (2023) 'Daniel Bernoulli', *Encyclopedia Britannica*, 13 March. Available at: Encyclopedia Britannica (Accessed: 10 December 2023).

2. 'Narrative – 33. Herman Branson – Linus Pauling and the Structure of Proteins: A Documentary History' (2023) Available at: Oregon State University Special Collections & Archives Research Center (Accessed 11 December 2023)

3. Nobel Prize Outreach AB. (2023) 'Nobel Prize awarded to women', *NobelPrize.org*. Available at: NobelPrize.org (Accessed: December 2023).

4. Putneysw15.com. (2020) Remembering the Night 81 People Died in Putney. [Accessed 2020, 2023]. Available at: http://www.putneysw15.com/default. asp?section=info&page=conhistory003.htm

5. ScientificLib.com. (n.d.) 'Friedrich Bessel', *ScientificLib.com*. Available at: ScientificLib.com (Accessed: 10 December 2023).

6. Viruses: From Structure to Biology. (n.d.) 'Rhinovirus Structure'. Available at: Viruses: From Structure to Biology – Rhinovirus Structure (Accessed: 11 December 2023).

7. Watson, J. (1962) 'James Watson's speech at the Nobel Banquet in Stockholm', *NobelPrize.org*, 10 December. Available at: NobelPrize.org (Accessed: 10 December 2023).

Laboratory notebooks and publications (reference only):

1. Crick, F. (1953) 'A structure for D. N. A.', Draft typescript with pencil revisions, PP/CRI/H/1/11/1, Francis Crick (1916-2004), Wellcome Collection. Available at: Wellcome Collection (Accessed: 2019, 2023).

2. Franklin, R. (1953-1954) 'Evidence for a 2-strand helix in structure A was obtained from a study of the cylindrically averaged Patterson function', Annual report, Turner-Newall fellowship, The Papers of Rosalind Franklin, Reports and Working Notes on DNA, FRKN 1/4, Wellcome Collection. Available at: Wellcome Collection (Accessed: 2019).

3. Franklin, R. (1951) Notes for Colloquium on Molecular Structure, The Papers of Rosalind Franklin, FRKN 3/2, Churchill Archives Centre and Wellcome Library. Available at: Wellcome Collection (Accessed: 2019, 2023).

4. Franklin, R. (1952) Laboratory notebook, Research on DNA, FRKN 1/1, b19832059, pp. 2, 3, 4, 11, (photos 49 ('v good'): filament 'burned', 51: 'interruption') Wellcome Collection and Churchill Archives Centre. Available at: Wellcome Library (Accessed: 2019).

5. Franklin, R. (1953) Laboratory notebook, R.E.F. DNA Crystallographic Calculus etc., FRKN 1/1, b19832059, pp. 28 (10 Feb. '2-chain helix' evidence), 40, 41, Wellcome Collection and Churchill Archives Centre. Available at: Wellcome Library (Accessed: 2019).

6. Franklin, R. (1951) Notebook on Stockholm Conference, The Papers Rosalind Franklin, FRKN 3/1, Wellcome Collection. Available at: Wellcome Collection (Accessed: December 2023).

7. Franklin, R., Wilkins, M., Ashton, J. (1953) Papers of M H F Wilkins: annotated copies of Rosalind Franklin's DNA notebooks, K/PP178/5/2, image 27/276, King's

College London Archive and Wellcome Collection. Available at: Wellcome Collection (Accessed: 2019).

8. Gosling, R. (1954) 'X-ray diffraction studies of Deoxyribose Nucleic Acid', Phd Thesis, KDBP/5/1, King's College London. Available at: King's College London Archives (Accessed: 2019).

9. Wilkins, M. (1992) 'The secret pattern', Draft text, K/PP178/6/5/8, King's College London Archive. Available at: King's College London Archives (Accessed: December 2023).

Letters and correspondence (background and reference only):

1. Corey, R. (1952) Letter to Linus Pauling, Pauling Papers, Correspondence series, box 67 folder 5, Oregon State University Special Collections and Archives Research Center, Corvallis, Oregon. (Accessed May 2021.)

2. Cowan, P. (c. Jan. 1953) Letter to F. Crick. Crick Papers Box 2, Folder 11, University of California San Diego, USA. As cited by Cobb, M. and Comfort, N. (25 Apr. 2023) 'What Rosalind Franklin truly contributed to the discovery of DNA's structure', Nature journal, comment. Available at: https://www.nature.com/articles/d41586-023-01313-5 (Accessed 11 December 2023).

3. Crick, F. (6 Dec. 1955) Typed letter to Leonard Hamilton. (Data 'almost entirely' RF's), Christie's lot, printed and manuscript Americana & Science, 27 Jan. 2023. Property of the Leonard D. Hamilton Estate. Available at: https://onlineonly.christies.com/s/printed-manuscript-americana-science/the-x-ray-data-which-jim-i-used-was-almost-entirely-rosalind-franklins-128/173829 (Accessed 11 December 2023).

4. Franklin, R. (1955) Letter to John Bernal, The Papers of Rosalind Franklin, Reports and Working Notes on DNA, 12313 Folder 2/31, Churchill Archives Centre,

digitised copy accessible at National Library of Medicine. Available at: National Library of Medicine (Accessed: 11 December 2023).

5. Franklin, R. (1952) Letter to John Bernal, The Papers of Rosalind Franklin, 12313, Folder: 2/31, Churchill Archives Centre. Available at: National Library of Medicine (Accessed: 11 December 2023).

6. Klug, A. (c. 6 Jul. 1994) Letter Aaron Klug to Maurice Wilkins. Wilkins, Reference: K/PP178/5/5. King's College London Archives. Available at: https://archives.kingscollections.org/index.php/k-pp178-5-5 (Accessed 11 December 2023).

7. Monod, J. (1961) Letter to Francis Crick, PP/CRI/D/2/26, Wellcome Collection. Available at: Wellcome Collection (Accessed: 11 December 2023).

8. Pauling, L. (1960) Letter to the Nobel Committee for Chemistry, Oregon State University Special Collections and Archives Research Center, Corvallis, Oregon.

9. Randall, J. (circa 13 Jan. 1969) Letter to Max Perutz. (MRC 'confidentially'.) Papers of M H F Wilkins: correspondence with Max Perutz, Reference: K/PP178/3/33. Wellcome Collection. Available at: https://wellcomecollection.org/works/fes89nuf/items?canvas=57 (Accessed 11 December 2023).

10. Randall, J. (1950) Letter to Rosalind Franklin, The Papers of Rosalind Franklin, 12313 Folder: 1/2, Churchill Archives Centre, digitised copy accessible at National Library of Medicine. Available at: National Library of Medicine (Accessed: 11 December 2023).

11. Randall, J.T. (1951) Invitation to university staff, believed to be stored at King's College London Archive within the Wilkins collection.

12. Randall, J.T. (1951) Letter to Linus Pauling, Linus Pauling and the Race for DNA, sci9.001.2-randall-lp-19510828, Oregon State University. Available at: Oregon State University (Accessed: 11 December 2023).

13. Schaffer, F. (n.d.) 'Correspondence on Rosalind Franklin and Poliovirus Research' (RF smuggling polio), Viruses: From Structure to Biology – Rhinovirus Structure. Washington University in St. Louis. Available at: Viruses: From Structure to Biology – Rhinovirus Structure (wustl.edu) (Accessed 11 December 2023).

14. Thomson, A., 2019. Email correspondence. Cambridge University. Gertrude Clark 'Old Hall', Rosalind Franklin, Jean Kerslake 'lived in Peile', Mrs P was 'Helen Palmer'.

15. Watson, J.D. (c. Dec. 1968) Letter from James D. Watson to Max Perutz. Cold Spring Harbor Laboratory Archives Repository, Reference: JDW/2/2/1401/14. Available at: https://libgallery.cshl.edu/items/show/83819 (Accessed 10 December 2023).

16. Wilkins, M. (c. 11 Dec. 1951) Copy of handwritten letter to Francis Crick. Wilkins, Maurice, 1916-2004, CSHL Archives Repository, Reference JDW/2/2/1995/3. Available at: https://libgallery.cshl.edu/items/show/81729 (Accessed 10 December 2023).

17. Wilkins, M. (1953) 'I think you're a couple of old rogues but you may well have something…', Letter to Francis Crick, King's College London and Wellcome Collection, K/PP178/3/5/7 and PP/CRI/H/1/42/4 (3.). Available at: King's College London Archives (Accessed: 11 December 2023).

18. Wilkins, M. (c. 1953) Note to Francis Crick. Papers of M H F Wilkins, Reference: K/PP178/3/5/9. Wellcome Collection and King's College London, Archives and Special Collections. Available at: https://wellcomecollection.org/works/hqpx6tvm/items (Accessed 11 Dec. 2023).

19. Wilkins, M.H.F. (1968) Note to 'Sir John' (Randall), (on 'confidentiality' of MRC report) Wilkins, Maurice, 1916-2004 Perutz, Max Ferdinand, 1914-2002 Medical Research Council, K/PP178/3/33,

Wellcome Collection. Available at: Wellcome Collection (Accessed: 11 December 2023).

Other documents and paperwork (reference only):

1. English Heritage (1992) *Plaque for Rosalind Franklin*. Donovan Court, 107 Drayton Gardens, Chelsea, London, SW10 9QS, Royal Borough of Kensington and Chelsea.

1. Medical Research Council, c. 10 September 1948. Biophysics Committee. Constitution and Functions. In: M. H. F. Wilkins, ed., Papers of M H F Wilkins: correspondence with Max Perutz. Reference: K/PP178/2/22. Available at: King's College London Archive and Wellcome Collection (Accessed: 2019, 2023).

2. Randall, J., December 1952. Report on Biophysics Unit DNA research, 1951-1952. Report to the Medical Research Unit. Wheatstone Physics Laboratory. Notes on current research prepared for the visit of the biophysics research committee 15 December 1952. In: Wilkins, M., ed., Papers of M H F Wilkins. Reference: K/PP178/2/22. Available at: King's College London Archives (Accessed: 2019, 2023).

3. The Women's Library, Papers of Hugh Franklin and Elsie Duval. (Elsie's death records associated with 'influenza'.) London School of Economics. Women's Library. Reference: 7HFD/A/4/06. Available at: https://archives.lse.ac.uk/Record.aspx?src=CalmView.Catalog&id=7HFD&pos=2 (Accessed December 2023).

Further reading:

1. Zack, M., 2015. What is the parallax formula and how is it used to calculate the distance between two stars? Socratic.org. Available at: https://socratic.org/questions/what-is-the-parallax-formula-and-how-is-

it-used-to-calculate-the-distance-between-two-stars
(Accessed 11 December 2023).

Photographs (reference only):

1. Excursion to the Stockholm Archipelago, 1951. Photograph of Rosalind Franklin, Beryl Oughton, David Shoemaker, Donohoe and Kenneth Hedberg. The Crystallographic Community. Second Congress and General Assembly of the International Union of Crystallography (IUCr). Stockholm, Sweden. 27 June – 3 July. Available at: IUCR.org (Accessed: 2020, 2023).
2. Franklin, R., 1951. X-ray rotation photograph of asbestos. King's College London Department of Biophysics. [Photograph] KDBP/1/1/0572. Source: Wellcome Collection [Accessed 19 December 2023]. Available at: https://wellcomecollection.org/works/emtbxrpj/items
3. Franklin, R., c. 1952. Photographic prints chiefly relating to x-ray diffraction images of DNA, 1951-1963. Images of negatives for RF's 'best' photo, including photo 51. In: Wilkins, M., ed., Collection: Wilkins. Reference: K/PP178/15/1/1. King's College London Archives. Available at: King's College London Archives (Accessed: December 2023).
4. Madrid International Union of Crystallography meeting 1956. Photograph of Anne Cullis, Francis Crick, Don Caspar, Aaron Klug, Rosalind Franklin, Odile Crick and John Kendrew. Early theories of virus structure – Scientific Figure on ResearchGate. (Accessed 11 Dec, 2023).
5. Sessions and Banquet at Uppsala, 1951. Photograph of Rosalind Franklin, John Rollett and Durward Cruickshank. The Crystallographic Community. Second Congress and General Assembly of the International Union of Crystallography (IUCr). Stockholm, Sweden. 27 June – 3 July. Available at: IUCR.org (Accessed: 2020, 2023).

Oral histories, plays and audio:

1. Caspar, D., 1 January 2001. Don Caspar on Rosalind Franklin. CSHL Digital Archives. Cold Spring Harbor Laboratory. Available at: https://library.cshl.edu/oralhistory/interview/scientific-experience/women-science/rosalind-franklin (Accessed 11 December 2023).
2. Crick, F., 9 September 2002. History of Neuroscience: Francis Crick. Society for Neuroscience. Available at: https://www.sfn.org/about/history-of-neuroscience/autobiographical-videos/crick,-francis (Accessed 11 December 2023).
3. Franklin, N. & Jill, 1979. Interview with Franklin, Norman & Jill. The Brian Harrison Interviews. The Women's Library. London School of Economics (and Political Science). Reference: 8SUF/B/187.
4. Franklin, C. & Charlotte, Interview with Franklin, Mr Colin & Mrs Charlotte. The Brian Harrison Interviews. The Women's Library. London School of Economics (and Political Science). Reference: 8SUF/B/155.
5. Gosling, R., March 2003. Raymond Gosling on working with Rosalind Franklin. CSHL Digital Archives. Cold Spring Harbor Laboratory. Available at: https://library.cshl.edu/oralhistory/interview/scientific-experience/molecular-biologists/working-dna-rosalind-franklin (Accessed 11 December 2023).
6. Gosling, R., March 2003. Raymond Gosling on Continued Relationship with Rosalind Franklin. CSHL Digital Archives. Cold Spring Harbor Laboratory. Available at: https://library.cshl.edu/oralhistory/interview/james-d-watson/discovering-double-helix/continued-relationship-rosalind-franklin (Accessed 11 December 2023).
7. Horton, G., Horton, Mrs Gertrude interview. The

Brian Harrison Interviews. The Women's Library. Reference: 8SUF/B/145.

8. Olby, R., September 1969. Interview with Gerald James Holton. (RF 'projected' DNA photos to show Corey during '52 visit) Oregon State University Special Collections and Archives Research Center. Available at: https://scarc.library.oregonstate.edu/coll/pauling/dna/quotes/rosalind_franklin.html (Accessed 11 December 2023).

9. Sinatra, F. 1943. You'll Never Know. US: Columbia.

10. Ziegler, A., 2019. *Photograph 51*. Directed by Helen Leedham. 9-13 April. ADC Theatre, Cambridge.

Books (background reading):

1. Brown, A., 2005. J. D. Bernal: The Sage of Science. Oxford: OUP Oxford.

2. Byatt, A. S., 1991. *Possession: A Romance*. London: Vintage Books.

3. Chargaff, E., 1978. Heraclitean Fire: Sketches from a Life Before Nature. New York: Rockefeller University Press. (If only he and Franklin 'could have collaborated'.)

4. Crick, F., 1988. What Mad Pursuit: A Personal View of Scientific Discovery. New York: Basic Books.

5. Garnett, E., 1937. The Family from One End Street. UK: Frederick Muller.

6. Glynn, J., 2012. My Sister Rosalind Franklin. Oxford: OUP Oxford.

7. Levi, C. (1945) Christ Stopped at Eboli. Translated by F. Frenaye. London: Penguin Books.

8. Maddox, B., 2002. Rosalind Franklin: The Dark Lady of DNA. New York: Harper Collins. (Mering letters 'destroyed'.)

9. Sayre, A., 1975. Rosalind Franklin and DNA. New York: Norton.

10. Watson, J., 1968. The Double Helix: A Personal Account of the Discovery of the Structure of DNA. New York: Atheneum Press; London: Weidenfeld & Nicolson.
11. Wilkins, M., 2003. Third Man of the Double Helix. Oxford: Oxford University Press.

Author interviews and correspondence:

1. Abbott, D., 2019. Discussions about Newnham College culture on the sidelines of the Greenwich Book Festival.
2. Dunitz, J., c. May 2019. Author interview conducted over the telephone. England. *On meeting with RF and DNA's space group*: 'Beautiful pictures,' Dorothy urged him to 'explain it to her (RF)' regarding DNA's space group, C2 'only possibility', biological molecules exist in 'one mirror image form'. *On location*: Offices in 'large room upstairs' 'on first floor of the museum', 'T-rex' at the museum. *On the MRC report:* 'Her report was given to Bragg, who showed it to Perutz, who showed it to Francis'. Crick 'immediately' saw a helix. *On Randall*: He handed DNA to RF, RF 'much better experimenter than Wilkins', problem 'solved faster' because of her.
3. Franklin, C., 27 November 2019. Email correspondence with the author. 'Rosalind's delight in mountain climbing', her 'wit', 'joy' in Paris, 'human side' neglected.
4. Franklin, C., 26 January 2020. Email correspondence with the author. On RF's 'delightful sense of humour', 'deeply brave' in sorrow.
5. Franklin, C., 29 January 2020. Email correspondence with the author. On Mering and RF ('no relationship').
6. Franklin, E., c. 5 February 2019. Email exchanges with the author. On Hugh 'utterly weak at the end of his second hunger strike'.

7. Glynn, J., c. January 2020. Email exchanges between the author and Jenifer Glynn. England. 'Hotel in Fjaerland.'

8. Glynn, J., 7 January 2020. Email exchange between the author and Jenifer Glynn. On Norwegian holiday, family 'Austin with a canvas roof', 'Evi did not come', heard of war 'from hotel waiter'. *On war*: 'Spitfires' while RF 'staying with family friends' in Sussex 1940. Also, RF gained '2.1' for BA. Mering and RF's relationship 'that of teacher and pupil', 'wrongly romanticised'.

9. Keep, N., April 2019. April 2019. Email exchanges. Birkbeck 'slums' demolished.

10. Nicholls, L., c. 15 January 2019. In-person interview with author. 'Controlled' experiments, Fourier Transform.

11. Sutton, B., c. 30 April 2019. In-person interview conducted by the author. *On photo 51:* Raymond 'jovial', took and developed photo 51, ran experiment for three days, 'power failure', RF 'drew the fibre' from a water gel, and saw photo 51's 'importance', RF thought 'water content was important', her insights into humidity and the camera. MW 'realised he shouldn't have shown it'. *On MRC report:* Watson and Crick 'don't know' about C2 without MRC report, C2 'gives a unit cell with the dimensions', 'rhomboid'. *On process:* crystalline DNA 'fluffy white powder', RF invented 'device' to draw DNA, DNA 'right handed helix', black-edged note 'a joke', Wilkins 'complained' Randall gave RF 'best' camera and Signer DNA, Randall 'autocratic'. Bessel functions 'waves' cylindrically average, atom 'middle' of electron map. *On conditions:* 'University museum room with no windows' (Dorothy's office at Oxford), RF worked in an underground 'lead-lined room'.